Praise for the Max Brown Tetralogy (+1)

"*How I Made $3,200,000 from My Hobby* is a sharp, witty debut from a deeply talented and engaging humorist.
—*Self-Publishing Review*

"Michael Bernhart draws you in page after page."
—Sarah Jean Alexander, author of *Wildlives*

"*How Speleology Restored My Sex Drive* by Michael Bernhart is just right. It hit hard and there was hope. It bounced back and reflected brilliantly."
—Stephanie Barber, author of *All the People*

"Bernhart's is a funny and engaging voice . . . sharp, witty . . . talented."
—*The Independent Review of Books*

"*How I Made $3,200,000 from My Hobby* is a big-hearted and resplendent book."
—Adrian Van Young, author of *The Man Who Noticed Everything*

"*How Moral Philosophy Failed* is a small miracle of hope and desperation. With unexpected grace, Bernhart's characters love, hate, and cope from page to beautiful page."
—Jonny Diamond, editor of *LitHub*

"What if a book upended everything you thought you knew about our world? *How Existentialism Almost Killed Me* by Michael Bernhart could absolutely do that."
—Gabe Durham, author of *Fun Camp*

"*How I Made $3,200,000 from My Hobby* pre-chews a charmingly irascible post-millennial W*eltanschauung* and gently funnels its essence back to esurient readers."
—Molly Brodak, author of *A Little Middle of the Night*

"A must-read final chapter in the action-thriller series, *How Moral Philosophy Failed* is a one-of-a-kind tale of crimes against humanity, and the few people willing to step up to fight against it. By the book's final pages readers will be left in shock as the final events begin winding down. This . . . captivating read is filled with action, suspense, and fantastic character development that readers will absolutely love. Be sure to grab your copy today!"

—Anthony Avina, author of *I Was an Evil Teenager: Remastered* and *Identity*

"*The Max Brown Tetralogy (+1)* is a significant contribution to literature. Bernhart's is the voice we all have been waiting for."

—Gina Myers, author of *Hold It Down*

"This book is very similar to art."

—Sommer Browning, author of *Backup Singers*

"Make no mistake about it, Dr. Bernhart knows how to write. Really write."

—Matt DeBenedictis, author of *Congratulations! There's No Last Place if Everyone Is Dead*

"This book (*How Moral Philosophy Failed*) is a spark in a dark place, a light in a desolate landscape. Unweaving the threads of love, family, loss, and disrepair, this novel pounds at the heart of humanity.'"

—Sarah Rose Etter, author of *Tongue Party*

"I always felt Dr. Bernhart was too good-looking to write something this brilliant."

—Michael Fitzgerald, CEO of Submittable and author of *Radiant Days*

"Move over, *The Crying Game*. This is the new best art."

—Amelia Gray, author of *Gutshot*

"I read *How Existentialism Almost Killed Me* by Michael Bernhart with great initial intensity and then, as I kept reading, with increasing self-loathing, for I became surer, with every page, that I would never write a book as lovely, as true, or as pure, as this."

—Karl Taro Greenfeld, author of *The Subprimes* and *Triburbia*

"*How I Made $3,200,000 from My Hobby* . . . is a great book for people who hate literature."

—Lindsay Hunter, author of *Ugly Girls*

"*How Existentialism Almost Killed Me* is as mystical as it is practical. Bernhart's manual will serve us deep into the millennium."

—John Dermot Woods, author of *The Baltimore Atrocities*

"If Stephen King read this, he'd regret the eight or nine times he's said 'If you miss so-and-so, you're missing a treat.' Yes, this is the one that truly deserves those words."

—Gabino Iglesias, author of *Hungry Darkness*

"This book (*How Moral Philosophy Failed*) is GOOD."

—Jamie Iredell, author of *Last Mass* and *I Was a Fat Drunk Catholic School Insomniac*

"Reading this book is like reading the hush of the crowd right before a Criss Angel performance."

—Kristen Iskandrian, author of *Mother, Motherer, Motherest*

"Who wouldn't want to read this book?"

—Michael Kimball, author *of Us* and *Big Ray*.

"Brave.... Stunning . . . A Triumph."

—Samuel Ligon, author of *Among the Dead and Dreaming*

"When it gets rolling Bernhart's text feels like one of those old carny rides at county fairs, when you're not sure it's supposed to be moving that fast but there's nothing you can do about it."

—Megan McShea, author of *A Mountain City of Toad Splendor*

"Are you ready for these words to live inside of you? The novel (*How Moral Philosophy Failed*) has no point of no return. Its labyrinthine narrative and rhythm will make your heart race and your palms sweat. Bernhart is ruthless in his execution . . . and grants no mercy to the faint of heart."

—Sade Murphy, author of *Dream Machine*

"A deceptively enjoyable book."

—Adam Robinson, author of *Adam Robison and Other Poems*

"This book is the pony you were promised but don't deserve."

—Jim Ruland, author of *Forest of Fortune*

"*How Ornithology Saved My Life* by Michael Bernhart . . . sensational!"

—Lucy K Shaw, author of *The Motion*

"Bernhart's latest (*How Speleology Restored My Sex Drive*) is an archive of the fresh, fierce language of our time . . . We need this book. We're lucky to have it."

—Matthew Simmons, author of *A Jello Horse,*
Happy Rock, and *The In-Betweens*

"Michael Bernhart is the greatest writer in the history of western civilization."

—Mike Topp, editor of *Stuyvesant Review*

"It's a well known fact that every book by Michael Bernhart is an improvement on another, making *How Ornithology Saved My Life* the best book by a writer on the verge of something even better."

—Colin Winnette, author of *Haints Stay*

"A must read (*How Speleology Restored My Sex Drive*) for fans of classic adventure tales that combine the thrill of an Indiana Jones story with the political climate of our world today."

—Anthony Avina, author of *I Was an Evil*
Teenager: Remastered and *Identity*

NIGHT SWEATS:
HOW MORAL
PHILOSOPHY
FAILED

THE MAX BROWN
TETRALOGY (+1)
#5

BY
MICHAEL BERNHART

Hough Publishing

This is a work of fiction. Names, characters, events, organizations, places and incidents are either products of the author's imagination or are used fictitiously. Any similarity to real persons, living or dead, is coincidental and not intended by the author. Except for Lawrence Kohlberg; he's real and his theory merits your serious consideration. Add Frances Kamm and Thomas Nagel, two other moral philosophers of note. Finally and sadly, Larry Foley is also not fictional; he was murdered in his driveway as described.

Correspondence concerning this book – or the others in the series – may be sent to MaxBrown@HoughPublishing.com. Constructive criticism is always welcome and, given that revisions can be incorporated immediately, will be acted on. Trolls, flamers and other dipshits whose aim is to hurt, not help? Keep your sad little thoughts to yourselves. If you can't, be forewarned that your emails may be published, with full attribution to their authors. No effort will be made to disguise how pathetic and illiterate you are. Seems fair.

Published by Hough Publishing, LLC, Jewell Mountain, GA

Inquiries to Hough Publishing, PO Box 811, Hiawassee, GA 30546, USA. Or, contact@HoughPublishing.com.

www.houghpublishing.com

Published in the United States of America

ISBN: 978-0-9976160-9-5

Dedicated to the memory of the 5,000 women who are victims of "honor" killings every year and to the uncounted thousands who are victims of acid attacks.

Daily Journal

Sally Taylor-Brown

24 September
Geneva

I'm worried about Max. Last night he drank too much, again,
and then couldn't sleep. A lot of recent low blows have him off
balance.

Maybe I should be worried about myself. I've become hardened
to the horrors that pass through our little clinic. Women with no
noses, or an eye burned out, most with sagging, mottled flesh.
Who are these savages who throw acid at their girlfriend or fi-
ancée or wife? When I started at the clinic I was paralyzed by
the sight of ruined faces and ruined lives. Now I've swung over
to "detached professional," processing the acid-attack victims
from intake to discharge, with little emotional involvement.

I'd better find a balance pretty soon. Or quit. I'm becoming
someone I don't like. Is it because I've never had to face up to
real adversity? Fate, if you're listening in, that wasn't a request.

27 September
Geneva

I started this journal to get into the habit of writing but it isn't
working. Max is the family wordsmith. It's easy for him, but he
says he'll never write anything again and it's up to me. It just
seems that when something important happens, the last thing on
my mind is to rush in here and write it in this diary.

1 October
Geneva

A relief – for me – but at someone else's huge cost. A frightened teenager arrived today. I picked her up at the airport and
signed the papers. Can you believe it? A child, disfigured by an

attacker? So young someone had to sign for her when she arrived. Heavily bandaged, but probably an eye gone, for starters. I tried to not think about what else was hidden beneath the bandages. I held it together until I handed her off to Hanan, our counselor, then I hid in the bathroom, bawling like an infant, revolted at the tragedy of that poor child's life, and relieved that I could still feel such sorrow.

3 October
Geneva

Today has been a "good" day around the Taylor-Brown house. Max didn't get dropped from a Board today – he's down to just one – and the Chancellor at the Université told Max he *might* be invited back to teach next term "if there is an opening." Max thinks he's being punished for writing all those negative things about Swiss banks and other big companies in his last book. The old fart suggested that at 68 Max should be ready to "relax and enjoy life."

How can you interpret that any other way than that you're being put out to pasture?

6 October
Geneva

I tried to keep a diary when I was 11 and didn't do any better then than I'm doing now. Maybe I can recruit Max to help out. At least he can read it so it's more of a joint effort. Of course I'll have to be careful about what I write.

11 October
Basel

A bad day for me. Came up to Basel for a memorial service for one of the women who had been treated in our charity clinic. A shy Iraqi girl, she underwent reconstructive surgery two weeks ago for the acid attack that disfigured her face, neck and left side of her chest. The surgery was only a partial success but she seemed okay, at least physically. Then eight days after she was released, she was dead. We only found out because she didn't show up for a follow-up appointment.

Two other Board members/volunteers came with me to the service. Max declined. I could really use his support.

12 October
Geneva

More on that Iraqi girl. I learned that there had been a debate about whether she should go back to her family in the refugee camp in Jordan. Schwarzherz, our clinic director, was pushing her to return "home." A good idea? That's where she was attacked. She never would tell us who did it. Now she never will. Her uncle appeared out of nowhere to claim the body and to give her a traditional Muslim burial. Boy is he a cold fish!

15 October
Geneva

Big emergency meeting at the clinic. I usually don't volunteer on Tuesdays but was called in. Schwarzherz seemed very upset and told us that loyalty to the organization was "primary." He said that talking to nosy authorities would jeopardize carrying out our work of assisting women who have been attacked. Who's been talking to anyone? Not me.

18 October
Berne

Why I would have to go all the way to Berne to be interrogated by FedPol is a mystery. Lots of questions about the dead Iraqi girl that I couldn't answer. Don't the Federal Police have an office in Geneva? Aren't they supposed to come to your door like Sergeant Friday did in Dragnet? I talked to the national guys and then a weaselly looking toad – although he has a great head of hair – from the Geneva office named Méchant wanted to grill me again. I think he was hitting on me. Sad that I can't be sure anymore. Is this just my vanity talking – or wishful thinking? I don't loiter in front of mirrors.

Anyway, I couldn't tell the fuzz anything. The poor Iraqi girl could hardly speak with the burns all over her face. Hanan, our staff interpreter, spent a lot of time with the girl. I suggested that FedPol should talk to Hanan. I got the impression they already had.

19 October
Geneva

Whooeee! Talk about a shit storm! I reported the meeting with FedPol to Schwarzherz and he went ballistic. When the police call me in am I supposed to tell them to piss in their hats? I used that phrase with Dr. S. It didn't help our conversation. That's the sort of wise-ass thing Max would do. Except he doesn't do much of anything anymore. I should focus on him. Rough patch, losing his job and all. That whole business of killing bad guys in Cambodia had a much harder effect on him than I realized at the time. He wants to be a good person, but is convinced he isn't. I've got to put the whole clinic/dead girl business out of my head and be there for my husband.

23 October
Geneva

Another acid-attack victim arrived from a refugee camp in Jordan. A different camp, perhaps along the northern border. Syrian girl. I hate the bastards who do this so much! This girl is in better shape, although she'll never win any beauty contests. Our people in Jordan are getting bolder all the time and they move to get a victim into treatment more quickly. Why don't the victims stay there for the reconstructive work? There's one really good Jordanian reconstructive surgeon I've heard about. Must be more. We seem to insist on bringing the women to Switzerland, usually on the argument that they'll be exposed to another attack in their home country. I wonder if it isn't just organizational ego. Or Schwarzherz's ego.

25 October
Basel

Hanan asked me to go with her to the Muslim cemetery in Basel. We spent an hour walking around. No recent burials. The dead Iraqi girl isn't listed on the cemetery register. We both got the strong impression the uncle was rushing things along so he could get the body interred within the 24-hour period required by Islam. Now that we know about these cemetery registers, Hanan called the Muslim cemetery registries in Berne, Lucerne, and Zurich. The girl isn't buried in any of those cemeteries. Where did she go?

1 November
Lausanne

Semi-annual Board meeting. I didn't want Max to know about it since he's been dropped by all of his five boards. But I had to tell him when he asked where I was going.

Surprising news. The clinic's finances are good, for once. It looks like there was a little more income from Botox and other minor procedures purchased by the aging Mesdames of Geneva who can't afford a high-class facility. Still, that seems like small potatoes; money must be coming from somewhere else.

But more surprising was the tragic report that *three* women we'd operated on had died within a few weeks of release. Someone suggested that depression was a contributing factor when the women realized they would never look really good again and they were afraid to go back home. "You know, these women blame themselves." I've heard the victims themselves say something like that but does it add up to suicidal depression?

We, the Board, directed the clinic to shift more resources into post-operative counseling. Schwarzherz will shit a brick.

3 November
Vevey

The signs seem clear. Max had his second driving accident in a month. He's rushing around carelessly, although we both know he has nowhere to go. A few years ago he wanted to make a difference in the world. Now he just wants to be useful. I don't know what to do for him. Not helped by my own minor health problems.

12 November
Geneva

Merde! A first for me: I've had to call in sick to the clinic three days in a row. Gut hurts, puking, nausea. Something I ate? Max has been doing more of the cooking, but he's probably a better cook than I am. And this has gone on way too long.

Here's something positive: A spark of interest from my boy. Max has been reading up on theories of morality, especially this Lawrence Kohlberg guy who came up with a stage theory about moral development. Max says he's going to propose a new course to the Université. But that's not what caught my attention. Kohlberg was in British Honduras collecting info for his theory and caught some intestinal bug. He lost a few pounds every month until there was no more of him. Scary. I've been losing weight.

14 November
Geneva

Max fixed dinner again tonight. I appreciate the effort, but wish he could make more appetizing stuff. I have no appetite to begin with. After dinner I went to massage his shoulders – he was just sitting there at the table, kind of moping. Shock! His shoulders are soft. He used to have tight muscles. I didn't expect him to get out of shape so fast. I think they're called trapezius.

22 November
Geneva

Gave in to Max's nagging and saw a doctor. Crohn's disease. At first I thought she said I had a crone's disease and I was ticked. Can't be cured but can be controlled. A few people need surgery. I looked online and there are some scary complications. Who needs this? Not me. Sure it will turn out to be nothing.

23 November
Geneva

Max went to the gym to work out today. I guess I just had to get sick for him to pull himself together. Or so it seemed for a while. He was back home soon, marveling at how flabby he'd become. I spent the day near the bathroom. Whatever that doctor gave me isn't doing the job.

24 November
Geneva

Happy Thanksgiving! Not really all that happy. I was hoping that our daughters would pay us a surprise visit. They're in London interning at The Economist so it wouldn't be a huge trip for them. We called them, but they didn't pick up. Must have been somewhere where they couldn't hear the ring.

Max tried to roast a turkey. At five o'clock it was still cold inside so he gave up and ordered Chinese takeout. Good thing the Swiss don't celebrate Thanksgiving. Otherwise where would we get our Thanksgiving moo shu pork? I suggested vindaloo as an ironic statement about the Native Americans being called Indians. Max has lost his sense of humor.

He was still upset about the turkey failure when we turned in. I've started sleeping in the guest bedroom since I wake up once or twice a night to move to a dry area of the bed.

7 December
Geneva

The medication seems to be helping and today was my fifth day back at work at the clinic.

Hanan? Is she going overboard? She's convinced something is going on with these dying women. Still only (only?) three have died but she called all the Muslim cemetery registries in the country. None of the women were buried in Switzerland. I pointed out to her that it is common to repatriate bodies for burial. She countered that these women had been dramatically disowned by their families and were running for their lives. Why would their families spend a lot of money to bury them back in their home country?

12 December
Berne

Hanan is on to something. She read about the charred remains of a woman that were found in the woods outside of Fribourg. The FedPol weenies agreed to let us examine the remains. Not a task I would have volunteered for, but Hanan was insistent. After I got used to the sight it was nothing special, just burned bones. FedPol said the victim was dead before being doused with gasoline and burned. How can they be sure? They're Swiss, so they're sure. But that's not the big news. They showed us the personal effects that hadn't burned. There was a ring with an Arabic inscription on it. Hanan is convinced it's the same ring that the Iraqi girl had. It does look familiar.

14 December
Geneva

The feces have hit the fan! Schwarzherz called Hanan and me into his office this morning and went nuts. He did everything but froth at the mouth. He said he should fire both of us for meddling and endangering the clinic's reputation. I reminded him that as a Board member and volunteer it would take more than his signature on a piece of paper to get rid of me. Hanan doesn't have that protection. He never told us what the problem was, but Gisele, the administrator, told me that Schwarzherz got a phone call from FedPol. Not surprising. We told them that the ring looks like one that had belonged to a woman who had been operated on in our clinic. Doesn't Schwarzherz want to get to the bottom of this?

25 December
London

If the mountain will not come to Mohammed . . .

We came up to London to see the girls. This city is just one big playground for young adults and they're taking full advantage. We hadn't told them anything about our little health issues. Margaret was speechless when she saw me. Do I look that bad? Skin is a little yellow and I'm down ten pounds, but I had a few spare pounds that I'd vowed to shed. Max just looks drawn and lifeless. What a change for him!

London is doing us good. The girls have laid on a full schedule. Exhausting. Now, Christmas day, things are slowing down. Presents are opened, dinner is in the oven. But then it's back into it tomorrow with a pantomime and an evening concert. Kind of looking forward to getting home.

Rats! While I was writing this I got a call from Gisele, the one at the clinic. I thought it was to wish me Merry Christmas. Another woman has died.

3 January
Geneva

Finally recovered from the trip and able to get back to work. Just no energy. Everyone is talking about the four deaths. Schwarzherz says these things happen. Less than two percent of the women who have come here from the Middle East have died after surgery. He's ignoring the fact that there were no deaths until the last few months.

Max says I should look into it. Transparent, Maxie boy. He thinks my health problems are because there's no big challenge in my life. He's projecting.

7 January
Geneva

Back to the doctor. After some humiliating tests she said Crohn's is looking less likely. Is this a good development?

8 January
Geneva

We have a houseguest. Another acid-burn victim, this one from Pakistan. She speaks a little English and I followed Max's advice and got "involved" by asking her to stay with us. The acid was thrown by her fiancé who thought some other man had been staring at her. God, I hate these bastards. They never see justice. She doubts her fiancé will want her now and she's sorry she allowed a man to stare at her. Like it was her fault? I want to tell her the fiancé's no loss, but I know that's not how those societies work.

Her name is Rania and she seems constantly embarrassed. I've tried to have a "normal" conversation, asking about her life, her friends, her family. Backfired. Any thoughts of that life must fill her with dread; she clams up. She wears a veil, not out of religious observance, but so as not to upset others by her appearance. It might be a mistake. The veil hangs directly down; Rania has no nose. We eat together, although I think she would prefer not to. She lowers her head and picks up the bottom of the veil to spoon in food.

12 January
Geneva

Rania, our houseguest, underwent surgery today. As big a jerk as Schwarzherz is, he does wield a knife well. I've been getting bolder and scrubbing in, although I remain in the back and simply take away dirty pans, gauze, and so on.

17 January
Geneva

Rania's bandages came off today. Pretty grotesque, but Schwarzherz says she'll look fine in a few weeks. He usually resists doing more than one "patch-up" surgery. If they look "good enough" that's the end of his job. At first I thought that was because he didn't think he had the skill to really restore the women's looks. Now it seems to be something else. Laziness?

I'm a bad one to accuse anyone of laziness. I just can't get into the habit of writing in this journal. It glares at me accusingly from my nightstand. Max agreed to "help" by reading it, but his feedback is a verbal pat on the head: "Very good. Keep at it."

I'm scheduled to see an oncologist tomorrow. I hate the thought. This is all a bad dream. I'll wake up and Max and I will both be just like we used to.

21 January
Geneva

Still no word from the oncologist. Assume it must be nothing or they would have been in touch.

22 January
Geneva

Cancer. Liver.

From Max Brown's notes on Kohlberg's stages of moral development

Stage 1. Might makes right. A person who operates at the bottom-most level of moral development believes an act must have been wrong if the perpetrator is punished. The harsher the punishment, the worse the transgression is perceived to have been. This gives rise to a perception that recipients of punishment, including innocent victims, are guilty in proportion to their suffering.

The rationale can be summed up in the often-heard explanation, "S/he must have had it coming."

This level of moral development is common – and expected – among young children but the number of people who continue to employ stage one moral reasoning through adulthood is depressingly large.

The men who throw acid at the women who come to Sally's clinic are probably at this level. It sounds like some of their victims buy into it as well; they think they must have had it coming. Perhaps interview some of the attack victims for teaching case material?

Sally needs a break

I'll take over for a while. Writing a journal has become a source of anxiety for my wife, not a relief or outlet; however, she feels that the story of the acid-attack victims needs to get out, so I'll break the promise I made to myself – as well as to those of you who read my past books – and fill in until our girl is back at full fighting strength.

Big issues first: Sally's cancer is still at an early stage. That good news didn't lessen the blow, the numbness that came over us, the unwillingness to accept that our lives have been shattered. The sun has lost its warmth and we've entered a cold, bleak, unrecognizable world.

A lot of wakeful nights, holding each other. When sleep comes it's a brief escape which segues to the cruelest time of the day. You have two normal, sane seconds after waking before the world caves in on you again.

I can't bear the thought of anything happening to my best friend and soul mate. She's taking this better than I am. If I can keep my mind occupied with something else – like the Kohlberg stuff – I'm okay. Then it comes back like a punch to the solar plexus and I'm staggered with guilt for thinking about anything other than her health.

We've learned that cancer of the liver, detected early, is not necessarily a death sentence. A transplant, accompanied by unpleasant radiation treatments, can extend life expectancy well beyond three to six months, numbers that jump out at you from the first page of almost every article on the disease. In comforting contrast, we found a graph on the website of the European Liver and Intestine Transplant Association showing half the recipients of a liver transplant were going strong after fifteen years. From this we conclude the real challenge is delaying metastasis until a replacement liver becomes available. The medical options for holding back the inexorable spread of diseased cells are no more than speed bumps.

After the initial shock we've gotten busy looking for a living donor. Yes, each human comes equipped with only one liver, but the organ has unusual regenerative powers. The donor can hand over the major part of his or her liver; what remains will grow back to its original size and functionality. Amazing, isn't it? The downside is that the recuperation period for the donor is described as "protracted and excruciating." Living donors aren't lining up.

That reduces the pool of willing living donors to three, but Sally's blood-type is different from mine or our daughters.

She's been assured that the cancer is not fast-growing, so there's no need for a frantic search, but the failure to come up with a donor within the family is a setback. They've got her on some experimental pills that are supposed to slow the spread of the disease. Radiation therapy is scheduled, but that's also a holding action to keep the disease in an early stage until a donor is found.

The other big issue, of course, is the string of deaths at the clinic. Sally's journal is skimpy on details, so I'll describe how the clinic operates. If I over-explain it's probably that 'keep the mind occupied' thing that governs much of what I do.

Over a decade ago the charity was founded to provide reconstructive surgery for people from the developing world who couldn't obtain it otherwise. (Plus a few local paying customers.) The early patients typically had cleft palates, harelip, deformed hands . . . those sorts of problems. Then honor crimes appeared in the media and, overnight, the clinic switched to treating female victims of "honor" attacks. Mostly from the Middle East and North Africa, but occasionally a woman from Bosnia or Chechnya would be brought to them.

You students of management will immediately spot the challenges this refocusing entailed. In the clinic's early days the clients would have suffered from the deformity for most of their lives; finding them could be leisurely – passive; and there was rarely any medical urgency to get them into the OR. The acid-attack victim is different. The crime is not broadcast. She often goes underground. And her chances for successful repair decline with each day she doesn't receive care. A network of community outreach workers was created in several countries and in-country facilitators were hired to help the victims get to Geneva.

Dr. Schwarzherz, who, to his credit was one of the founders of the NGO, was unwilling to slow purchases of his ever-expanding arsenal of surgical tools so that more resources could be allocated to community outreach. This led to a pitched battle at about the time Sally joined the Board of Directors. She brought no special expertise so both sides may have felt they could recruit her to their cause. Sally voted for expanded community activities to speed victims into surgery – not a glitzier operating theatre – and earned Schwarzherz's enmity for life.

The most serious 'honor' crime is honor killing. The family believes that the stain on their honor can only be cleansed by removing the offending woman – guilty of some real or imagined amorous misdeed – from the face of the earth. Estimates of annual deaths range from five to twenty-two thousand women and girls.

The underlying motivation for 'honor' justified acid attacks is different. Fear of sexual inadequacy and infidelity usually figures in. Here are examples of women who came to Sally's clinic:

- A man seemed to be showing interest in a young Iraqi woman who already had a steady boyfriend. Easy fix: the boyfriend made her unattractive – to the point of revolting – with a splash of acid in the face.
- A Bosnian woman declined an older man's advances and offer of marriage. He made sure she won't get further offers.
- There were several cases of women who were attacked purely out of sibling rivalry. A woman feared that her fiancé was attracted to her younger, and prettier, sister. The younger girl was falsely accused of some vague romantic impropriety, became disfigured, and no longer a rival.
- Sadly, a mother appears to have been an instigator. She suspected her daughter might have engaged in pre-marital sex.

At a minimum the girl seemed to be enjoying life way too much. The older woman was threatened by this behavior and encouraged the men in the family to make a cautionary example of her own daughter.

The list of trivial and tragic reasons recounted by the victims – those that survive – is endless.

Sally's clinic has not dealt with honor killings because the victims they receive are disfigured, but alive. When four died, clinic staff asked: had the victims' attackers decided that the sentence had been unjustifiably commuted through reconstructive surgery, and a stiffer punishment had to be imposed? Was the clinic only patching up acid-attack victims for their execution?

For me, that doesn't compute. An 'honor' *killing* is usually a family decision, sometimes carried out by a minor who will receive a lighter prison sentence. A perverted sense of honor may actually figure in somewhere. The honor-justified *acid attack* is more often the work of an individual: a rejected suitor, a jealous husband, a cuckold. It's rash, impulsive. Here feelings of sexual inadequacy figure large. A follow-up fatal attack, conducted on foreign soil? It doesn't fit.

Sally tries to maintain her usual schedule at the clinic, but she really can't. She hasn't mentioned her diagnosis for fear that it would be interpreted as trolling for a donor, and she feels her problems pale compared to those of the women who are brought for treatment and surgery. I think she's wrong.

Right now it falls to me to monitor goings-on at the clinic and report them to my wife. After the ring belonging to the Iraqi girl was identified by Hanan and Sally, FedPol closed the clinic for two days last week while they rooted around in filing cabinets and interrogated staff. Captain Méchant, Sally's lubricious 'weasel', supervised the rooting. Schwarzherz distinguished himself with rabid ravings about patient confidentiality.

Sally was spared the inquisition, presumably because they'd met with her twice before. Not so Hanan, who was taken down to the FedPol station in Geneva to make a formal statement. She's the only Arab on the staff and Sally's convinced that's the reason the pigs focused on her, despite the fact that Hanan is the staff member who's been trying the hardest to get someone to pay attention to the deaths and disappearance of bodies.

Hoo boy! I just read what I've written. I didn't mean for it to be that formal – or windy. Sorry, folks. I guess that's how a man tries to get some distance from the awfulness that life has become. Maybe my writing will settle down later, if Sally needs me to fill in again.

A last quick word on her: Is she in denial? It's obvious that I'm skating back and forth across that boundary. Trying to step back and gain some perspective: I don't feel we're doing everything we can. I wonder if she's even put her name on a list for a donated liver. She said she was going to fill out the paperwork but I haven't heard anything more from her about it.

She'll squawk and drag her feet, but damn it, we have to be more proactive. Ignoring cancer is not a winning strategy.

From Max Brown's notes on Kohlberg's Stages of Moral Development

Stage 2. What's in it for me? The second level of moral reasoning is expressed in self-interest, with little regard for the needs of others.

Concern for the opinion of others is not based on morality or respect, but on an assessment of what others can do for you.

"You scratch my back and I'll scratch yours."

Is that Schwarzherz? I don't know him well enough to say for sure, but . . .

I hadn't thought about it before, but this reciprocity is the Golden Rule - 'do unto others as you would have them do unto you.' It shows up in every major religion; for example, you find it dozens of times in Islamic writings (Koran, Hadiths), usually along the lines of 'love others as you would be loved.'

Interesting. This ubiquitous religious basis for morality comes in at a primitive level in Kohlberg's system.

Daily Journal

Sally Taylor-Brown

2 February
Seattle

This trip has been a waste of time. Max won't listen to reason or anything the doctors are telling us. We went to Mayo in Minnesota and heard exactly the same story we heard in Geneva. Max was angry with the people we met and all but accused them of being quacks. His parting words at Mayo: "If it were your wife, you'd be taking this all more seriously!"

Today we were able to meet with a respected oncologist at the Fred Hutchinson Cancer Research Center. Tomorrow we'll go back after he's had a chance to look over my file. Meanwhile Max is stalking around our hotel room, smacking his fist into his palm and muttering that, at last, we're getting somewhere. I hardly recognize this behavior.

4 February
SeaTac Airport

Same story from Hutchinson: keep doing what I've been doing and get on a donor recipient list – which I am – while the disease is still in this early stage. Max thinks there are some alternative-medicine therapies practiced in India and China. I found him on Expedia looking at flight schedules to the Far East.

7 February
Geneva

I'm so upset I don't know how to write this. Hanan has been "taken into custody," but that's not even the worst of it. A sweet, once pretty, Bangladeshi woman arrived at the clinic just as Max and I set off on our fruitless tour of cancer treatment centers. Gisele said the surgery went well and was not that extensive. When the woman didn't appear for her routine follow-up appointment Hanan went to the apartment. The scene must have been revolting. The woman was dead, and everything was missing from her torso. Stomach, lungs, other organs. Gisele said it was like someone had used a huge ice cream scoop to disembowel the poor woman. I didn't witness the death scene and, still, the image is indelibly etched in my mind.

Max and I went down to post bail for Hanan or do whatever we could. We asked to see that weaselly lecher, Méchant. The idea is nauseating but I thought some eye-batting might get him interested in Hanan's case. The weasel was "unavailable." Maybe I would have gotten further if I'd gone without Max.

No bail. No hearing has been set. We were allowed to see Hanan for a few minutes. She's frightened out of her wits. First, she was the one to discover the body, and now this?

I asked Schwarzherz to pull whatever strings he has to get Hanan released. He shrugged.

9 February
Basel

Max vociferously disagrees with what I'm doing so it can't be completely wrong.

Gisele made photocopies of all the info in the dead Bangladeshi woman's file. This afternoon we went to the address the woman had listed as an emergency contact. The area is the Muslim ghetto in Basel and I expected the shop signs would be in Arabic. They're all in Bosnian or Turkish or Chechen, or some language like that.

There was no one at the "contact persons" apartment although it might have been occupied recently since the heat and electricity were still turned on. A woman across the hall let us into the apartment. Gisele flashed her clinic employee ID as if it meant anything and we were in.

But not for long. We'd just started looking around when a big bearded man stormed in, shouting at us in fractured German

(Gisele's opinion; I wouldn't know). Gisele told him who we are and he seemed even madder. We left since I was getting worried we might be attacked. Gisele explained that the man was threatening us not to interfere in things that don't concern outsiders.

We didn't really have a chance to investigate. What was I expecting? Bags in the refrigerator filled with body parts?

10 February
Geneva

I had to put my foot down. Max has completely taken over my medical care. This morning he announced that we would be leaving Friday for Delhi where there's a doctor who has "discovered an exciting herbal therapy."

When I told him absolutely not he got red and stormed out. Then he came back, damp eyed, and asked my forgiveness. He's more desperate than I am to solve this problem.

I'm already on one experimental treatment, the pills that might slow down the progression of the disease. One experiment is enough. Max says, no, "We have to throw the kitchen sink at this thing."

Max, you seem oblivious to the strong hints I drop so let me put it in writing. I am trying to tell you the following:

I am still Sally, your loving but currently exasperated wife. I am not cancer victim #123. I am the woman whom you've slept beside for 25 years. Who bore our daughters. I understand that, right now, you can't watch me in the morning with that same old poorly disguised expression of lechery on your face – your trademark – as I rush to the bathroom. But, goddamn it, Max! I won't let a fistful of unruly cells define me and neither will you!

12 February
Geneva

Major news! Last night someone broke into the clinic and made
a mess. It looks like several patient files are missing. An upset-
ting scene for the cleaning woman who comes in early. Chairs
thrown around, file cabinet drawers pulled out onto the floor,
Schwarzherz's cabinet of precious tools tipped over – some of
them missing, the surgical lights smashed, the operating couch
slashed.

At least they can't blame it on Hanan. They still have her locked
up.

Great news! Gisele just called to say that Hanan is being released.

Wow. Just think how lousy everything must be if I label the release of an innocent person as "Great news."

13 February
Geneva

Gisele confirmed that the missing files include those of the four
women who died. Three other sets of files were taken. Gisele is
trying to get the addresses of those three women. We need to
find out if they're okay.

Driving home from the clinic someone tried to run me off the
road in an old Peugeot. It looked like a large guy with a beard.
Am I getting too jumpy? Could just be a bad driver, and beards
are pretty common around here. As are bad drivers. But it
seemed intentional.

Valentine's Day
Geneva

Sweet Max brought me breakfast in bed – a heart shaped Whitman's Sampler and a bowl of yoghurt. His dislike of big Swiss
companies means he won't allow any of their yummy choco-
lates into the house. Whitman's is okay, of course.

I don't have anything for him. Amazing how your priorities change. Not too long ago my biggest concern was whether I should continue using a rinse to keep some red in my hair and the grey at bay. This is the first time I've thought about that since January 22nd.

From Max Brown's notes on Kohlberg's Stages of Moral Development

Stage 3. Conformity to the expectations of society and others. The third level of moral reasoning is based on a person's eagerness to be seen as a good person - one who fulfills his obligations.

In the immediate case there is the social contract among people with whom there is a close family or working relationship. "I owe it to my wife/father/mother/children/etc. to behave in an expected manner." Further out in the concentric social circles the standards of conduct are set by generally accepted social norms. The approval of others is the incentive.

"See? I'm doing my duty to my family /neighbors/society."

Maybe some role plays with the students to spark discussion about the differences among the levels?

This is insane. My wife is dying before my eyes. How can any of this matter?

Max speaking

Sally's leaving too much out. (She says she's happy to have me add to the running narrative, but she really wants this to be her writing project; I'll keep my inputs to a minimum.) The clinic break-in isn't just about files, although that's an unnerving part of it. The operating theatre was trashed. Schwarzherz says they'll be out of commission for several weeks, much of that due to foot-dragging by the insurance company. And there was a threatening passage from the Koran spray-painted on the wall of the waiting room. "Where ye are, death will find you, even if ye are in Towers." Hanan was reluctant to translate it for us.

Captain Méchant, the FedPol a-hole, (should I condense that to FedHole?) seemed openly pleased; he ran a hand through his outsized grey bouffant and smiled as he digested each revelation. Cementing my dislike of the man, he taps his fingertips together in front of his chest before speaking, the universal signal that the Most Important Person in the Room is about to render a Pronouncement of Great Consequence.

It looks like someone is trying to shut down the clinic and make sure Muslims are blamed. It seems too pat. Everyone knows that quotation from the Koran; it was widely referred to when the twin towers came down on 9/11. And Hanan said the Arabic letters were poorly formed. Islamophobia is depressingly widespread in Switzerland and Muslims are easy targets.

Aside from that – and I won't pose as a forensic expert – the door to the clinic didn't look like it had been forced. Whoever broke in was practiced at picking locks, or had a key. My suspicion usually goes straight to Schwarzherz, but not in this case. He loves his surgical toys too much to harm them.

One more thing about the break-in: Gisele says the petty cash box is gone, in addition to the files and some surgical instruments. Who puts a clinic out of operation, writes a threatening religious message, and steals a few francs on the way out? The last part seems more in the character of a young punk, perhaps hired and given a key.

On another front, I checked to see if Sally's name is on the European Liver Transplant Registry. They wouldn't tell me how many are ahead of her on the list. I stressed that she's in a very early stage and her prognosis is better than most – *if* she gets a healthy liver ASAP. They still need her signature on some forms that they're faxing to the clinic. If she balks, I'll just forge her name. She seems – I don't know – not resigned or fatalistic, but just not as engaged with this disease as a person should be. Her parents didn't live long and she's assumed she would also have a comparatively short run. She's fourteen years younger than I and we've both assumed (without talking about it) that we'll check out at about the same time. A sweet thought until checkout time draws nearer.

Daily Journal

Sally Taylor-Brown

15 February
Geneva

We (Hanan, actually) contacted our community outreach workers in Jordan and they went to the homes of the three women whose files have been taken. The outreach workers were told that all three women were back home, but they weren't able to see them. Vague reasons were given such as "at the market" and "resting." Should we believe the three women are okay?

16 February
Geneva

Gisele is a bulldog. She got on the phone to all of the Muslim cemetery registries. The name of one of those three women – the ones whose files are missing – is on the registry for the cemetery in Zurich. The date of interment is ten days after she had her last appointment at our clinic. I'd like to get a look at that body (not actually, but you know what I mean).

I called the FedHoles (thanks, Max – I like it) to report the Zurich burial. Whoever I was talking to thanked me for my trouble, but said that so many Arabs use the same names it is surely just a coincidence. What bullshit. Arabs have a long string of names that includes their father, their father's father, their family or tribe, and their given name. Hanan told me her full name is Hanan bint (daughter of) Omar ibn (son of) Khalid al-Tafile. Not a whole lot of people have that name. But the FedHoles! Eager to pin something on a Muslim. Less interested in them as murder victims.

Tomorrow Hanan will call one of our Jordanian community outreach workers again and see if she can find anything more about the woman who is both "at home" in Zarqa and buried near Zurich.

17 February
Geneva

Bad day. Puking constantly.

Max again

The drug to hold the cancer at bay (sorafenib) is making Sally sick. That's what the oncologist says. There's no doubt in the good doctor's mind what to do: keep taking the tablets – up the dosage if indicated. Docs are all the same: mildly interested in finding the cure, indifferent to patient comfort.

I may need to do more of the writing. Sally's so focused on the deaths of the acid-attack victims she barely has the time or energy to tell me what's going on, much less write about it. She drags herself to the clinic. Drags herself home. Collapses. Sleeps 10 – 12 hours. Repeat.

Plus, Fearless Sally's one of those people who's intimidated by the sight of an empty page.

Updates:

19 February. The woman who's moldering in the Muslim cemetery in Zurich, while also enjoying a family reunion in Zarqa, may be doing neither.

I caught an early train to Zurich and went to the cemetery. The custodian took me out to the gravesite, but he acknowledged it didn't look like anyone had been planted there. Undisturbed grass and weeds signaled no digging had been done for several months, well before the woman's reported burial. On the other hand, the marker looked new and consistent with the burial date in the registry. Who would buy a burial plot and headstone, and not use it? Someone crafty? Or stupid.

Gisele said the Jordanian outreach worker reported in and the family in Zarqa continues to stonewall about the woman. A neighbor, when asked, said she'd seen no sign of the woman since before the acid attack.

Where did she go? Thin air? More charred remains waiting to be discovered in the woods?

20 February. Expecting that it would be a waste of time, I went to the FedHole station to report my findings, afraid I'd be inter-

cepted by Captain Méchant. We keep hoping we'll stumble onto the one conscientious officer who'll take these disappearances seriously. Agent Henri Verteux may be the cop we've been looking for.

The desk officer half-listened to my report and announced, with a smirk, that Agent Verteux was just the person for the case. He led me to a remote corner of the building and, with a muttered introduction, waved me into an immaculate office.

Henri doesn't fit in; the antithesis of the rumpled TV cop. His desk was clean, books were placed vertically on two shelves, his trench coat was carefully suspended on a hanger, and his posture was military. I wondered if he had anything to do other than keep his pencils sharpened (a half-dozen sharpened yellow pencils stood at attention in a clear-plastic holder).

Henri made notes, looked at the pictures I'd taken of the gravesite and asked that I forward copies to him. He wasn't optimistic about finding someone who may simply be in hiding or has been killed in another country. Nevertheless, he did start a file.

Can you believe it? Except for the burned and disemboweled women, there were no active case files on the other disappearances. And these are anal-retentive Swiss. They have files for everything!

21 February. It looks like I'll be the one to maintain the written record a while longer. Sally underwent the first radiation treatment this morning at the Hôpitaux Universitaires de Genève, a sprawling complex of grey concrete and glass, ironically acronymed HUG. She'll stay there two nights while she rides out the worst of the side effects.

I can't stand to see her like this. Aside from a few scrapes she's always seemed invincible. Now she's the one in trouble.

22 February. Sally seems more comfortable this morning. I tried to decipher her medical record, especially the meds. We always suspect hospital staff will dope a patient to the gills just to keep

them quiet. My interest in Sally's paperwork was ill seen. An officious nurse didn't know how to take it away from me, but later, when I came back from the loo, the record was no longer in the box at the foot of Sally's bed.

Since Sally's asleep most of the time I dropped in on Agent Henri to ask about developments. He said he couldn't discuss the details of an active investigation with the general public, but he glanced around as he said it. When I was sure no one was within earshot I ventured that the public, especially the large foreign contingent, had shown inadequate appreciation of the work of the security forces. I would be honored to buy him a beer after work. He accepted, but couldn't meet until the following evening. So far, so good. It seems significant he's accepted my invitation; he doesn't look like the kind of guy who needs a free beer and awkward conversation with an aging ex-professor.

23 February. Brought Sally home this morning. She was still groggy, but not nauseous. She's wondering if she'll lose her hair. We'd failed to ask.

When I told her about my brief encounter with Henri and the scheduled rendezvous she snapped to full alertness. And of course she insists on accompanying me. Not gonna happen, babe.

Meeting with Agent Henri. A slow, casual start. Chitchat about family; he has a girl friend (11 years) and vacillates between marriage and trial separation. I get the impression he thinks he should be sowing a few more wild oats before settling down. Would strait-laced Henri know how?

Midway into the third beer I opened the subject I assumed we both wanted to discuss. I'll try to recreate the dialogue. Not the exact words – we spoke in French – but the gist:

"Agent, we're very concerned about the young women who've disappeared and, in at least two cases have been murdered. The clinic is the one factor that connects these women. Perhaps you and I can share our thoughts and information."

Agent Henri's brow furrowed; he drank slowly. Perhaps he was deciding how much to divulge. I knew if I could get him started he'd spill the beans. Why else would he be here? I tried another angle.

"Something that's been troubling me, Agent, is the absence of any other connecting factors. The women are from different countries, their emergency contacts in Switzerland are in different cities, and their prognosis varies a great deal. But after they leave the clinic, within a few days or weeks they're dead or disappeared."

That did it. Dangle a crime puzzle in front of a young detective long enough and he'll eventually take the bait.

"Well, it is not an easy case. We have done the obvious. The airlines confirm that none of the bodies were shipped back to their homeland. They also confirm that the three women whose files are missing did not travel as passengers. Of course, now we suspect that one of them may be deceased – the girl from Zarqa. The easy conclusion? The women never left Europe.

"What happened to them?" He was growing expansive and leaned back. "Well, it is possible that those whose bodies have not been found are hiding. They were attacked once. Perhaps they fear they will be attacked again. Or, they may have been murdered by the same man or men who attacked them before. We do not think they are being trafficked for sex – for obvious reasons. That leads us to a dead end. What other purpose could be served?"

"Organ harvesting," I blurted.

"Ah, you are thinking of that unfortunate whose insides were removed."

No. I've been thinking about organs for a different reason.

"Our experts tell us that was too crude a procedure. Some valuable organs were not completely removed. Others may have been damaged. There is a black-market in organ sales – it's called a 'red-market' – but that is dominated by imports smuggled from Asia and Africa. Still, I suppose we must not rule out the possibility. Just because a crime is poorly committed does not mean it is not a crime."

He finished his beer and looked around for the waitress, probably to ask for the check. I wasn't getting what I wanted.

"Agent, you employ the first-person plural when describing the efforts of FedPol. I'm going to take a guess here and that is, you're working pretty much on your own."

He settled back in the chair and ran a hand through his short blond hair. "Not only alone, but unofficially. I have some latitude to spend my free time on an unassigned case. I feel it is my duty to investigate crime, whether or not others are equally interested." He drained his mug and looked like he regretted he'd said that. I wonder how much "latitude" he really has. I suspect he has plenty of free time.

He seemed, again, about to leave.

"I would be honored to assist you in any way I can." Henri looked uneasy. "I have a personal interest that you're unaware of." I described Sally's situation, our lack of success in finding a transplant donor on our own, and the uncertainty about her rising to the top of the Registry in time to save her life.

Henri digested this for a minute. Then he did signal the waitress, but to order two more beers.

"I am so sorry to hear that. You and your wife have my deepest sympathy. But you understand that FedPol cannot assist you in any endeavor to obtain an organ outside the normal channels. The regulations are clear."

I had left that implication hanging.

"No, that's not why I wanted to talk. Our interest is personal on many levels, one of which is we're starting to appreciate the desperation that fuels this market in human body parts. We'd like to help."

"I don't see how you can? You are foreigners without the resources of a professional police force."

"A sting operation."

He looked perplexed.

"Henri, we may have enough elements to put together a credible sting. First, we need to broadcast that I'm prepared to pay handsomely for a liver. Then I think we can assume that the people involved have been able to stay in business because they have connections and means." Henri nodded agreement. "They might be able to determine whether Sally's name is on the Registry or find a record of her radiation treatment. You see, Sally provides credibility to the sting that FedPol doesn't have unless your superiors decide to make a major investment in this case. I gather they don't."

Agent Henri put down his beer, perhaps in the hope that a pause in drinking would restore clarity of thought. The prospect of an off-the-clock scheme to entrap organ vendors – and perhaps murderers – was a lot for the young cop to digest and he started to meander.

"I don't know . . . I can't even consider . . . I said I had latitude but if I participated in such a plan . . ."

I broke in to help him out. "I know, Henri. I'm not looking for an answer tonight. I wanted to alert you to the possibility and to assure you that there are some people who support what you're doing and are deeply grateful."

He relaxed. We contested the bill, I paid, and hurried home to brief Sally.

From Max Brown's notes on Kohlberg's Stages of Moral Development

Stage 4. Law and order. Moral reasoning in stage four goes beyond the need for individual approval that is central to the reasoning employed in stage three. Rules, laws, and norms prescribe what is right and wrong. If one person violates a law, then everyone will; thus there is an obligation and a duty to uphold laws and rules. When someone does violate a law, it is morally unacceptable. Kohlberg's testing found that most people remain at stage four where morality is predominantly dictated by acceptance of the rules of the society.

Is this particularly strong in Swiss society? Would Henri let me write a teaching case about him and FedPol? Disguised, of course.

Daily Journal

Sally Taylor-Brown

24 February
Geneva

My boy, Max. Either idling in neutral at the curb, or tearing around the racetrack. I wish he'd discussed the sting thing with me. I approve, of course, but it seems like he's still treating me as less than I am. If you're reading this, Studly, back up a few pages and reread that bit about not treating me like I'm only a cancer case.

Men can be so pigheaded.

25 February
Geneva

Agent Henri called the house a few minutes ago. Max is out, but I was able to convince the cop that I spoke for both of us. I suspect Henri might have refused if I weren't a "cancer victim" who needs to be handled with kid gloves. What the hell. Why not use my "special status" when it suits me? There aren't many upsides to cancer.

Despite all his roundabout disclaimers, backpedaling, cautions and caveats, I gather that Henri is in. He doesn't want to meet in the station or any place we might all be seen together. I suggested our apartment. He agreed. Now I'll have to clean up. Apparently neatnik Henri's standards are higher than ours. Housekeeping has been low priority lately.

26 February
Geneva

Max tried writing down a conversation (pretty well, I thought), so, here goes. This, as best as I can recreate it, is the conversation we had with Henri this evening. His English is good and I don't think I'm correcting anything.

Max and me: Welcomes, offer of coffee or stronger, usual apologies for the mess. Although I'd busted my buns cleaning up. Max watched. Perhaps that's part of his attempt to treat me like the old Sally? Okay, he did vacuum a little.

Henri: "No coffee, thank you. Your apartment is lovely."

I suppose it is. I can't see it for the other thoughts clouding my vision.

Henri: "This is all very unusual, and without precedent for me. I'm only here because our office has not taken adequate interest in what may be a very serious crime. Or crimes. However, I need to warn you that if my involvement is suspected by my colleagues, I may have to withdraw. We are encouraged to follow up leads on our own, but if there is suspicion of a serious crime we must inform our superiors so that all the resources of FedPol can be employed. It is often difficult to know where the line is. Although the disappearance of several women seems to go beyond 'suspicion' of a crime."

Max: "We understand and appreciate the position you've put yourself in. We assume you feel as strongly as we do about the killing of innocent women who've already suffered a great deal."

Me: "Since I work at the clinic, Agent, I've met these women and feel a personal connection. Your help is especially important to me."

Then I screwed up. I placed a friendly hand on his arm to emphasize my gratitude. He flinched and recoiled slightly. Jesus Christ! I'm a leper! Henri was obviously embarrassed, but the damage had been done.

Unflappable Max to the rescue: "But tell us, Henri. Any new leads since yesterday?"

Henri was still recovering from the arm touch *faux pas*. His filters – as Max would say – were out of service and he spoke rapidly. "Yes, of course. I was able to find a few things. Maybe there is a pattern. I have focused on the seven women whose files were taken. Their contacts were all in or near Fribourg which is unfortunate as the Fribourg Cantonal Police do not co-operate easily with FedPol. As you know, our cantons often place their autonomy above the national good." At this point Henri requested a beer. He sipped the foam off – rather daintily – before resuming.

"I have one friend on the force in Fribourg and he visited the addresses your administrator gave us as emergency contacts. In four cases neighbors said the contact person – always a man – was remembered by neighbors but had not been seen for some time. The neighbors could not specify a date when the contact person moved out, but, in general, it seems to have been around the time your clinic records show the woman was operated on. The other three? My friend isn't sure they even existed." He picked up the beer, inspected it (for what, pray tell, Agent Ver-teux?) and deciding it was okay, raised it to his lips.

Max and I, together, raised our eyebrows to signal interest – which was genuine – so Henri put the beer back down and con-tinued. "Passport control says two of the four men your clinic listed as contacts left the country on international flights. I have asked the airlines for the destination of those two and whether they were accompanied. The others may still be in Switzerland, or simply left by land and then took a flight from another coun-try. I cannot ask German or French immigration control for in-formation. That request would have to be official and come from the office director."

I was letting Max take the lead with Henri: "It seems, Henri, that the trail of the seven disappeared women has gone cold. No bodies. The only known contacts have left Switzerland or dis-appeared themselves." Henri nodded agreement. "That takes us back to our conversation of a couple of days ago. The clinic will be closed for repairs until late March. No more acid-attack vic-tims to shadow until then. We do, however, have the sting op-tion. Sally's in agreement. If you had good contacts in the Mus-lim community you could let it be known that a wealthy foreigner desperately needs a liver donor. Blood type AB negative."

Notice the choice of words? ". . . *if* you had good contacts . . ." Clever Max put Henri on the defensive. Henri had to demonstrate he was a full-fledged cop, with informants.

He took the bait: "Well, of course I have such contacts. But they are the imams and community leaders that help us identify potential terrorists. They are not men who would be involved in killings and organ sales."

Max: "No, they wouldn't. But even good people like to pass on interesting news when the conversation lags. They will tell their friends, with a disapproving headshake, about the offer of money for a liver. The friends may be more or less ethical, but equally talkative. Soon the offer will be widely disseminated. Of course, we're assuming organ harvesting is involved somewhere. That could be wrong, but for the moment it seems one avenue to pursue."

Henri: "Since the men involved in the previous disappearances left Switzerland, we can then assume there is someone who remains here and is the coordinator, or mastermind." He said this triumphantly, although it seemed a pretty obvious conclusion to me – and only accounted for two of the seven contacts. Max rewarded him with an approving smile. Agent Henri took this as a signal for celebration and, finally, sipped at his beer.

Henri has been doing his homework and was eager to share. He told us a viable liver on the "red market" will bring as much as $157,000. That's enough money, he thinks, to support a stable organization of corrupt surgeons and donor-finders. He emphasized surgeons plural. "Normally four specialists are needed for a transplant. Simple removal, of course, can be done by one general surgeon – if the survival of the donor is not important."

I'd heard enough but show-and-tell wasn't over. Max hadn't warned me Agent Verteux was such a pedant. "The red market operates on the standard business model; keep costs down and revenues up. Since it is, by necessity, an unregulated market, the selling price is set by demand. Where these butchers can increase their profits is at the point of supply. A few of them buy kidneys from desperate and ignorant people in the third world; some have arrangements with coroners and mortuaries to swoop in and grab whatever is viable; but the truly dangerous ones simply steal organs from the unwilling or unsuspecting, killing the poor person in the process. You see? The big money is finding a source of free organs."

We saw. Is our clinic a source of free organs?

I haven't wanted to become too immersed in the details of the operation – just wake up with a new liver and a bluebird singing on the windowsill. But Henri wasn't finished. "In Europe alone there are more than 4,000 people waiting for a liver transplant. The average waiting time is three and a half years."

C'mon, Henri. I definitely don't need to hear those numbers. Time to change the topic. Max to the rescue. "Impressive knowledge, Henri. Let's hope Sally's progress up the list will be more rapid."

Henri reddened. He realized he'd been showing off – and insensitive. "Of course," he mumbled, "every case is different. The wife of a FedPol officer required a liver transplant recently and now she seems to be fine." We both looked at the cop hopefully. Was there a shortcut? "I do not know the details, but I am certain no laws were broken." No shortcut. Although Henri didn't look certain.

Me: "Max, there's one other place to dangle this bait of an easy sale." I think Max wanted to follow up on the 'no laws broken' angle, but turned toward me.

"Schwarzherz."

Crap! I can't write any more. Feel I'm going to barf.

Max again

Sally's back in the hospital. Was it the house cleaning? This is not the time for us to be playing cops and robbers.

It's February 27, 3:20 PM. Sally's been here for four hours. I brought her over when she was nauseous and weak to the point of falling down. No sign of the oncologist, but an internist made a cameo and decreed the cause was the sorafenib. Is he sure? These are also symptoms of hepatocellular cancer on the move. But Sally doesn't exhibit some of the other major symptoms. Her skin is no longer yellowish.

Same day, 8:15 PM, back at home. At Sally's insistence she left the hospital Against Medical Advice. Before we were able to fight our way free – it took two hours – it was made clear there's no graver sin in the world of medicine than to self-discharge.

She's stronger tonight, but at least stays in bed and, grudgingly, allows me to hold her arm when she gets out.

While at the hospital I called the Registry to see if there was any movement up the list. "We will inform you, sir," was the icy answer. I argued that advance warning is needed to schedule the surgery. No dice. The woman was obdurate. They shouldn't have someone so unfeeling in that job.

Same day, 10:20 PM. Sally's asleep. I sit by the bed watching her.

I can't bring my emotions under control. Weepy Max. God damn it, this is so wrong!

I wish I was stronger. She deserves better.

Daily Journal

Sally Taylor-Brown

1 March
Geneva

What would we do without Gisele and Hanan? They're bricks! I told them about my situation and they thanked me for sharing my problem with them. They said they had been aware that I was not 100 percent. I told them about the sting operation and how I wanted to put out the word through Schwarzherz. Of course Gisele thinks no better of the director than I do. Hanan keeps her thoughts to herself.

Phone call from Gisele. Schwarzherz came by the clinic at noon to see how repairs are coming. Gisele briefed him on my cancer and told him, "The husband is going crazy and it's said he'll even pay someone for a viable liver." I was eager to know how Schwarzherz reacted. According to Gisele he only said, "That is not legal" and his expression didn't change much. Can we read anything into that?

Hanan is going to put the story out among her contacts in the Muslim community, but she's pretty integrated into Swiss society; she may have few Muslim friends. Wise for her, given the hostility.

2 March
Geneva

Agent Henri called to say that he'd planted the organ purchase story. He was almost whispering so he must have been calling from his desk. Is he going to get cold feet at a critical point? He is kind of a wuss, for a cop.

4 March
Geneva

Oh my God! This is a problem we hadn't counted on. Max received four (4!!!) telephone calls from men peddling livers. The telephone numbers were all blocked. That response seems too fast. And how do we know if one them is involved in the deaths of our women?

The calls were pretty similar. The callers wanted to confirm that Max was serious. Only one caller discussed price – around $80,000 – but they all said the transaction would go quickly and only cash would be accepted. All said they'd be back in touch very soon after they'd lined up a donor; we should get our financial ducks in a row.

It's evening now and Henri came by so we could talk. Max actually has done some picking up around the place. Henri isn't surprised by the response we've received. He doubts any of the offers are more than scams. He says that Max will be asked to make a large earnest-money payment – in cash – and we'll never hear from the vendor again.

Max has a recording feature on his phone that he'll use for all future calls from blocked numbers.

Henri made an interesting point. We should have thought of it ourselves. Did any of the callers mention what happens after the liver is delivered (could I work that into a pun?)? Let's say we have a fresh organ in a beer cooler. How does it get inside me? The Hôpitaux Universitaires wouldn't be receptive. I'm on their shit list anyway. We need not only a corrupt organ vendor; we would also need a corrupt surgeon, or team of surgeons according to Henri.

6 March
Geneva

Pay dirt? There have been two more calls from organ peddlers. One of them was the usual quick inquiry and a high-pressure pitch to lay down money. "These livers go fast. Pity if someone died because they didn't act in time." Not exactly those words, but that's the general idea.

The other caller said he had nothing available at the moment, but expected a healthy liver in late March or early April if we'd still be interested. By a wonderful coincidence late March is when the clinic is scheduled to re-open. Max thought the caller was a native Swiss-French speaker. Or someone who's lived in this part of Switzerland for a long time. And here's the good part: The caller wanted to know how we're fixed for a team of surgeons and a facility to perform the transplant. Sounds like he has it all.

Max clarifies

Sally's dislike for Schwarzherz may be influencing how she interprets the 'pay dirt' call.

I immediately informed Henri – we're careful to keep him involved – and during our conversation he said that one of the distinguishing features of bogus calls was the promise, or implication, to provide an organ immediately. Or to fail to inform the purchaser that the organ wouldn't be available for a while. In his view, the caller who spoke of delivery in a few weeks may be the first genuine inquiry we've had.

The question about whether we had a surgeon on standby? Henri says that might be a simple attempt to sell a package deal or it might be someone who's testing the genuineness of the buyer. He says the European press corps is bursting with eager journalists, all looking for an exposé and constantly trolling for a juicy story. A journalist, baiting the hook, might not have thought through all aspects of the crime and would stumble if asked any details.

Thinking back, I don't believe I handled that very well since I hadn't thought through all aspects. In the future I'll be prepared to answer, 'yes, we do have the transplant procedure covered, but cannot, for obvious reasons, divulge the details.'

One more point: The 'pay dirt' caller was the first to ask about blood type.

I didn't tell Henri, but if a package deal came along – liver and transplant in a good facility – I'd be for it. Sally probably wouldn't.

Daily Journal

Sally Taylor-Brown

7 March
Geneva

I asked Gisele what's happening to the women who need reconstructive surgery while we're closed. It's her understanding that most of them are going to the Jordan Hospital in Amman. That's probably where many of them should have been going all along. Gisele thinks Schwarzherz is uneasy about this and is haranguing the medical supplies guys to get our clinic back into operation. They're waiting on the insurance company.

At Max's urging we're going to look into the availability of corrupt surgeons. Not sure what this gets us, but Max needs to be doing something, even if it isn't a high percentage play.

8 March
Lausanne

An eventful day. Two things worth writing down:

1. That internist at HUG called in a prescription to help minimize the side effects of the sorafenib. Felt better within an hour.

2. With my restored vigor, Max let me accompany him to a clinic in Lausanne that Agent Henri said had been suspected of borderline medical practice. He didn't know details but guessed it was about prescribing the wrong stuff and performing unnecessary procedures. Max only let me out of the house, I'm sure, to lend credibility to our story about needing a transplant.

The clinic looked like any other from the outside. And the inside too. As expected, the receptionist wouldn't let us talk to the physician without an appointment. Max wheeled and cajoled to the point where I thought he was going to win her over. He's one of those depressing men who get *better* looking as they grow older while us, their wives, get steadily worse looking. So unfair.

That's off the point. The receptionist held firm but a glance at the sign-in sheet revealed the doctor had been seeing patients since 8:00 AM. It was already four in the afternoon so we left and went around to the parking area. There was a beautifully maintained vintage Jaguar XJ12 with an MD sticker on the back. Those are remnants of the days when doctors would make house calls and the sticker protected them from tickets if they had to park illegally.

 A little after 5:00 the doctor came out and we pounced. I'll try to reproduce the dialogue again.

Max (his French is much better than mine): "Dr. Levy. Pardon for ambushing you like this but it's an urgent matter." Levy couldn't have appeared more annoyed. I think he was looking around for someone to help him, perhaps a cop. But my boy isn't deterred easily. "My wife and I have had some bad fortune, and some comparatively good fortune."

Dr. Levy: "Congratulations on your good fortune; condolences for the bad. As you can see, I am in a hurry and you should make an appointment if this is a medical matter." He fished out his car keys.

Max: "Then I'll be brief. My wife has cancer of the liver. Still in stage 1, maybe early stage 2." I looked at the ground. I don't like to hear my condition talked about in public. "We believe a generous family member will soon be a liver donor. She has a severe cardiac condition and is failing daily. It's her dying request that her organs be used to extend the lives of others. Unfortunately the official transplant sites are linked to the European Registry. The rules are that any organ received goes into the general pool and is made available to those who have been on the list longest. Family wishes are not considered."

Levy: "If you are asking whether I will assist, two points: First, I respect the rules of all the organ registries. Second, I am not a transplant surgeon and have neither the training nor the facility to conduct such an operation." With that he turned toward his car, but fired a parting shot. "So you see, you have wasted your time coming here, and now you are wasting mine."

Me: "Do you know anyone?" I think I looked desperate, but that may have been because I needed another hit of the new drug.

Even a physician who deals with ill and dying people every day has trouble brushing off a desperate request.

Levy: "Look, I am not indifferent. Family should come before bureaucratic rules. I understand there are some who do work outside the registries. I will make a casual inquiry. If I learn anything I will leave the information at my reception to the attention of Mrs. Jones. You may start checking with the receptionist sometime next week. Now I really must go."

And he did, the fancy Jag shooting a small spray of gravel in our direction.

Max watched this showy departure, shaking his head with disapproval. "Curiouser and curiouser, Sal. He's ready to make a referral."

What does this all mean?

10 March
Geneva

Oh oh. Agent Henri is getting cold feet. When I reported on our conversation with Levy, Henri didn't seem to want to hear about it.

11 March
Geneva

More radiation therapy. Yuck.

Max

Pinch-hitting again while my soul mate sleeps off the after-glow of radiation.

11 March. I assumed Levy would have a name for us quickly – he didn't really need to ask around – so I called his clinic just after they rolled a drowsy Sally off to her room. An envelope for Mrs. Jones was waiting to be picked up.

Half an hour later I was at Levy's clinic where the receptionist was unwilling to relinquish the envelope; I was clearly not Mrs. Jones. She made a call to the back, after which she handed me the envelope. I tore it open in the car and a typed card fell out.

I didn't see this coming –

```
Dr. Emile Schwarzherz

Chemin de Blandonnet 8
1214 Vernier
Genève
```

That's Sally's clinic.

Daily Journal

Sally Taylor-Brown

13 March
Geneva

Schwarzherz! I wanted it to be him. But I really didn't want it to be him. Maybe it isn't. He might be only helping families carry out a dying request, like the scenario Max put to Dr. Levy. Or, maybe Levy is wrong and he gave us Schwarzherz's name by mistake.

Should I tell Gisele and Hanan? Max was reluctant to tell me but he knew he had to. There's one thing Gisele can check. What happened to the clinic's old OR equipment when Schwarzherz bought new? That's reason enough to let her in on this news.

14 March
Geneva

Gisele was even more shocked than me. She's always disliked Schwarzherz, but never thought he could be killing women for their organs. She recovered, however, to describe how she thinks it works.

"Don't you see how it all fits together, Sal? He doesn't bother to fix them up right in the first place because he knows they won't live long. He has all their medical info so it's easy for him to line up matches. Then, when everything is set, the woman will be asked to go to his 'other' clinic – conveniently equipped with our second-hand things. The woman won't resist. Schwarzherz probably tells her he's going to make a few improvements – they all need more work – and, presto, she's unconscious, and he's mining her body for everything they have an order for."

When she finished I felt sick, and it wasn't the meds.

15 March
Geneva

Henri. What should we tell him? Have to discuss with Max.

Later. Just finished another evening meeting with Agent Henri. We make less of an effort cleaning up each time. Hope Henri doesn't judge us by the mess we live in. The regular housekeeper is under the weather, right?

Henri thought that Gisele's description of how Schwarzherz might be involved is plausible. Gisele confirmed that our clinic's discarded OR equipment is always carted off by Schwarzherz. He says he's distributing it to needy clinics but he's never brought back any receipts.

Henri says it's all very interesting, but pointed out that what we have is pretty thin: an accusation by a corrupt informant. Henri says Levy is so tainted that we can't put much weight on something Levy says that casts another physician in a bad light.

Max asked if Henri could raid Schwarzherz's house and see if there is a small surgery there. Henri said he would need a court order and that meant going through the hierarchy in FedPol. He doubts Méchant would approve the request and that would be the end of his involvement. And career, we suspected. Max is pretty sure that Henri has exceeded his 'latitude,' probably due to pressure from us.

We talked about putting Schwarzherz under surveillance – Max, Gisele, Hanan and me rotating the shifts (Henri didn't volunteer) – but gave it up. Without any more women coming out of our clinic Schwarzherz wouldn't be doing anything and it would be exhausting for us. And he might spot us.

Max and I talked far into the night (Now I'm writing this the next day, but trying to put the right dates on events). It doesn't all fit together, no matter what Gisele says. There's the crude disemboweling of one woman. What's that all about? Someone else trying to get a piece of the action? Another inconsistent thing is the trashing of our clinic. That's putting Schwarzherz out of business for almost a month. Not something Schwarzherz would have arranged unless he contracted with some jerk to do the job and it went sideways. And Levy. When observant Max was picking up the 'Mrs. Jones' envelope he looked around the waiting room. Levy *does* have a certificate from the Swiss Medical Board to practice thoracic surgery. It's hanging proudly among the other certificates doctors love to decorate their walls with. He lied.

16 March
Saint-Cergues, France

You know how you realize that something's a bad idea and still, you go ahead with it? I mean, a *really* bad idea?

Max is not to blame. I was the one who wanted to scope out Schwarzherz's house. He lives just across the border in a French town, probably to keep his tax bill down. We were all invited to his house for a New Year's party two years ago, but I was brand new on the Board and didn't pay too much attention to the layout.

Max agreed to snoop around the director's house because he said if he didn't go with me, I'd just go by myself when he couldn't prevent it. That's what 25 years of marriage will do for you. Perfect predictability.

We waited until it was pitch dark and the only light in Schwarzherz's house was the flickering of a TV. He was probably dozing in front of it. Max parked down the street and we crept around to the back of the house. We assumed the most likely place for his surgery would be in the basement and in the back. There were three casement windows, but when we shined our flashlights through them we saw a laundry room, a storage room, and some (little used, I'm sure) exercise equipment.

What we didn't see were the detectors that were planted somewhere around us. First clue: a light went on inside, and then went off. Second clue: a robotic voice announcing our presence. Third clue: floodlights abruptly bathed the backyard in their sickly glow.

That was enough clues. We were sneaking around the corner, about to dash across the front lawn when the back door opened and Schwarzherz came out, a shotgun in his hands.

I don't think he got a good look at us. We ran toward a line of cedars and then to the street. Max is usually pretty steady, but it took him forever to get the key into the ignition. As we drove away we heard two shots, Schwarzherz blasting at shadows or just warnings. We won't do that again.

17 March
Geneva

Gisele APPROVES of our caper! Maybe that's why we get along so well. Neither of us has any common sense. She did scold me for our clumsy execution.

She says she's taken papers out to Schwarzherz's house and been in several rooms. She thinks that if there's anything there it would be upstairs, maybe in the attic. She doesn't think Schwarzherz would have a clinic that's not in his home because he's too cheap to pay for one, and a free-standing clinic's visibility and unusual hours would attract the attention of the congenitally snoopy Swiss.

But she finds it's odd that Schwarzherz has a gun, since permitting is a nightmare in France, and why he would blast away at shadows. She thinks he must be really nervous about something.

The Liver Registry called. Max almost wet himself with excitement when he saw the caller ID. They only wanted to know if we still needed an organ. Duh?

Then it hit us. A lot of time has passed. Many on the list are dead by this point. They were only checking that I'm still alive. Max is back in berserk mode.

I'm in berserk mode?

<u>18 March</u>. Sally underwent more radiation today. They've increased the frequency. The oncologist is watching the calendar too.

If I get a genuine offer of a compatible liver for her, there's no question in my mind how I'm going to respond.

Daily Journal

Sally Taylor-Brown

23 March
Amman, Jordan

Why are we doing this? It seems to be a habit. We substitute movement for progress. But, since I've got some energy back there was no point moping around Geneva. Max was against it. He's still babying me but I know I'll feel better trying to do something about the women who are being killed than watching lame Swiss soap operas.

Besides, Max the diligent academician has read that my blood type is more common in the Middle East than in Europe. He's hoping we'll stumble across an unemployed liver that's my size.

We arrived in Amman yesterday and visited the Jordan Hospital. Nice facility. We met with the surgeon, Dr. Zuheir, who's doing the reconstructive surgery while our clinic is closed. A little bit stuck on himself, but he is apparently very good. We learned that one of the benefits – probably the only one – of America's clumsy invasion of Iraq was that it provided Dr. Zuheir with an endless supply of maimed patients to practice on and hone his reconstructive skills. He was surprised to see us, but took the time to answer our questions.

Max (berserk) went straight to the point (his): Jordan Hospital is listed as a transplant center. Where do the organs come from?

Answer: Mostly motor vehicle accidents. Sometimes from a Palestinian who's been shot by Israeli soldiers and doesn't make it; Jordan Hospital provides free care to any Palestinian injured while standing up for Palestine. Organs are only rarely taken from older donors/cadavers.

Is there a registry that distributes the organs?

Answer: Yes, but . . .

Are organs taken from victims of honor killings?

Answer: Only once. Big stink as some people alleged that the hospital had something to gain from the honor killing.

Something about the way Dr. Zuheir answered made me wonder if there was more to the story, but he was checking his watch – and we were imposing – so I cut it off although Max could have grilled him longer.

Now it is the 23d and I'm writing in the car. We're on our way to Zarqa to try to meet with the family of the woman who's buried (?) in Zurich. One of our community outreach workers is with us, the only one who speaks English. She doesn't look excited about this. What's she worried about?

Evening. Same day.

We're still alive, miraculously. Here's what happened:

Zarqa is pretty overwhelming. Narrow, crowded streets, honking, pollution. People staring at us with no warmth in their expressions. The outreach worker directed the driver to the address. It's in one of the many refugee camps that were set up fifty years ago when the Palestinians were either being driven out of their homes, or giving up and leaving. The camp doesn't look like a camp, it looks like the rest of Zarqa, but the residents think of themselves as displaced and only temporarily there despite pretty overwhelming evidence that they're never going back to their homes in what used to be Palestine.

The outreach worker knocked on the door. She really didn't look happy. The door opened a crack, and there was a muted discussion inside. Finally the door was opened halfway by a woman about my age. Several men were visible down the hall.

"Max, we have to get out of here." He was on a mission and slow to move. "Now, Max. Damn it! Now!"

The outreach worker didn't need any urging. She bowed and said something apologetic to the woman holding the door. I grabbed the arms of my traveling companions and pulled them toward the car.

"Jesus, babe. What the hell was that all about?"

"Those men down the hall? One of them chased Gisele and me out of that apartment in Basel."

"Really? This is big, Sal!"

"Bigger than you think, Studly. When Gisele and I went to Basel we were checking on a woman from Bangladesh. This guy was the Bangladeshi's contact, but, lo and behold, today we find him at the home of another disappeared woman in Jordan."

This has to be a major break, but what does it mean?

24 March
Amman, Mukhabarat HQ

Henri suggested we contact the General Intelligence Directorate, Mukhabarat, if we needed support. He said they have a great reputation for effectiveness, although their methods may be a little rough.

The building was imposing and it took a while to get in and find someone who would talk to us. Persistent Max is good at threading these needles. Finally, a portly officer named Majid appeared. He listened patiently to our story, then excused himself to do some background research. On us? Or the people we were telling him about. After thirty minutes he reappeared with several file folders.

It turns out that that house in Zarqa sees a lot of interesting people go through it: the occasional religious extremist, some garden-variety activists for greater democracy, and even a kid who was busted for pot. Majid said it was not really a home to any one family. The woman, who is supposedly in the Zurich cemetery, hadn't lived there. Majid thinks she may be from Mafraq and he seemed a little embarrassed that omniscient Mukhabarat wasn't sure.

That's all he was willing to give us for free. There has to be a lot more in those file folders.

He asked what we intended to do and we explained, again, that we seemed to have stumbled onto an international ring to kill women and loot their bodies. We didn't know what to do. That's why we'd come to Mukhabarat.

He drummed his fingers on the unopened folders.

"You should not continue. You have, as you say, stumbled onto a complex situation. Much of the information is unavailable, even to me, and so much of the rest is unconfirmed that it is not responsible to reveal it. What you have told me about the doctor in Switzerland is a helpful piece of the puzzle. But you should not continue. If you haven't realized how dangerous these people are, think for a minute about what they are doing."

We did think about it. I did, anyway.

Max always figures out a way to keep the discussion going. "Majid, thank you very much for your time. I wish we could walk away, but we can't. We have a personal connection to these women. I doubt Mukhabarat is recruiting geriatric foreigners as undercover agents (hey! speak for yourself, old man!), but we did work for a while for the CIA and might be able to provide some small assistance."

It seemed obvious from his reaction – actually, his lack of it – that Majid already knew about our earlier CIA connection. We were pretty darned effective spooks, not that we got any thanks from the Agency. It's all in Max's fourth book.

Majid: "I appreciate your offer. This is an active investigation. Jordan will not sit by while our daughters are murdered in Europe. I cannot order you, a foreigner, to step aside, but I can tell you that we are working on this."

Which is a lot more than can be said for FedPol.

At this point the door opened and a woman with more impressive insignia than Majid's entered. Was she watching from behind the large mirror on the wall? She introduced herself as Major Nouf and led us to her office. We knew our fortunes were improving when she provided tea and biscuits.

Major Nouf explained the 'complexities.' Honor crimes are a source of embarrassment and sorrow to His Majesty but the fractious nature of the politics in the country results in slow progress. Just to illustrate, she told us that the previous king, Hussein, narrowly survived 12 assassination attempts and seven plots to overthrow him. Keeping an uneasy coalition together means treading water on some issues, while keeping them on a slow boil. Nouf tends to mix her metaphors.

It looked like Nouf was going to enlarge on her complexity thesis when Max moved things along: "Major, you brought us to your office for a reason other than a lesson on Jordanian politics. We're ready to go to work. We have some intel background, and we're motivated. What can we do for Mukhabarat that doesn't involve stepping aside?"

Major Nouf was ready with an answer: "If you're determined to keep going, the role for you is obvious. You are the logical people to follow up on the women who came from Jordan to your clinic. Foreign NGOs do this all the time – send their managers around to view the good work of their organizations and accept the gratitude of those who received services. Seventeen women and girls from Jordan went to your clinic during the last 24 months. We believe there are at least eight who are missing."

Holy Toledo! Eight? Some must have died that we never knew of. We don't keep in touch with them after their follow-up visits if they've listed a local contact who will take care of them. I have to get Gisele and Hanan checking on all the women Schwarzherz operated on.

"You can go to these women's homes and express your interest. As representatives of your clinic, you are making a follow-up visit. This, by itself, is not suspicious behavior. I suggest you try to speak with all seventeen since you are concerned about unauthorized organ removals. Some may have given up an organ and survived." The major stopped and selected a biscuit for herself. Biting it in half, "One thing: there's an excellent chance you'll be harmed."

She chewed thoughtfully, and added, "Perhaps killed."

Max gets a word in

It's still March 24th as I write this. Sally's sleeping. As she got older she had increasing trouble sleeping. Now she's catching up.

Major Nouf outfitted us with pistols and a phrase book. I'm such a bad shot I intend to focus on the phrase book; my odds are better at talking my way out of trouble than shooting my way out. Sally, on the other hand, is an excellent shot, which is one of the reasons the Taylor-Browns are alive and living in hope.

There's one (only one?) thing I'm worried about: A person who sees the odds moving against them tends to take more risks. This is a fact. Would Sally rather succumb to a long debilitating disease, or go out in a hail of bullets? You see what I'm saying? This is not a depressed or suicidal woman. Anything but. That granted, even a person like her will be aware of a reordering in the personal outcomes available when those outcomes change dramatically. Just something I think about. And worry about.

Before we left Mukhabarat's large complex we were introduced to a woman, Nour, who would pose as a community outreach worker and serve as guide and translator. Her English is perfect, the accent difficult to place but definitely British isles. She's a study in contrasts. She'd obviously spent considerable time on her makeup this morning, but was dressed in baggy olive drab pants, a floral print orange and blue blouse, and a dark green vest. We privately expressed the hope that Nour's intel sense is better than her fashion sense. I suspect the vest is needed to conceal a gun, perhaps in a holster in the small of her back. Major Nouf explained that Agent Nour has a special and personal interest in honor crimes. I hope it isn't too personal. And Nour doesn't look like she'd be an easy target for an 'honor' attack.

Our travels together will be a fishing expedition. Tomorrow we go to Mafraq to look for the home of the woman "buried" in Zurich. Her name is/was Tara.

Daily Journal

Sally Taylor-Brown

25 March
Mafraq, Jordan

Mafraq turns out to be a dusty little town in the north of the country. Not many people out. We've asked about Tara at every official and unofficial level. Nobody has any information on her. They don't remember anyone of that name or recognize her photo. By noon Max and I concluded that all-knowing Mukhabarat had this one wrong.

Max wants to return to that same house in Zarqa we went to two days ago. And he worries that *I* have a death wish?

I agreed on the condition that we take a side trip. I didn't come all this way and miss the sights. Ninety minutes west of Mafraq is one of the hundreds of fascinating archeological sites. This one is called Umm Qais. It's ancient biblical name was Gedara.

Where we made a wonderful discovery: Nour is a history buff! Which gives us something to talk about since Nour clams up when we ask about her family or herself. She led us around the ruins, tracing the progression through different rulers and peoples by showing us their architecture and religious buildings. Max was under-whelmed. For an over-educated guy, he doesn't show much interest in interesting stuff.

Umm Qais started out as a Greek center of culture. Then the Seleucids of Syria controlled it for a while, followed by the Ptolemies of Egypt. It changed hands a lot. Finally the Romans took it in 63 BC. It should be most famous to us for a Bible story, but Max and I don't recall hearing about it in Sunday School. You'll see why it doesn't get the same airtime as Lazarus, Jonah, loaves-and-fishes, water-into-wine, and the rest. But it does figure in all four of the Gospels. Here's the story:

Jesus climbed up to Umm Qais/Gedara from the Sea of Galilee (after calming both the waters and his wussy disciples) and encountered two men possessed by demons. JC slipped right into messiah mode; He exorcised the demons and cast them into a herd of pigs who were minding their own business nearby. The pigs reacted just as you might expect anyone would when they find themselves suddenly inhabited by demons: they went bananas and ran off a cliff. Is that where 'when pigs fly' comes from? Anyway, it was a farming community and the locals weren't thrilled to see valuable livestock disappear over a cliff. They took up pitchforks and chased Jesus and his little band out of town. No recruits to Christianity that day. Apparently even messiahs have a learning curve.

Zarqa

The detour to Umm Qais put us behind schedule and the traffic was terrible. It was dusk before we arrived at the house in Zarqa. I was uneasy. We took our pistols off safety – our 'guide', Nour, did too – and cautiously approached the door. A car backfired and I almost lost it. Nour – I think she wants to show us she's made of the right stuff – threw open the door and dropped to one knee, her pistol pointed down the hall. The house had been vacated.

The neighbors told Nour that everyone had been gone by yesterday morning. Apparently they all moved out right after Max and I showed up.

We all three agree this is important. These people know they have something to hide and they know we're after them.

Are they after us?

26 March
As-Salt

There are two women who came to our clinic from Salt half a year ago. Salt is a town right by Amman and has a mostly Christian population. I suspect Nour wants us to see that honor crimes are not just a Muslim thing.

The first visit was an upper. We actually got to meet the woman and she looked pretty much okay. She says she's getting a certificate to teach. The home looked nice. We were invited to stay for lunch, but declined. Success story. I have to send it back to Gisele who can put it in the next newsletter to our financial supporters.

The second visit? Not so much.

There were omens. Salt is hilly and our car wound up a narrow one lane road. Nearing the top, an on-coming bus forced the driver to reverse all the way back to the bottom. Salt could use some traffic engineering.

The address is a compound, surrounded by a mud wall eight feet high. Glass shards are embedded in the top of the wall. We knocked and the gate was finally opened by a small boy, maybe ten. He looked us over and closed the gate again. After waiting a few minutes, we pounded on the gate some more, this time more forcefully. We could hear voices inside. Nour shrugged; she couldn't make out what was being said.

Nour shouted out something. I think it must have been about the purpose of our visit. Someone shouted back.

"They want us to leave. They say only women are present. That is not a reason to keep us out. They have a Christian name."

Max pounded on the gate. He's getting frustrated.

Finally an older woman, dressed in traditional Palestinian garb, threw the gate open and glared at us. Nour began talking quickly. The old woman's expression seemed to shift from anger to fear and back to anger.

Max noticed it too. "Nour, she's afraid of something. The polite thing would be to go, but the stakes are too high." As he said that he kicked the gate back and darted through. And could have been shot by the boy who was holding an old rifle.

Nour is quick. She grabbed the gun out of the kid's hands before he could react. Now the old woman looked *very* frightened.

I told Nour to tell her we've come to talk to Lama – give her all that BS about this being a courtesy follow-up call, etc., etc.

"There is no need," said the old woman. First cultural lesson of the day: many Palestinian Christians speak English. "I already know you come to see Lama. I already hear that someone is in Jordan looking for women who go to Switzerland. Lama is not here and you cannot speak with her. We will not change our answer."

A curtain moved in the window of the nearest small building in the compound. Since Nour had taken care of the rifle, I ran into the building and saw a woman go out the opposite door. I caught up with her. She tried to pull away, terrified. Lama? Not the girl I'd seen in our clinic. Schwarzherz had fixed Lama up pretty well. This woman was hideously disfigured.

Max and Nour caught up, pursued by the protesting old woman.

"What's the matter, babe?"

"This can't be Lama."

Max glanced at the scarred face and turned away. The hole in the right cheek through which brown teeth and purpled gums were visible, the glass eye, mottled skin that sagged like dripping wax. He shook his head, still unable to look directly at her.

His voice was thick, "Unless she's been attacked again.

The old woman grabbed my arm in both her hands: "Please leave us in peace. There are others who can give you what you want. My daughter has suffered enough."

Nour started to ask something in Arabic. Max held up his hand to stop her. We've learned that a person will reveal more when struggling to speak in an unfamiliar language. Keep the conversation in our language.

Max asked, "What do you think we want?"

The old woman looked as confused as I felt. "Anything more will kill her."

Unlike Max, I could look at the disfigured woman. I guess you get hardened to this at the clinic. "Lama, is that you?"

No response, which in the circumstances meant yes.

Lama's blouse hung crookedly. Something seemed to be wrong with her torso and she was hugging her forearm to her right side, protectively. Taking her hand gently, I slowly lifted the corner of her blouse. An ugly red scar ran around her waist and up out of sight under the blouse.

"Oh my God, Max. I think her right kidney is gone."

Max stared at the floor. "And they think we're here from the clinic to harvest the rest of her."

An upsetting day

Sally's devastated, but she's trying to call Agent Henri to keep her mind occupied. This seems like more than circumstantial evidence, and it keeps mounting. Henri isn't picking up. Strange, for a cop.

Lama spoke with us for no more than two minutes, but it was enough. Three weeks after her surgery in Geneva she was told to go to another clinic, not Sally's clinic and not Schwarzherz's home. She was met by someone wearing a surgical mask. Her sketchy description doesn't sound like either Schwarzherz or Levy, but it's also hard to rule out either one. Two people were in the OR, both with masks. They spoke to her in English and told her she had an infection from the acid attack and needed more surgery. One of the men said they might be able to improve her face too. She didn't protest.

When she woke up a strange man who spoke like he was from Jordan was there. He took care of her for two weeks, then brought her back to Salt. He said his name was George. Nour explained that's a common first name among Christians in Jordan.

Lama went to a doctor in Salt who told her there was no reason to remove a kidney for "an infection." She had been tricked. One month later her original attacker threw acid on her again. She's afraid to return to Switzerland.

Daily Journal

Sally Taylor-Brown

27 March
Amman

Major Nouf is unavailable this morning. Too bad since our news seems pretty big. The Mukhabarat people look grim and preoccupied. Max thinks they've caught wind of a planned terrorist attack. Of course he doesn't know and Nour isn't telling us anything – if she knows anything.

We were just informed that today we'll have to provide our own car and driver. Maybe Max is right. Something big is going down. Worried that Nour will be reassigned, we quickly leave Mukhabarat with her for a car rental place.

Fourteen more women on our list. First up is Dania in Ma'an.

Ma'an

It's a two hour drive south to Ma'an, halfway to the Gulf of Aqaba. I got Max to agree to another detour. There's a completely intact Roman fort a few miles west of the Desert Highway. Perfect, and no one knows about it, but Nour does. A garrison of 200 men stayed there. High walls and towers at each corner. Really neat. Better than any Hollywood movie set.

Max stayed down in the central courtyard while Nour and I investigated the ramparts. It embarrasses him, but he's deathly afraid of heights. He took up flying as a cure; it didn't work. He's comfortable in an airplane, but his courage still fails on the fourth rung of a stepladder.

As we clambered around I tried to imagine what life was like for those men. Lonely and short. I'm not lonely. The only sign of "life" was the carcass of a goat that had been dinner for wild dogs or jackals. Could have done without the discovery of a gutted corpse.

Back on the road. Ma'an is supposedly in a conservative area. It's pretty depressing. Mud walls and mud houses. A few of the better homes are built from cinder block. Goats and camels wandering around looking for something to eat. Lots of luck finding anything, guys. The place is parched and barren. What do people do here to survive?

We quickly find Dania. She must not have heard of the people from the Swiss clinic who have come to pick up a few more organs. Her mother welcomes us in. Dania looks okay. She's married but her husband is working in "the gulf." They say he's an engineer on a construction project in Oman but this doesn't look like the home of an engineer. They may be exaggerating his title.

Nour asks if Dania has a scar on her body. She does, and she shows it to Nour and me (not Max). Bad news. Another kidney.

Just like Lama, she can't describe who did the second surgery. She's glad she went back because her face was improved. She's not sure what the scar around her waist means.

We're starting to think that the two men behind the masks have different specializations, one facial reconstructive surgery, the other thoracic. We know two doctors who fit the bill.

Tiring trip, but worth it.

28 March
Back in Amman, Jordan Hospital

I was ready to keep going, but Max freaked out. Dr. Zuheir arranged for a radiation quickie. Yuck and double-yuck.

Time is running out

I'm not freaking out. Time is *running* out for my soul mate. We have to keep this thing in stage one, or close to it. Sally deserves those fifteen-plus years. The universe owes it to someone this good.

She's always been an inveterate tourist, from our first trip together in England and continuing for 25 years. Now I worry she's trying to pack all the living she can into her remaining hours, like those people with a terminal diagnosis who set off on the extravagant trip they'd never had. Is part of her giving up?

28 <u>March</u>. When everyone's speaking an unintelligible language it undermines my confidence, but the staff at Jordan Hospital seem to know what they're doing. They get a lot of medical tourism: sick Americans and Europeans (and their insurance companies) looking for a bargain. The radiation procedure seems to go at about the same pace as in Geneva and Sally was wheeled off to a recovery room by mid-morning.

<u>Same day</u>. While Sally's resting, Nour and I are going to cross another one off the list. She's an Iraqi woman who was living in a refugee camp near the Iraqi border when she was attacked. Nour has an address for her in East Amman. Most of the Iraqi refugees spent little time in camps and took up residence in cities. Her name is Fatima; Nour informs me that was the name of the Prophet's daughter.

We arrive at a five-story apartment building. Long rods of rebar stick up out of the roof and tops of walls. This is a common sight and Nour explains that the presence of the exposed rebar means the building owner can claim the building is under construction and exempt from property taxes until completed (never).

Fatima's address is on the top floor. Slogans are spray painted on the walls of the stairwell. Nour, who's been a cornucopia of irrelevant information to this point, declines to translate.

More graffiti on the door of Fatima's apartment. Nour checks the safety is off on her pistol. Overly dramatic? I check mine.

No response to our knocking, but Nour isn't convinced the apartment is empty. She signals we should retreat up the steps toward the roof. We can monitor the door to Fatima's apartment while remaining out of sight. Nour's wearing a heavy perfume of some cheap sort. Is that a good idea for a sleuth?

She turns out to be right. Within a few minutes we hear sounds of the door being unlocked. The door opens a crack. We hold our breaths. The door opens fully and a veiled woman steps out, uneasily. I think there's scarring around her left eye. She's followed by a man holding a pistol. He grips her arm tightly and peers down the stairs. Nour looks like she's about to spring into action and I signal she shouldn't. With two hands I try to mime one person walking behind another. I feel silly but Nour gets the message: we should shadow this pair.

The man and veiled woman proceed slowly down the stairs. Their intentions are obvious: get out of the building undetected. My intention is to not get shot. I worry about Nour's.

Voices from below. Good. Covering sound. Nour and I move quickly down two flights. A teenage boy comes up the stairs toward us and exchanges *sala'ams* with Nour. Is that good? We're either established as legitimate users of the stairs . . . or as someone sneaking up from behind. A metal door bangs – the door to the street – and we run down the last flights. Nour eases the door open. The man and veiled woman are no more than ten feet away, waiting at the curb. They're going to be picked up. How do we get into our own car so we can follow them?

"Be ready," Nour whispers. She pulls a red-checkered *keffiyeh* up over the lower half of her face and walks out the door and down the hill toward our parked rental. She's only halfway to our car when an old Mercedes comes to a quick stop at the curb and the driver signals, with rapid hand gestures, to our quarry to get in. They're off and turning a far corner when Nour pulls up. I jump into the back – the nearest door – and we're in pursuit. Nour is able to keep them in sight for a few turns, but traffic and traffic lights conspire against us and we lose sight of the old Mercedes.

Nour drives aimlessly in the direction the Mercedes was last seen. "You know what this means," she says. "They could see us through the door. They recognized you and now they have seen me."

"Can you continue now that you're blown?"

"Anyone who is seen with you is immediately blown. It makes no difference. We will just keep looking for these women. Some will not know about you like the girl yesterday. Others will and perhaps someone will make a mistake."

Not us, I hope.

Next day (29 March). Sally's still out of it, but unwilling to accept the fact. The radiation takes a toll. I try to find Dr. Zuheir but he's unavailable. We need a status update on my girl.

Nour has another name and address. This one is in Abdoun, the wealthiest section of Amman. The well-heeled are throwing acid at one another? The victim's name is Mariam ("Mother of Jesus" says Nour) and she lives in a walled fortress, just like everyone else in Abdoun. I tell Nour that this makes no sense. A woman of these means doesn't need to draw on the resources of a charity in Switzerland.

The victim is a servant, not a woman of means. She's from the Philippines and, according to Nour's file, the suspected acid thrower is the lady of the house. "These foreign house workers have few protections." I wonder if the man of the house had taken a shine to the unfortunate Filipina.

We get nowhere. After long arguments with a woman (the lady of the house?) the gate is slammed shut and no amount of pounding will reopen it.

Back at the hospital. Sally has been seen by an oncologist. The doctor skirted questions, but Sally got the impression that a transplant needed to be imminent. I called the Registry on the excuse that we were traveling and concerned we might have missed a message. "No," same frosty tone, "you have missed nothing."

Daily Journal

Sally Taylor-Brown

30 March
Amman

Gisele is the most efficient person I know. She recruited Hanan who recruited two imams. The four of them checked the registries of every Muslim cemetery in the country. Of the 68 Muslim women operated on during the past year and a half, 16 are buried in Switzerland. Incredible! And we knew nothing of it. Talk about heads in the sand!

Maybe I should write "buried" in quotes since the Zarqa girl is listed as buried in the Zurich cemetery, but Max concluded that she isn't.

The two imams are trying to follow up on the victims' local contact addresses. They're making a note of those instances where they run into a stone wall. A prayer leader can usually expect cooperation from a fellow Muslim. When he doesn't get it, well, that smells funny.

Max's new crime-fighting buddy, Nour, is also efficient. The license plate on the old Mercedes they followed was hammered out in somebody's garage. It isn't registered. She says that Mukhabarat will get the phone records for Lama, the disfigured woman in As-Salt. She's the one who knew we were going around visiting women who'd been to the clinic. Who tipped her off? My money's on that big, bearded guy I saw in Basel and again in Zarqa.

Then the efficiency drops off. I tried Agent Henri again. This time I left a message about the 16 "buried" Muslim women. I also left Gisele's contact number. He should be taking action. I'm going to ask Gisele to contact him directly.

Hooboy! Fast turnaround. Gisele just responded. She was able – through persistent efforts – to get Henri to pick up the phone.

Seems Henri and his Main Squeeze are having a tiff. Is his love life more important than 16 buried women?

Zarqa

Back to Zarqa. There's something about the city that unnerves me. We're looking for Manal who was in our clinic six months ago. I remember her. Long beautiful hair and those enormous dark eyes that Arab women are famous for. Nour has them. Is Max attracted to Nour? He used to make a big deal of my "big green eyes." He assures me that older men don't want young women; they just want to be wanted by younger women. It seems he's told me that more times than was necessary.

The acid attack had destroyed half of Manal's nose and etched deep scars on the left side of her face. Schwarzherz did a decent job grafting skin onto the cheek, but the nose was less of a success. She was one of the few that was talkative, almost to the point of out-going and you had to admire that, given what had happened to her. She spoke enough English that I was able to have short chats with her without Hanan's help. We felt good about sending her back home since the uncle who had disfigured her had been arrested and locked up. I'm not crazy about Zarqa, but am looking forward to seeing Manal again.

The address is on the outskirts of the city so we were spared creeping through congested narrow streets. Patchwork growth of the city. Whole blocks are vacant, awaiting development, while the next few blocks are packed with houses. Manal's address is a modest house, probably pretty good by local standards. Nour seemed relaxed. No gun out.

Manal herself answered our knock. She didn't look happy to see us, which surprised me. She seemed uncertain whether to let us in and kept glancing over her shoulder. Disappointing. It didn't look like we'd be staying long and chatting, but we did need her to answer one question: do you still have all your internal plumbing?

Nour picked up on Manal's nervousness and pushed past her through the door. As she ran in, she reached behind her for her pistol. Good thing. An older man stepped into the hallway with a butcher knife in his hand. Max and I fumbled for our own guns; Max, of course, only did it after he saw I was getting my pistol out.

The man quickly backed through a door. We caught up with him in the kitchen where a large cutting board was covered with vegetables. He'd been chopping up dinner. Max and I put our guns away. Not Nour. I guess that goes with her profession. It's one thing to be suspicious to the point of offensiveness. Another to be trusting – and dead.

I tried to make the situation more normal than it was. "Manal? Do you remember me, Sally, from the clinic in Switzerland?"

Manal looked terrified. Was this someone else who'd been alerted we were on an organ-collecting tour? "We're only here to make sure that you're alright. I think you've been told some-thing different."

Manal didn't respond, but looked to the man.

Max asked Manal if she had a scar around her waist. She looked puzzled by the question, but finally shook her head, no.

"Show us." That's Nour. It was a demand, not a request, and it was accompanied by a flick of her pistol. A little strong, I thought.

Manal backed away. The man continued to hold the knife. This was going completely wrong.

Thank God for Max. He put his hand on Nour's pistol and gen-tly pushed it down. How does he get away with it? But he does. The man put the knife on the chopping block. "Now," said Max, speaking slowly and clearly, "do you know why we are here?"

Manal didn't answer. Max explained. "We have learned that some of the women who came to Sally's clinic were harmed by doctors in Switzerland. We are trying to find those doctors and the others who help them. They must be punished."

I was surprised when the man spoke in English. "If bad doctors are in Switzerland, why are you looking here?"

That's a very good question.

The answer

There's a very good answer, Sal: the trail has gone cold in Switzerland. Our best leads are in Jordan.

Daily Journal

Sally Taylor-Brown

Still 30 March
Mukhabarat HQ, Amman

We came back to Mukhabarat HQ so that Nour could check two things. Who was the older man with Manal, and had she received a call from the same number as Lama had? That would help find who was trying to poison the victims' reaction to us.

While waiting for Mukhabarat's techies to check Manal's telephone record, Nour ID'd the man with Manal: it's her uncle – the one who'd attacked her. His file shows he served six months, then had been released on the petition of the family. Nour says that's the usual pattern for honor crimes. He'd given us a bogus name and the national ID card he showed Nour was consistent with it. Nour suspected the ID card was a phony when she saw it.

Max asked if the file had anything on the uncle's motive for throwing acid, since the usual pattern is it's the work of a disappointed suitor or jealous boyfriend/fiancé/husband.

"The file says that Manal was going out with friends a lot and the uncle claims he was afraid she would be compromised."

That makes me wonder if uncle's feelings for Manal had progressed beyond protectiveness to something seedier.

So, where are we going? Back to my favorite city.

Zarqa

Late afternoon and traffic is a problem again. Will the uncle have taken off? If he's figured out that Nour is with the big scary Intel Directorate he'll realize he doesn't have much time and will vanish. She hadn't flashed any ID, but waving a service pistol around isn't the norm for social workers.

At last, an overdue smidgen of good luck. The uncle was shoving stuff in the back of his small car when we pulled up. Five minutes later and he would have been gone.

We shared our theory with Nour that people will reveal more when forced out of their first language. Our presence gave her the excuse to interrogate Manal and her uncle in English.

Nour used an interesting tactic, but I guess every good interrogator uses it: accuse a person of a huge crime and he'll willingly confess to a lesser one. She first put Manal's uncle on the defensive by confronting him with his true identity. Then she ramped up the pressure.

"You are wanted for murder. Eye-witnesses have placed you at the scene of the murders of four women."

Uncle (making his first mistake): "Four? Where? When?"

Nour: "Thank you. You're not denying your involvement in the murders. You just want help establishing your alibi."

Uncle (second mistake): "No, I'm not a murderer. Four women you say? Eye-witnesses?"

Nour: "So you are disputing the number. If not four, how many do you say you killed?"

Uncle: "None. No women. Not men either. I am many things, but I am not a murderer."

Nour: "Your little crimes don't interest me. People say bad things about you and it is all connected to the murder of women."

Uncle (he can't keep his mouth shut): "No, I have done bad things to women. But I have never killed one."

Nour: "Really? How bad can they be if so many say you are a killer."

Uncle: "No, I threw acid to defend our honor. I did it twice. But no one died."

Manal's head shot up; she looked away from her uncle. The confession of two acid attacks was obviously news to her.

Nour: "You were punished for one acid attack. You are now confessing to another attack for which you have not been punished?"

Uncle: "Yes . . . no. No murders. I know the other woman did not die and here is Manal, as you can see."

Max (unexpectedly joining in): "And the kidneys that were cut out of women? I suppose you're not guilty of that either?"

Nour looked annoyed that her line of questioning had been interrupted, but she let it go. We all glared at the uncle.

"No. It is all the opposite. I refused to cooperate. They told me that Manal must be punished more and the punishment was to give her organs to women more honorable than her. I refused. I have always felt I made a mistake with the acid. That is why I live here and take care of my niece."

Manal tossed her head dismissively.

Nour took interest in the organ lead: "Who asked you about kidneys? If you are trying to shift the blame onto someone else, it will go very hard on you."

"A big man with a beard. I met him once. I refused when he called me and he insisted we meet in person. I still refused."

Bingo! Or maybe not. The country is full of big men with beards.

Nour pressed her advantage, "We need the phone number of that man. Perhaps he will support your story."

This sent the uncle searching through the record of calls on his phone. After a few minutes he showed Nour the screen. "I think this is the number."

I asked Manal if it's the same number she was called from to warn her we were in Jordan and we intended to harm her. A minute later she confirmed that it was.

There were still several loose ends. Nour wanted to know why the uncle had used a false name and ID. He switched into Arabic for the answer. By Nour's expression, the explanation wasn't convincing. She also wanted to know why he was packing his car when we arrived. Again, Arabic. Nour translated – with a snort – that he was going to Karak to visit a relative.

"We will check on this 'relative'. If you are lying again the prison sentence will be long."

The uncle looked defeated. He sat down. "Can you not see that I am worried for the safety of my niece?"

Max rejoined the interrogation, "A little late for that, isn't it? Look at what you did to her." Then I could see Max regretted he'd drawn attention to Manal's ruined face.

Uncle: "I am only trying to make things better. This is a big problem."

Nour: "We agree on that. A very big problem. Now tell me everything about the big man with the beard. What did he say to you?"

Uncle: "He say that many women who dishonor their families escape punishment when their face is made good again. This is against the will of the family and it is against the will of Allah."

Max, sputtering with anger: "And merciful Allah is okay with doubling down on the punishment?" He turned away in disgust.

Uncle looked confused. "He say dishonorable woman could provide health to another by giving part of her body. He say many women do this and become honorable again."

"And that's okay?" Max shouted. "We know of 16 headstones in Swiss cemeteries of women who paid for their return to grace with their lives." He waved his arm and addressed this to the room. His face was flushed as he turned and leaned toward Manal's uncle. Nour looked annoyed and cocked her head toward the door. I led a fuming Max into the hall. Things upset him more easily than before.

Me, in the hall: "And that was your 'bad cop' act?"

Max: "Sorry, babe. It's just that trying to put a moral justification on . . ." He glanced back through the door at Manal; she'd moved near a window and the deep scarring on her face was highlighted. Max held up his palms in defeat. I think his eyes were damp.

While Max cooled down, Nour learned that the uncle had this conversation with the BBM just before he turned himself in for the six-month wrist slap. The BBM wanted him to contact Manal in Switzerland, beg for forgiveness, and provide her with the name of a person who would take care of her while in Switzerland. Fortunately for Manal, her uncle refused.

We need two things: Who is the BBM? And who is in the network in Switzerland? Uncle had no answer to either question.

31 March
Mukhabarat HQ, Amman

No surprise. Nour told us the BBM's telephone number led to a burner, and it hadn't been used for several days. Apparently he had put out the word on us, then ditched the phone.

What next?

Al-Karak

Karak, that's what's next. The city's about halfway down the country. Like everywhere else in Jordan, Karak has a fascinating history. The Crusaders built a castle where Raynald de Châtillon held sway in the twelfth century. He was about as lousy a guy as you might encounter in the twelfth century (which was famous for its lousy guys). He liked to throw his prisoners off the high castle walls down onto the rocks. For some reason he thought it more fun if the victims had their heads locked in a box so they'd be flying blind. He reneged on every deal he made. He was there for the money.

"A boodler," was Max's judgment. De Châtillon's primary adversary was Saladin, a very chivalrous man. The Christians often came off second-best in comparisons of morality. By the way, this is not Nour trying to make a point. I got this out of a guidebook I read during the trip down.

We passed by de Châtillon's castle. The drop from the parapet to the rocks hadn't been exaggerated. A victim would have plenty of time to think about what was coming during the descent.

We're looking for one of the three disappeared. I'm wondering why we didn't start with them. Nour let us look at her file. Big help. All in Arabic, but it did have a picture of the victim. I recognize her. And there's a picture of the man who threw the acid – a distant cousin – although there's some question about whether he actually did it or just sold six months of his life (in prison) to allow someone else to walk.

We were waiting at a traffic light and a man on the sidewalk said something in Arabic to us. I was curious and asked Nour. She didn't reply but the driver, breaking his customary silence, translated, "May Allah take you." Not everyone loves us.

Different tactics. As soon as we got an answer at the door, Nour flashed her Mukhabarat credentials and pushed into the house. The family – five of them – were seated for lunch which made me uncomfortable. The two women at the table quickly covered the lower halves of their faces when they saw Max. The acid-attack victim was not present.

Backup would be comforting and I was glad to see the driver appear at the door. Did I mention we had a Mukhabarat car and driver again? I assumed the driver was armed and trained. He looked competent.

There was an exchange in Arabic. Nour translated, "They say she's visiting friends in Cairo." Another exchange in Arabic. "I threatened them, but they're sticking to the story. They insist she's fine and traveling."

I was watching the younger woman, maybe just a teenager. No doubt about it. Tears were forming in her eyes.

"Nour, the woman we're looking for is dead." I nodded at the crying girl. "Ask her where the body is."

Nour must have translated that directly as it undermined the younger woman who started convulsing with sobs. One of the men put his hand under the table and our driver responded by putting his hand into his vest. You know what I was thinking at that moment? Maybe Max has something. Maybe this is how it ends: a hail of bullets. No more radiation, no waiting on a registry that doesn't move, no slicing me open. I'm worn down. Am I really ready to quit?

Max caught me under the arms as I sank toward the floor.

April fools

We're locked in a room in the basement. As you can tell by the existence of this written account, it's a furnished room, including paper and pens in a little desk. This isn't a normal time to sit and write but, a) there's not much else to do, and b) it seems to be important to Sally. No, we are not transcribing her dying words. I'm simply keeping her narrative up-to-date.

It's April first. Sally's fainting spell disrupted everything. Nour, the driver, and I were all tending to Sally. The three men at the table were all getting their guns. When we finally turned our attention to them we were confronted by one pistol, one shotgun and one Kalashnikov. They locked us up down here in what is a small apartment with a bathroom and three beds.

Sally's doing better. She says it was just low blood pressure brought on by the various drugs and the fact that we'd gone past her regular lunchtime. I desperately want to believe that. The yellow is returning to her skin.

The four of us have talked about our predicament. We're a problem for our captors. They over-reacted and locked up two Americans and two Mukhabarat agents. The Jordanian spooks will soon be missed, setting off a manhunt. Our general destination was recorded before we left Amman, and at some point the absence of the file Nour took will be noticed.

Mukhabarat will go all out to find their people, but Sally and I are even bigger problems. Nour told us about an American aid official, Larry Foley, who was shot in his driveway four years ago. They turned the country upside down. Every soldier, every cop was required to work fourteen-hour days until they found the perp.

Our captors have to either move us, or get rid of us, or surrender. These are not good options for them.

Ah, here they come, holding blindfolds. Looks like a move. I hope.

1 April
???????

I feel so stupid. If I'd held it together we wouldn't be in this fix. Max tried to reassure me it wasn't my fault, but then he asked if I'd remembered to take my meds this morning.

Only guessing but it seemed like we rode in the back of that panel van for around two hours, most of it at highway speeds. Jordan's a small country so we could be anywhere. Blindfolded again before we got out of the van. We went down some stairs. A few street noises. Now we are in a basement room and the little casement windows have been covered over on the outside. We could be anywhere.

Max and I are in a different room than Nour and Anwar, the Mukhabarat driver. I guess we present different challenges. Our captors treat us with some care. For example, they let us keep the paper and pen. They read what Max wrote, but I don't know that they understood it very well, or care. Is this Arab hospitality? Or maybe indecision over what to do with us. As near as I can figure, the options have to be kill us or they have to go underground. I can see the three men doing that – maybe slipping over to Iraq to join some insurgent group. The Sinai is also a possibility. The two women?

I know it seems strange that I'm writing but it does provide distance from what's going on. I can see why Max intellectualizes when things get tough. Now that I've thought that, I expect him to take over at any minute.

Since fifty percent of the available options are for them to kill us, shouldn't we be trying to escape? Max seems lulled by the small courtesies, like being allowed to write, decent bed, a bathroom. Me? Why am I not more concerned? Do I really believe to my core that I'm carrying a death sentence and what these people do to me doesn't change that outcome?

A clue about our whereabouts. Dinner was from a fast-food place, like a McDonalds or something similar. We conclude that we're in a decent sized town – although not much noise – and there's a tourist business. Where? Ajloun? Petra? Aqaba? Probably not the last one; we'd sense the nearness of the sea. Irbid would be too far.

We've checked the windows and doors. No easy way out. The walls seem thick and the faintness of the street sounds means our shouts would not be heard.

Max doesn't think they can keep us here. He thinks that by this time Mukhabarat has gone to battle stations and the Army and police will be close behind. They'll go house-to-house throughout the Kingdom until they find us. Our captors have been around long enough to know that's coming. Also, Max is sure they can't move us on the road again. Roadblocks everywhere. The desert is pretty flat and movement is visible for miles; no walking, at least during the day. A cave, maybe?

I wish we could reason with them.

Max banged on the door until the three men showed up; one pistol. They were annoyed at the summons.

The oldest of the three spoke decent English. I guess because the place was a British protectorate until around 1950. The conversation was brief.

Max: "We have a mutual problem." He left it there. I think he didn't want to state the options.

Oldest man: "This is not what we planned but it is what has happened. We have friends who are working to help us. We do not want to harm you, but we all understand the situation. And do not say something stupid like, 'We will walk away and never speak to anyone about this.' Perhaps in the morning we will know more. You should sleep. There may be difficult days ahead."

They filed out.

Me: "They sound almost like we're partners."

Max shrugged: "Mutual problem."

Private

After I write this it's going straight into my pocket. Sally can't see it.

If I were these guys, I know what I'd be thinking:

1. They had a nice, quiet, middle-class life. A family living peacefully in Karak. One of the three men had probably thrown the acid; then they went along with the organ donor stuff, not expecting the girl would die. An unwelcome surprise when she did. But, except for the younger woman, they got past it.

Boom, we come through the door. They panic. They take prisoners.

2. They want to go back to that comfortable life. They don't want to subsist, hunted, in the Sinai desert, or in some rebel hideaway in Iraq.

3. They have to get rid of us in a way that throws suspicion off them, and they have to get rid of both us and the two spooks.

4. Too late to stage an accident that takes out four people. Whatever they do at this point is going to look like murder.

5. Who are we always ready to blame for a violent death in this neighborhood? The jihadists/terrorists.

6. Videotape a beheading or turn us over to someone who will do the job.

7. Send the tape to Al-Jazeera.

8. Some splinter branch of the jihadi movement will eagerly claim responsibility.

That's my analysis.

I need to convince them it won't work. Mukhabarat will discover the absence of the file that Nour took. It leads directly to their door.

2 April
Same place, wherever that is

Decent breakfast.

Good Lord! I'm commenting on the catering?

We're told to drink lots of water. We assume we'll be walking through the desert.

Guess who just showed up! BBM. I don't think we are supposed to know he's here, but I recognize his voice from that time in Basel. I have a knack for that. No idea what they're saying on the other side of the door, but voices are raised. That's not good. To me it means there's one side calling for strong action and the other side urging restraint. I'm pretty sure what the strong action would be.

The oldest of the three Karaki men came in. He looked pretty flustered. No pistol. He told us to rest, drink water, and we'd leave in the late afternoon. Who won the argument? The hawks or the doves?

Lunch was so-so. Holy-moley! There I did it again!

Petra!

We're in Wadi Musa, the tourist town just outside Petra, the most famous place in Jordan. Petra's an ancient Nabatean city, protected by high mountains on all sides. Access is through a long narrow canyon called a *siq*. I know it's Petra because the paper put on the outside of a casement window peeled off and we could see the Crown Plaza Hotel not too far off and beyond that the cliffs I've seen so often in my guidebook.

Max says it makes sense. Thousands of tourists around. Who would notice a mixed group of seven Jordanians and Americans? Also, since this is the big dollar earner in Jordan, there will be a light hand when it comes to roadblocks, searches, and shakedowns.

Oh my God! I have to jot down one more thing although they are gesturing for us to leave: I think Manal's uncle is here! The one from Zarqa who said he had repented and was taking care of his niece. (But I think maybe he has the hots for her.)

Muthlim Siq
Petra

You know what? This is just plain nuts. I've overcome my fifty year-long writer's block, and now I can't stop. WTF. Go with it.

We're taking a long rest stop so I have a chance to describe where we are.

This place is so fabulous I keep forgetting our predicament. We have been "walking" down the alternative entrance to Petra. The walls of the main *siq* are more dramatic and the path is smooth so all the tourists take that. *Muthlim siq* is the riverbed the Nabateans diverted the water down. It's cut deep into solid rock – in some places we're looking straight up at 100-foot rock walls on both sides – and we're picking our way over giant boulders and sliding down dry waterfalls as we work our way along this narrow passage. The entrance to *Muthlim* is also far from everyone else so there hasn't been an opportunity to signal for help.

Nour says it's about two kilometers before we get into Petra itself. She also says – some information she should keep to herself – that any rain will flood *Muthlim siq* and drown everyone foolhardy enough to be in it. The ground for miles and miles around is solid rock. Water doesn't soak in; it roars down gullies, creating instant rivers twenty to thirty feet deep. Every few years there's a drowning in *Muthlim* which is why the authorities discourage use of it. As luck would have it, everyone seems to have heeded those warnings and we're the only people in it today.

Nour says Jordan is still in its 'rainy' season. Shut up, Nour.

I hear distant thunder.

Whew. Out of *Muthlim* at last and in a deserted part of Petra, near the Christian burial grounds (according to Nour). There were a few sprinkles, just to scare the pee out of me, but no flood. Now we seem to be stalled again, so I'll write although Max is dropping broad hints that I should save my energy.

Manal's uncle and the BBM are not with us. They split before we left our 'prison'. They kept out of sight, but I'm positive I recognized their voices. We don't know what to make of the uncle showing up. It seemed like he was trying to put some distance between himself and all this 'honor' bullshit.

The oldest Karaki came into Petra on the smooth *siq* and carried things in two large bundles. I think he must have rented a horse because he brought a lot and was waiting for us when we emerged from the *Muthlim siq*. We're being given small backpacks to carry supplies, although they haven't given us anything to put in them yet. I'm amazed at how they arrange this stuff. They're in big danger, and still they seem to think through the logistics.

Max asked Nour if the Tourist Police won't find us as they shoo people out for the night. She says it's not likely. Petra is huge, cliffs and mountains everywhere so you can't see in any direction for more than a few hundred yards, and there are caves to hide in. The Tourist Police go through the motions, but people spend the night in Petra all the time.

The good news is that it looks like the three Karakis only brought one pistol which they pass around. The youngest guy has it now. Maybe we can jump him.

They gave us some sandwiches which the older guy bought at the Crown Plaza. Night has fallen quickly and they're signaling we should finish up. I thought we might spend the night here but we're about to move out. Half-moon just came over a cliff to the east. I suspect unreliable light from it as the cliffs are so high that only the widest valleys in Petra will have more than a few hours of direct moonlight.

I'm ready to stop for the night. Why are we moving? And to where?

The Monastery is where. After stumbling along over dark ground for half an hour Nour just told me we're about to enter the narrow path up to the Monastery which is the highest point in Petra. She warns: lots of drop offs, most of them several hundred feet. Don't step unless you're sure of where you're putting your foot.

We're allowed a quick rest stop before starting up the mountain. Surprise. There's a restaurant here. It's closed for the night, but the bathrooms are open: actual toilets and sinks with running water. A sign above the tap warns – in four languages – against drinking from it. I'm thirsty; it's hard to resist the water.

And I'm tired. I don't think I've ever been this exhausted. If I just lay down on the ground what would they do? Would they kill me?

I have my Max. He'll see me through.

Now they're giving us hand gestures to move out.

I'm very sorry to write that that was Sally's last journal entry.

Panic time

That was the most terrifying night of my life, and there may be more to come. Sally collapsed halfway up the mountain. My Sally. I grabbed her before she hit the ground. It was one of the few relatively flat and wide spots on the path so there was no danger of her pitching off into the dark abyss.

That's two collapses these guys have seen. Aren't they getting the message? She hasn't had access to her meds for 36 hours. Weakness and fatigue are side effects of radiation therapy; it knocks the stuffing out of a person. We got some water into her and she revived enough to hold onto my shoulders and wrap her legs around my waist while I carried her. The path was steep – mostly steps carved into the rock – and I had to trade off with the Mukhabarat driver twice.

There was one significant development during the trip up the mountain. The middle of the three Karakis – in age – misstepped and went down the steep cliff face, clawing futilely as he disappeared into the darkness. We think he's dead. Screams as he went down. Silence after he hit. The other two debated whether to go looking for him, but decided they couldn't in the dark. They brought everything except fresh batteries for their flashlights which petered out after fifteen minutes. Did the dead guy take the pistol over the side with him?

The accident gave the rest of us time to catch our breath. When we resumed Sally walked/climbed for a while, but I could see she was unsteady and I insisted I carry her again. She resists being carried but the path is often too narrow to walk by her side and support her. The only thing she said was, "Aren't you glad this disease knocked a few pounds off me?"

The most wonderful person in the world. I can't bear the thought of losing her or her losing the full life that's her due.

Hey, God. Could you transfer the goddamned cancer to me? I'd take it if I could. I've given this some thought and I'm serious. She'd do better on her own than I will without her.

If not God, maybe some other deity. I'd cut a Faustian deal right here – on the side of this miserable mountain. *Mephistopheles? Asclepius? Vejovis? Any takers?*

No response.

We climbed for over an hour. At the top of the path is the Monastery, a huge edifice fifty meters high cut into the mountain. An overwhelming sight, even in our frightened and exhausted condition. Small fires signal that there are people camped inside the Monastery and others are scattered around the area. Just kids back-packing their way around the world. None of them armed and probably unable to help us.

We were herded past the Monastery and across the rolling mountaintop until we were far from everyone else. Out in the open, the moonlight made walking easier. I was wondering if I'd be able to sleep on a rock surface. It wasn't a problem. The final event of the evening was to tie our ankles together with small chains and padlocks. They arranged us lying in opposite directions. If we wanted to go anywhere, we would have to roll together. My ankle was chained to the driver's, Sally's to Nour's. Muslim sensibilities.

The younger Karaki seemed to be crying. Nour said it was his brother who took the plunge.

Food and water. I wrote the preceding while we were waiting for the older Karaki to make a round trip to a canteen/restaurant in front of the Monastery. If you're wondering why I'm writing during all this, it's to keep Sally from doing it. She's gone from a fear of writing to an addiction. But it's hard to keep up and this may be the last thing I'm able to write for a while. We have bigger problems than keeping a running account going.

Breakfast is sandwiches teeming with toxic organisms and two Cokes apiece. Diarrhea? What the hell. It can't get worse.

Perhaps to distract us Nour has slipped into tour guide mode. "To the west is Mount Harun where Aaron is buried. He was Moses' brother. It is written that Moses and Aaron went there often to talk with God. Because of Aaron's tomb it's been a shrine forever. Back during the crusades Christian monks lived in the caves around the shrine. It's also holy for Muslims and you can see the mosque."

Well, yes, you can see it, but because of the distance it's just a white dot. Lying between us and Jebel Harun are several miles of the nastiest terrain I've ever seen. A hellscape of vertical walls two thousand feet high, great jumbles of boulders, not a flat space anywhere, not a single green blade of grass or weed or shrub. Forget trees. You think that's the bad part? No. The great rounded sandstone mountains of Petra abruptly give way to jagged black volcanic up-thrusts. The rocks look razor sharp and impassable. On the far side of the volcanic activity, which extends for maybe one kilometer, the smooth rose-colored sandstone reasserts itself.

Steep drop offs, jagged rocks, no hint of a path. Who would ever venture into that?

Ah fuck! *We* would. "Finish eating and we start to Jebel Harun," announced the older Karaki. Compounding this bad news, the pistol was stuck prominently in his belt.

Time to speak up. "You've seen my woman collapse twice. She cannot walk that distance in these conditions."

"Is she sick?"

"Yes. She has cancer of the liver. She does not have her medicine and if she does not receive a new liver soon, she will die." Unfortunately I had to say this in front of Sally.

The man thought about this. "I see now that it is true. You are here to take more organs."

I'm stopping the running account. The writing has been a useful distraction but now it's too much of a drain. It's impossible to focus on anything other than survival.

If something follows this, it will have been written after the fact.

Hellscape

Our captors weren't novices. They kept us just hydrated enough so we could keep moving, but in a weakened state. For every small bottle of water we were allowed, the Karakis drank two. I would probably have done the same, had our roles been reversed.

I'd expected the Mukhabarat agents to make a move. The driver had seemed to be on the verge of doing something several times. He'd shuffle around, staring blankly at the ground as he edged nearer to whichever Karaki had the gun, but every time he got within five meters the Karaki would whip out the pistol and the driver would have to retreat.

It was miserable going. A rough path led off the top of the mountain down into the jumble of giant boulders. We frequently had to hoist one another up a rock face, or assist someone sliding down. The Karakis always made us back away when they were helping each other.

Long stretches of the path traversed steeply slanting sides of a mountain. In those areas the 'path' was reduced to scrape marks. We tried to place our feet in the occasional indents to gain a more secure toehold in the smooth rock and watched for pebbles or sand that might become ball bearings that would send a person roller-skating down the rock face.

The air was cool, but the sun intense and the altitude – over 4,000 feet – was a further drain. Nour said it was normally a six-to-seven-hour hike to Mount Harun but I don't think we were moving at a normal pace.

And why there? It's a holy site, one of the holiest in Jordan. Wouldn't pilgrims come up there? It seemed a poor choice to hide out. Maybe they planned to hole up in one of the monks' caves until the heat was off. Or maybe we wouldn't get that far. What little we could see of the path ahead, there appeared to be several promising places to push an unwanted captive over the edge. A body in those ravines wouldn't be discovered for a long time. I thought of de Châtillon airmailing his captives onto the rocks, their heads encased in boxes.

Sally was holding up better than I'd expected. They let her have more water than the rest of us. But she still stumbled frequently and pushed my hand away when I tried to hold her arm. *I think that's called counter-dependence, Sal.* We hadn't gone far when the Karakis announced the first rest break in front of one of the caves along the path. The cave was shallow but provided shade. More lethal-looking sandwiches.

The older Karaki, who'd been silent since we started walking, decided to share some family history. "When I was young boy my father bring me to Jebel Harun. It is magic place. Sometimes pilgrims come to get energy or to have babies. I think maybe my father and my mother go to Harun and that is why I am here. Now different. There is sometime guard because tourists come. Tourists have no respect for holy place."

Guard? If there was an official guard that the Karakis knew about, it seemed less likely they would want us to make the complete trip. What was their plan? A cave away from the shrine? Over the edge into the abyss? Or a different destination? I noticed Nour's eyes dart in my direction, then she resumed staring at the ground. I hoped her listlessness was an act to lull the Karakis into lowering their guard.

"I feel magic at Jebel Harun every time. After my niece die in Swiss country I come to Harun and pray for her soul."

Were we supposed to admire this act of piety? We were, however, learning one thing from his reminiscences: he knew his way around these mountains.

"What's your name?" That's me, trying to establish a chummier relationship with our captors. "It looks like we'll be traveling together for some time." I hoped that our time wouldn't be cut short.

"Mohammad. My nephew," he nodded at the young Karaki, "also have name Mohammad. Nephew who fall last night name Badr."

Our conversation was interrupted by the sound of an approaching chopper. Mohammad Sr. waved us further back into the shallow cave with his pistol. The helicopter went directly overhead, out of our sight, following the path toward Mount Harun.

As the clatter of the chopper receded to the west, I cocked an eye at Mohammad the Elder. "Mohammad, we have a difficult situation here."

He looked away.

"If you haven't figured it out, when we left Mukhabarat we took a file with your information in it and we told people we were going to Karak. Someone in Mukhabarat will realize that we haven't come back and the file is missing. It might be a coincidence, but I think the appearance of that helicopter means the search has begun."

Still no response.

"The file we took has your names and address. A bureaucracy like Mukhabarat will have backup copies. I'm guessing they've already gone to your home in Karak."

Mohammad Sr.'s eye twitched. Had the two women stayed in the house?

"It will be difficult for you to escape. If you surrender you will go to Suwaqa prison for kidnapping. You have four hostages and you might be able to negotiate a more lenient sentence in exchange for our release. If you kill us . . ." I couldn't help myself; my gaze drifted to the drop-off just a few feet in front of our cave. Recovering, "If you kill us, you will hang."

Neither of the Mohammads was interested in engaging in this conversation. Mohammad Sr. abruptly gestured for us to resume walking. I was hoping they'd discuss my proposal between them. They didn't.

Hard landing

As we started out, Nour, for no evident reason, resumed her tour guide chatter which consisted solely of descriptions of rock features. Why not? That was the only thing visible. She moved closer to me, and as her hand gestured at the mountains, she said quietly, "That was an Army helicopter. Perhaps they are already looking for us, but if they are they will not come back here soon because they have swept this area." Was there an alternative explanation? There was, and Nour continued, "Or, it could just be a normal patrol. We are close to the Israeli border and the Army has to watch for militants who want to provoke an incident with Israel."

Then she pointed at indentations in the sandstone and loudly explained the contribution of lightning strikes to the topography of the area.

We came around the side of the mountain and were confronted by the great upheaval of black volcanic material we'd seen from a distance. The smooth sandstone we were crossing looked reassuring and forgiving compared to the jagged spires of basalt in front.

"There is a path," said Nour brightly; her expression conveyed less optimism, "but it is difficult. Try to not fall down because the rocks will cut you." She, like myself, was scanning the hellscape for evidence of the promised path.

Our little band of hikers was becoming spread out. Mohammad Sr. led the way, either by dint of seniority or because he knew the land. Mohammad Jr. brought up the rear. He had the pistol; we were constantly in his view. The driver appeared to be having the most trouble. He wobbled when he walked and on two occasions sank to one knee. When he fell Nour would start toward him, to be waved away by gun-toting Jr.

Mohammad Sr. was becoming increasingly impatient with our progress. Nour had an explanation. "It is soon time for other pilgrims to appear on this path. They will come all the way from Wadi Musa which is two more hours, but they will walk faster. They will catch up."

"Are there a lot of pilgrims?" And are they young, combat trained, maybe armed?

Nour shrugged. "Most pilgrims come up the other path – from Wadi Araba. It is hotter, but not so dangerous. Only a few pilgrims and tourists come this way. Every year there are deaths."

I risked a look toward the edge of the precipice and an idle thought floated through my mind: would the ravines below our path fill with bodies to the point where, one day, the landscape would become level? I was getting dehydrated.

Mohammad Sr. was making angry arm gestures to signal his displeasure with our slow pace.

We entered onto the last traverse across a steeply slanted sandstone face before we reached the volcanic area. The rockface sloped down to the left; the angle must have been at least 40 degrees. You have to hand it to those pilgrims.

I was carefully watching where I placed my feet while staying within grabbing distance of Sally. Her breathing was labored, but her walk seemed steady.

Behind us we heard a soft thud and groan. The driver had dropped on all fours. That was too much for Mohammad Jr. who approached him gesturing and shouting. It looked like Jr. was about to deliver a motivational kick. The driver slowly rotated in Jr.'s direction, and, as Jr. pulled back his foot, the driver sprang at him. We'd been waiting for that.

But so had Jr. who dodged to the side, pulled the gun, and fired at the driver who spun and fell.

Jr. inspected the driver. The bullet wound appeared to be in the man's neck. Jr. looked questioningly at his uncle, who shrugged. Jr. echoed the shrug, then pushed the driver hard, sending him rolling down the steep rock face.

We watched, sickened by the sight of the lifeless body tumbling and flopping inexorably toward the vertical cliff that was twenty meters below the path. The rolling body accelerated, then lurched to a stop just short of the drop-off.

The Mohammads exchanged looks, then both turned to me. Jr. gestured with his gun in the direction of the driver. It was clear they wanted me to ease my way down to the twisted body, free it from whatever was holding it – inconveniently in plain sight of passersby – and dispose of it over the edge. My return up the steep rock face was optional.

I shook my head, no. Jr. stepped behind Sally, wrapped his arm around her neck and pressed the pistol against her temple. Sr. nodded, yes.

I started to inch my way down backwards, trying to place each foot flat on the unreliable sandstone. The slope was too steep to get more than the front third of my shoe flat against the mountainside. If I went sliding, arms windmilling, to my death, to whom would the body-disposal assignment be given next?

Sally spoke, her voice constricted by the arm around her neck. "No, Max. You're doing it wrong. You have to lie on your stomach and try to keep as much contact with the rock as you can."

I tried it. She was right. I did feel more in control, but I expected that at any second I'd feel myself slip and start irrevocably toward the cliff. Would my route carry me into the driver? Was his body's purchase on the rock-face strong enough to halt my slide? Not questions that needed to be put to the test. Sweat was making my hands slippery and I tried to wipe them on the rock as I continued the slow descent, afraid to lift my head high enough to check progress.

My feet encountered something soft. I'd arrived at the destination. Twisting my head, I could see no impediment holding the driver in place. Must be something under him. All I had to do was get a toe under him and boost him slightly. I looked back up the mountain. Jr. held Sally tightly, nodded yes, and smiled thinly. Hammurabi? This man's life for his brother's?

I inched my foot under the driver and lifted. Nothing. I pushed my foot further under the body and looked back at him. His eyes were open and pleading. He blinked, but made no sound. I looked up at Sally; she appeared to be having trouble breathing in Jr.'s choke hold. I edged my foot further under the driver and lifted. He rolled. There was the soft sound of the body making one more rotation, then silence. I kept my eyes fixed on Sally.

Jr. released her, proof I'd accomplished my assigned mission. Raynald de Châtillon would have been proud.

Lengthening odds

"The negotiated surrender option is off the table now."

"I know, Sal. They've murdered a government agent. If they're caught, they'll swing."

"When they figure that out we'll just be dead weight."

Sally and I were keeping our voices low. I'd hauled and clawed my way back up to the path and we were resting while the Mohammads talked. I was trying to suppress the image of the driver's face and pleading expression. The Morse-code blinking to signal he was alive. The terror in his eyes. An image that will never fade.

Two years since I'd killed anyone. I thought I was done with this. How about a big board like they have in hazardous factories that can be updated daily:

> **~~732~~ 0 Days Since Max Brown Killed A Fellow Human**

For a man who preached non-violence, I was a lousy practitioner.

I looked down the mountain to where I'd sent the driver over the edge. No outcropping was visible that might have snagged his body. What had held him there? Will power?

And what a waste of perfectly good organs. What was his blood type? Odds of it being compatible were pretty good in this region. These thoughts were interrupted by a sound I hadn't heard for over two years: Sally crying.

"Goddammit, Max. I'm so sorry. This is all my fault."

I gathered her in my arms, trying to ignore how frail she felt. "Your fault, babe?" I'd just killed a man; that's hard to top.

"I insisted we come to Jordan. When you were down by the edge of the cliff I was so afraid you were going to fall. I knew if you did, I was going to jump after you." Before I could respond my wife pressed her head into my neck and let it out.

The mind is a strange device. My only thought was: is it better to let her cry and release what's tormenting her, or should I try to pull her out of this before she uses up any more of her dwindling reserves.

I didn't have to choose. Sr. signaled we should reverse course back along the path we'd just come. Sally got unsteadily to her feet and looked at me pleadingly. I had nothing.

Our change of course seemed unlikely to augur anything positive, but it did mean we wouldn't have to go into the jagged spires of basalt. I looked questioningly at Nour. She shrugged. Sally allowed me to hold her arm as we retraced our steps.

We'd made it halfway back to the Monastery when we were directed left, along a path to the north.

"Little Petra is this way," said Nour. "It's a smaller and less popular version of Petra. But still there will be people there."

It sounded like she didn't understand the logic of this new direction. Or why the death of her fellow Mukhabarat agent had forced a change of plans.

I didn't either. If they were going to kill us, they weren't going to find a better opportunity than to send us over the edge to join the driver. Apparently we still had some value. This possibility, put on infinite replay, helped and I shared it with Sally. She shrugged acknowledgment. Was she too exhausted to experience hope, even fleeting rays of it?

Our captors' new plan required coordination with their accomplices. Every few minutes Sr. checked his cellphone. As we entered the path to Little Petra he signaled a halt and while Jr. watched us, Sr. walked out of earshot and placed a call. The frequent waving of his free arm suggested the new plan wasn't receiving unqualified support. The conversation over, he returned and gestured that we should resume walking.

After half an hour the terrain relented and a few scrub pines grew defiantly out of crevices. We took shelter from the sun in a grove of three stunted oak trees. Sandwiches and water were distributed.

Sally and I didn't talk much. The only conversation starter I had was, "How you doing now, babe?" a question that became tiresome with repetition. We had no idea what was going on so avoided endless and pointless speculation. Strange – to be in this situation with her, and have nothing to share but our fear. We'd been in difficult situations before, but rarely when both of us were captives. There had always been some kind of action one of us could take. Jr. was quick and accurate with the pistol so we were reduced to waiting and hoping they'd make a mistake before we were too exhausted to seize on the opportunity.

My soul mate put her hand on my arm. "That was a bad one, wasn't it." I knew she was referring to the Mukhabarat driver. "When I was in the Army the infantry guys bragged that any idiot could be a sniper. You squeeze, two hundred yards away something crumples, you don't even hear them cry out. You're not involved. But cutting a man's throat, or stabbing him with a bayonet? That's personal and it's not easy. The result is the same – someone dies – but the effect on the person who kills him is different."

She was right. Killing someone with a gun had been easy. Is that why it happens so often? But taking the life of a person whose humanness is pressed against you? Even if only against your foot? God grant I never end a man's life with a knife.

A second shot at negotiations. The Mohammads had finished their sandwiches and were repacking the knapsacks.

"Mohammad, we need to work together. It's still a mutual problem." This declaration brought a look of scorn from Jr., but Sr. did turn toward me, with an expression of forced patience.

"We're your captives, but all of Jordan is looking for you. If I were you I'd be trying to leave the country. We're slowing you down so your options are to kill us or lock us up somewhere we wouldn't be found until you had a good head start. My bias is obvious, but I'd advise against killing us. If you did that, the American government would be very persistent and would put pressure on other governments to find our murderers."

I was hoping I'd made a good case for the second option: locking us up. Mohammad started to say something, stopped, and turned up the path.

Four dreaded words

We resumed our trudge toward Little Petra. Periodically the path would disappear, but Sr. knew the way; after crossing unmarked terrain for several minutes the path would reappear in front of us.

The driver must have been their greatest concern; in his absence their vigilance relaxed. Sometimes the Mohammads would walk together ahead of us, checking over their shoulders to make sure no one was scurrying off across the rock face.

The path was usually wide enough that Sally and I could walk side-by-side. She seemed to be doing okay, but was withdrawn. Of course she was. There was a lot to think about.

"Max," she fixed her eyes on me. "We need to talk."

"Ah, babe. The four words every man dreads."

No smile in return. Levity couldn't penetrate the fear and fatigue.

"I'm listening. The topic? I'm guessing my name is in the subject line." That was aggressive and I regretted saying it. "Sorry, Sal. What's on your mind . . . aside from the fact that we're captives and our captors don't have many options other than killing us and we're weak from dehydration and you need a replacement part?"

She did smile at that. "You're right; your name is in the subject line." I smiled too, but my heart wasn't in it. She paused to gather her breath; the path had sloped up slightly.

"You're a combat pilot, Max." Four decades ago I was a combat pilot.

"You're courageous and resourceful." Also past tense – if ever.

"We're in deep shit here and I can't contribute much." At last something I could agree with – the deep shit part.

"It's time for my boy to step up."

That was it. That was all she had to say. Is there a response? I didn't have one ready. Sally cocked her head, waiting for a reply.

Isn't vanity great? My immediate reaction was pride. My woman looks to me to sweep her to safety. After this pleasant rush, pride gave way to the realization that her confidence was misplaced. Cancer's surprise arrival had undermined my usual Panglossian outlook. I had no ideas, no energy, and no faith that things were going to work out. But this wasn't the time to bring up those doubts.

"You're right, babe. It's good that the search parties may be out, but we need to do more." She nodded encouragingly; I was going in the right direction. "Junior's the problem. He's good with the gun, but even without that I don't think I could take him. He's young, he's fit, and he isn't weakened by dehydration."

Sally's expression was changing. She didn't need a recitation of the obvious. She needed a plan of action. I changed tack.

"Senior might be where we find leverage. I'll try to draw him into a discussion again about locking us up while they hotfoot it to another country."

Nour had slowed her pace and dropped back to join us. She shook her head. "They won't let you go. You are their only bargaining chip. If it is just me, they might. They must know that the security forces will not negotiate for my safety. I'm no good as a hostage. But you two are different."

Sadly, it made sense. I could talk to Sr. forever about the advantages of ditching us. We were too valuable to be let go.

"Of course you're right, Nour. Sally and I were trying to come up with a plan, but it's complicated by the fact that these guys aren't very good at this which makes them unpredictable, which makes them more dangerous."

Nour considered this. I wondered if she didn't, out of professional habit, attribute more intelligence to our adversaries than they deserved. "From what I could overhear, it looks like we're heading to a rendezvous. Perhaps Manal's uncle and the big, bearded man will be waiting for us." She caught her breath. "I think the fact of the search helicopter finally got through to them. We turned around when they killed Anwar, my colleague, so I thought there was a connection, but it was probably the realization that we would be out in the open for another five hours if we continued to the shrine on Jebel Harun. Little Petra is much closer and we will be there in just . . ."

"Too much talk!" shouted Jr. He waved the pistol for emphasis. Our planning meeting was recessed.

Shell game

Human behavior. Tourists who seek out distant and less known places don't go there to associate with other tourists. Apparently any contact with other foreigners contaminates the experience. This was driven home as our group entered the long passage into Little Petra. People we'd see ahead would evaporate into the caves or ancient ruins up off the path. No chance to enlist help or signal our distress. After passing several ruins, we made a sharp right turn up a steep path. Nour, perhaps to her embarrassment, didn't recognize the landmarks and shrugged. Sr. seemed to take satisfaction from this.

"Wu'eira Castle was most strong of all Crusader castles. You see it is on top of high cliffs."

It must have seemed impregnable in the 12th century. Any approach was straight up one hundred feet of rock.

The climb was arduous. I tried to provide upward pressure on Sally's arm, without being obvious. After five minutes of slow progress up the steep steps cut into one of the cliff faces we arrived at the castle entrance. If it was once a formidable redoubt, you wouldn't know it today. Crumbling mud walls, some arches and a few large intact, but roofless, rooms. The only vestiges of impregnability that hadn't been erased by time were the vertical cliffs that descended on all sides of the ruin. Conspicuously absent: no place to lock us up and leave us behind.

The castle was deserted but for two tourists, a young couple, who slipped out a far archway as we entered the largest room. The Big Bearded Man was waiting.

There was an immediate argument between Sr. and the BBM. Nour whispered, "The man says this is not a good place to come to. We have to go. He says Mohammad was wrong." Nour delivered this with some satisfaction. Sr.'s knowledge of Jordan's ancient monuments wasn't so great after all.

Sally sank to the floor and sat, cross-legged, resting her head in her hands. Jr. was inspecting the pistol. I was hoping for water.

Sr. and the BBM spoke more quietly. Abruptly the BBM signaled the conversation was over and headed toward the main entrance, gesturing that Sr. should follow him. Brief instructions were barked at Jr., who first appeared dumbfounded, then displeased.

Sally and I looked at Nour.

"We have to go to a car," she explained. "The young man with the pistol is to take us down the back way that was closed years ago because it is dangerous."

Jr. herded us through a side archway and along a crumbling rampart toward the opposite side of Wu'eira castle from where we'd come in. When we reached the end of the rampart the reasons for abandoning the old access stairway were evident. It was two feet wide, at best; some of the steps had eroded and were now ramps; and the drop off was nearly perpendicular. We pulled back from the dizzying view. Jr. was no more enthusiastic about this route than we were. Could this be exploited?

Jr. seemed unpredictable and hot-headed, but if we were valuable commodities, as Nour had said, we might be able to press some small demands. I retreated a few more feet from the edge and pulled Sally back. I'm more nervous when she's standing near a drop-off than when I am – and I'm the family acrophobe. "Water," I announced, and took off my backpack and pulled out three small bottles. Jr. scowled, reached into his pocket for the pistol, checked for tourists, but mainly looked indecisive. I pulled out a fourth bottle and offered it to him.

"Mohammad, I'm very sorry about your brother, Badr." This seemed a good time to remind him of the perils of venturing too close to the edge.

No reply, but none was wanted. "Were you close?" He didn't seem to understand this and looked at Nour who translated. Jr. sipped at his water – the rest of us had downed ours in a few quick gulps – and looked away. He wiped his eyes and turned fiercely on us. Embarrassed to be seen crying?

"We go now," he barked. "You go first." He pointed at me. Sally had been seated again. I helped her to her feet; she sagged back to the floor. Panic was overcoming me when she winked, her back to Jr.

"Mohammad, this isn't going to work. If we go down the back steps we will fall and you will not have your precious hostages."

Nour started to translate, but Jr. waved her off. He'd understood. His mouth was working. He took another look over the edge at the eroded steps, perhaps to weigh my claim, and repeated, "You go first."

I inched toward the edge of the rampart with small sideways steps. *Don't look down.* That's what they tell you.

'They' are wrong; fixing your gaze on the distant horizon doesn't work. You need to see where to place your feet, since the survivable foot-placement options, in this case, were few.

Gingerly . . . one foot on the top step. It held. I moved the other foot onto the same step, then edged a foot down to the second step. So far so good. Maybe whistling would help. Third step – first foot, second foot. The step crumbled; I tried to throw my body back onto the parapet which was chest high. My left foot was still on what remained of the sandstone step; my right was flailing in empty space and my arms were stretched across the floor of the parapet. My left foot slipped off the step and I felt myself sliding backward, the sand-covered floor of the parapet providing nothing to grab onto.

Then, two realizations: 1) Someone had stepped on my wrist, halting my slide; 2) I was still whistling.

An unlikely savior, Junior, had pinned my arm to the floor, his pistol trained on me. Why the pistol? If he couldn't keep me from falling would he shoot and spare me the terror of the fall? Sally and Nour sprang into action, each taking one of my hands as Junior stepped aside, and hauled me unceremoniously back up over the edge.

I lay, trembling, on the floor. Vertigo swept in and the floor seemed to be tilting. I gripped the floor again, searching for a handhold.

"It's okay, Max. I think you've demonstrated the folly of that route." The sound of her voice is always calming – except when she's mad at me. The floor leveled out. I crawled to the center of the room and sat up. Would retracing our steps down the front entrance be any better? Another attack of vertigo on those stairs and . . .

Junior signaled his impatience – acrophobia is a not an excuse note to the teacher – and we returned to the front of the ruined fortress. I looked over the edge at the stairs we'd come up. Better, but not a stroll in the park. I resumed whistling.

We started back down the narrow stairs. Jr. coming last, with Sally in front of him. He must have decided she was the leverage that would keep Nour and me from trying to get away. I was unlikely to bolt down the treacherous steps under any circumstances. Louder whistling.

"Max, you okay?"

"Hm hm."

"I'm not a music critic, but *Ode to Joy*? Positive message, but a little manic. Maybe something calmer – down tempo."

"Hm." I considered alternatives and switched to *Off We Go to the Limpopo*. A lilting tune and the lyrics are about forward movement.

It was midday and the tourists had either taken shelter from the sun or were breaking into their picnic lunches; none were near enough to signal. As we approached the exit of Little Petra we saw a guardhouse, presumably a ticket booth to check that tourists had paid the entry fees. No guard. I was getting more desperate for an opportunity to make a break for it. Sally must have picked up on that. "Patience, Max, "she whispered, "this guy's a good shot."

Rounding a turn, our fortunes soared. An Army Humvee was parked, engine idling, at the end of the path. I tried to signal to Sally that we should start running before Jr. noticed the Humvee, but he seemed aware of it and allowed us to continue directly toward it. Why?

Because the BBM, wearing army fatigues, was in the driver's seat. Manal's uncle sat beside him. They'd stolen the vehicle.

Jr. herded us into the back of the Humvee where Mohammad Sr. was waiting. No windows, but if the vehicle were pulled over at a roadblock, certainly we'd be discovered. The Jordanian Army would quickly be aware of a missing Humvee and start looking.

Nour must have been reading my thoughts. "Parts of the identifying numbers on this car have been covered with mud. If you're thinking we'll be freed at a roadblock, we'll probably just be waved through." Jr. captured this, and smiled.

The Humvee lurched forward. We really needed to up our game.

Thirty minutes later the Humvee stopped. Manal's uncle opened the back hatch and we climbed out into the bright afternoon glare. He avoided looking directly at us and retreated to his seat in the Humvee as soon as we were all out.

The BBM was already perched atop a ten-foot-tall chimney-shaped structure by the road. He was banging on something with a rock; it looked like there was a metal lid covering the top of the chimney that he was trying to open.

"This is a better hideout." Nour said, a note of admiration in her voice. "Look up." We did, shielding our eyes from the sun. Another towering castle sat on a cone-shaped mountain above us. The cliffs were not as steep as at Wu'eira, but they were higher. "Sho'bak Castle," announced Nour. "The best hiding place in Jordan."

Why? It looked more accessible than Wu'eira. A two-lane paved road wound around behind the mountain. There'd be no hugging a sheer cliff face as we inched up stairs carved out of crumbling sandstone. I pointed this out to Nour.

"That road goes up to the castle. We're going *into* the mountain." She paused for a reaction. It was becoming increasingly obvious she was a know-it-all, which must be a burden for someone in an intel service where the inviolable rule is that you keep your mouth zipped.

Getting no response from us, she resumed. "To withstand a siege the builders of the castle dug a tunnel down through the mountain to a water source. They found a spring and pool about half-way down through the mountain. Then they continued digging the tunnel down to the base for an escape route. This is where it ends. They used to let tourists go into the tunnel, but someone slipped and fell to his death (there's that 'falling to your death' thing, again). The water in the tunnel destroys the steps, and tourist traffic was also damaging. I have always wanted to come here. This is very exciting."

I couldn't share in her excitement.

The screech of hinges signaled the BBM had broken the lock on the door covering the entrance to the shaft. We climbed up metal rungs set in the side of the chimney – Jr. bringing up the rear – swung our legs over the top and descended down another set of rungs on the inside of the chimney. The BBM watched, impassively, and when we had all descended to the bottom, he threw down a bag and swung the metal hatch shut. Sounds of fumbling were followed by a click – presumably a replacement padlock being latched. We were sealed in.

Pitch black. A narrow streak of orange was visible along one side of the metal door above us, but no light reached the tunnel floor. An opportunity? If I could be sure which of the forms around me was Jr., I'd try to take him out and liberate the pistol. The person nearest on my right was Nour; no mistaking that perfume. Where was Jr?

"Sally, are you okay?"

"Right behind you." She knew what I was doing. Two accounted for; two to go.

There was a soft rustling to my left. I swung a wild haymaker. Would it connect with air, or a Mohammad? Fifty:fifty chance it would be the Mohammad with the gun. My fist grazed fabric, nothing substantial. There was shuffling and my wild swing was answered by a counter-punch to the chest. Recovering my balance, I lunged forward, trying to grab whoever was in front of me and had returned my punch. Nothing. I lurched into a dirt wall.

A flashlight switched on. Sr. was holding the bag BBM had dropped in. It contained fresh batteries and Sr. had reloaded.

Jr. shook his head dismissively and spat on the floor.

"You will die the way you live"

Those are the words I spoke to Mohammad Sr. He looked up sharply, interrupting his reading of the Koran.

We had climbed up the crumbling slick stairs through the mountain until we arrived at a subterranean room, perhaps twenty feet in diameter and eight feet high. A shallow pool of water occupied half the space, the remainder of the floor was wet and black, but firm. The Karakis distributed small bags of peanuts. Nour opined the water in the pool would be safe to drink. We scooped up water, settled in – with no idea for how long – and waited for an opportunity.

The Mohammads took turns praying, then set up shop on the far side of the pool where it would be more difficult to rush them. My failed attempt had put them on notice. A gas lantern came hissing to life and Sr. produced a small book with gilt lettering on the cover. He started reading, his lips moving. Jr. glared at us.

"You will die the way you live," I said, then waited for a reaction.

"You quote the Prophet? Peace be upon him."

"If someone does not show mercy to people, Allah will not show mercy to him." And then I ran out. I was pleased that I could come up with two passably relevant sayings by the Prophet.

Sr. pondered this. "Are you Muslim?"

"I am a man committed to non-violence," although I'd recently taken a swing at them, "and an admirer of any man who promotes peace, such as the Prophet, peace be upon him."

I didn't look at Sally, who might have found my new-found piety ridiculous. What the hell. We had little to lose. Perhaps I could invent a credible saying to promote our case. I was working on something pithy I might attribute to Prophet Mohammad that urged freeing captives when Jr. spoke in Arabic.

Nour translated quietly. "He's warning his uncle not to be deceived. He says you are a devil."

In which case, better not take chances with specious quotes.

Sr. resumed reading. That was my third failed attempt to start a dialogue. We sat in silence.

An hour or more later the clank of the metal hatch from far down the shaft signaled that company was coming. Jr. extinguished the gas lantern, knowing I couldn't rush them in the dark without splashing noisily through the water. A faint glimmer of light advanced up the shaft. It grew brighter, and then a voice called out. The Karakis turned their flashlights on; apparently it wasn't a rescue party.

A minute later Manal's uncle, breathing heavily, struggled up the last few steps and dropped three plastic shopping bags on the ground.

"Provisions," guessed Nour. "We'll be here a while."

Good that there was no immediate plan for videotaped beheadings. Bad in that Sally didn't have a lot of 'whiles' left in her. Without her meds she would feel terrible and the cancer would metastasize unchecked. I gave dialogue another shot.

Addressing the three men who were now clustered on the far side of the pool, "I've said it before. We have a mutual problem. You need us as bargaining chips if you are to have any hope of leaving Jordan alive. As for us, our situation is clear. We're captives. But we have a special problem that affects you. My wife is ill and her medicine is in that car back in Karak. If she dies, I will have no reason to continue living." My voice became thick. "I will want to die also and may succeed in taking one of you with me."

Manal's uncle looked alarmed. The Mohammads had heard some of this pitch before and were less impressed. There was a whispered conference among our captors – Uncle glancing frequently at Sally – then Uncle retreated, cautiously, back down the slippery stairs. Several minutes later we heard the clank of the metal hatch.

Wordlessly, Sr. examined the contents of the shopping bags. He was about to distribute the bounty, then thought better of it, selected a shrink-wrapped package of cold cuts for himself, and signaled with a hand wave that we were free to take whatever we wanted.

Manal's uncle had brought an interesting selection, but we weren't choosy. Chips, olives, packaged dates, processed meat, oranges . . . and it all tasted good. I was still eating when Sally's head slumped onto my shoulder, asleep. Moving carefully, I maneuvered us toward the wall.

My soul mate. The best I could offer her was a shoulder. With each passing hour her chances dimmed. I ran through the full gamut of negative emotions, starting at self-recrimination, through anger at a cosmos that would allow this to happen, and ending at deep sorrow. Eyes damp, I dropped off myself.

Sometime later we were both awakened by the distant clank of the metal door announcing another visitor.

Again, the precaution of dousing the gas lantern; again, the shout from below; and again, Manal's uncle appeared, this time bearing a small bag with the name and logo of a Geneva pharmacy on it. He handed it to Sally with a triumphant smile.

"Thank you . . . thank you so much." Beaming with relief, she opened the pill bottles, threw two capsules in her mouth, and scooped water from the pool.

I studied Uncle. "You did that for her, didn't you? Not for your own benefit."

He smiled. Had we found an ally?

Jr. was watching this with growing incredulity. Shaking his head angrily, he waded through the pool and grabbed for the bag of medicines. I beat him and held the bag behind me. Sr. shouted at his nephew, but it had no effect. Both of the older men seemed to be of the same mind. Manal's uncle stepped in front of Jr. and Mohammad Sr. splashed across the pool to join the confrontation. The shouting match between Jr. and the two older men rose to a crescendo, then wound down to gestures and muttering that signified final warnings were being restated, it having been agreed to disagree. Jr. retreated across the pool, in full sulk.

With calm restored, I asked Uncle, "Your name, sir? Your real name?"

He looked in Nour's direction. The Mukhabarat agent answered for him, "Khalid. His real name is Khalid al-Masri."

Khalid nodded.

"Thank you, Khalid. The medicines keep my wife alive while she's waiting for a liver transplant. And no, we are not in Jordan looking for an organ. Just as I said before, we're here trying to find who's involved in the illegal removal of organs from women who went to Switzerland for surgery after an acid attack."

Sally asked, "Where did you find my medicine?"

"In car."

That's where we'd left it.

The implications were clear. Should I share them? Why not? It had been my repeated contention that our problem was mutual.

"Does everybody understand what that means?" If they hadn't figured it out already, my question would get them thinking about it. "It means one of two things: Either Mukhabarat has not yet figured out that we're missing and has not gone to your house in Karak. Or they were watching that car – it's a Mukhabarat car – and will be arriving soon."

A flurry of competing voices in Arabic. Nour scowled at me. If it were the second option, I'd just complicated any rescue attempt.

"In either case, you might want to move. If they're coming for us you don't have much time. If they aren't, it means you have an opportunity – which will not last forever – to get across a border."

Sally looked dumb-founded, and whispered, "Whose side are you on?"

I would have to explain later. *For starters, Sal, I don't want a rescue attempt to take place inside the mountain.* The chances of us becoming collateral damage seemed higher than if we were out in the open. The other option: If there was an opportunity for them to leave the country, Uncle Khalid's act of kindness encouraged the hope that we'd be released when our captors reached safety.

Or, I might have just made a fatal mistake.

A missed opportunity

The steps up through the shaft were in worse condition than the lower ones we'd climbed earlier in the day. "Damage from tourists," Nour explained. All of us, except for agile Mohammad Jr., lost footing at least once and found ourselves pitched forward onto hands and knees, scrabbling for a purchase on the wet rock to prevent an accelerating descent. I stayed close behind Sally in case I had to stop her slide before she gained momentum.

Escapism? My mind wandered back to our first travels together in England. I'd insisted she go first up paths and staircases so I could study the sensuous curves of her backside. *We've come a long way together, babe. Who would have thought it would lead here?*

These thoughts were interrupted by our arrival at the top. Sr. held up a hand and went ahead. After the climb, we were glad for a chance to catch our breath. Sally slumped against the wall.

A gunshot reverberated through the tunnel. Was this the rescue attempt? It couldn't start off worse. Sr. had been shot and Jordanian commandos would come storming into the shaft, automatic weapons blazing. I grabbed Sally's arm, prepared to pull her onto the ground beneath me when the bullets started flying.

Not a rescue attempt. Sr. returned down the steps, shouting angrily in Arabic.

Jr. acknowledged Sr.'s outrage with a shrug, and tilting the pistol forward, signaled we should resume climbing. We looked at Nour, who shook her head; this wasn't the time for conversation among us.

The treacherous steps turned into a dry path that leveled out until we emerged into late twilight. I hadn't been aware of the passage of that much time. In the gravel parking lot in front of us sat the panel truck that had transported us from Karak two days earlier.

Lying face down to our left was a uniformed guard, a trickle of blood pooling in the dirt beneath his open mouth.

Manal's uncle, Khalid, staggered backward, his hand over his face. He took a second look at the dead guard, started to say something, but could only stammer.

BBM was holding a Kalashnikov with which he waved us toward the open side door of the van. As Nour passed him, he stopped her with the gun, and looked her up and down. He said something to Jr., who laughed, then he let Nour continue.

Closed in the back of the van, Sally looked at Nour. "Well?" Sally demanded.

Nour shook her head, no.

"He was talking about rape, wasn't he, Nour? Do you think he's serious?"

"He made the threat in front of others."

Sally was on the case. She had always placed rape at the top of the hierarchy of heinous crimes. "What did he say?"

"I do not want to tell you."

That wasn't good enough for Sally. She was in full prosecutorial mode and wanted all relevant information placed in evidence. She maintained an expectant look at Nour . . . who caved after a few minutes. "It is disgusting." We'd expected that much. Nour stopped there, but Sally had to know all the details. To determine the punishment she'd mete out?

Nour resumed, haltingly, "The big man said he wonders if a Mukhabarat's pussy is as tight as her ass. He said he should try both to be sure of the answer."

Sally's cheeks lit up with more color than I'd seen in months. While our prospects hadn't improved, the BBM's had worsened.

Not wanting to embarrass Nour by showing interest in what she was confiding to Sally, I kept my gaze fixed on the area beneath the bench seat opposite, where I noticed something unwanted: A video camera on a folded tripod.

After at least three hours on smooth highway, we slowed and bumped for a few minutes along a dirt road, then came onto a smooth surface that hissed beneath the tires.

"This has to be Wadi Rum," said Nour. "Or somewhere near it. We're driving on sand."

I glanced at Jr. who was riding in back with us. He showed no interest in our conversation.

Sally, who'd been dozing, lurched awake. "Wadi Rum? I've wanted to come here for years."

Like this? Apparently the same question occurred to her and she sank back into silence.

"Any idea what this means, Nour?"

"This is the easiest international border to cross. At night there is a steady stream of small trucks bringing contraband from the Aqaba Free Zone and Saudi Arabia. There is no serious effort to patrol the hundreds of kilometers of open desert that is the frontier. What happens when we get to Saudi? Who can tell?"

The presence of the video camera suggested one possibility.

"This is a good choice for them," continued Nour. Her professional filters had her constantly appraising – and praising – the tactics of her adversaries. "Since Rum is wide open with no trees, any pursuit will be seen far off. We can be in Saudi by daylight. The Saudis will not mobilize a manhunt unless your government gets involved. That assumes anyone knows we are missing."

After half an hour, Sally spoke to Jr. "Can we stop for a bathroom break?"

It had been several hours since we'd greedily scooped up water out of the underground pool. I was ready. If Jr. understood, he elected to feign non-comprehension.

Sally pulled open the small hatch between the cargo area of the van and the front seat and shouted, "How about a stop to pee?"

There was some inaudible discussion, but we left the track for softer sand and a slight incline. And didn't get far. Within a few minutes the van's wheels sank into the sand and we lurched to a stop. The driver wasn't giving up easily and gunned the engine; the smell of roasting clutch came through the floorboards. Should I let him burn out the clutch? Were we better off stranded in the desert? Not mine to decide. Someone else was wise to the fragility of clutches; there was a shout and the engine was turned off.

The sliding door opened onto a predawn landscape of breathtaking beauty. Endless tracts of sand, interrupted by towering monuments that reached up a thousand feet or more. This is Wadi Rum. Sally, the inveterate tourist, was transfixed. Well, I was too. Amazing that such majesty can, momentarily, lift you out of your current state of mind.

Nour had seen it before. "Come;" she said, "ladies' room is over there," pointing to a rock large enough to shelter a squatting pee-er. Sally followed Nour, turning to cock an eyebrow at me. Signaling something?

I looked at BBM. His eyes followed Sally and Nour. His threat was serious?

It seemed like Sally and Nour were gone a long time – I'd completed my business and at 68 I'm not fast – but Khalid and Sr. were indifferent to the extended absence of the two women. They were arguing about how to extricate the van which was sunk to its axles in sand.

BBM was not indifferent, and continued to watch the ladies' room. He appeared to start toward it on two occasions, then hesitated. Finally the women emerged.

Nour was not the same. The top two buttons of her blouse were undone. She walked stiffly, uncertainly. She brushed her hair back over her ear – mechanically. Her eyes, unblinking, stared straight ahead. She shot one quick sidelong glance at BBM, then resumed her forward stare and awkward gait.

Sally was at Nour's elbow, as if she were coaching her. It took a moment to realize what 25 years of living with Sally had taught me: Her response is always direct confrontation. Take-the-fight-to-'em Sally Taylor-Brown. She'd convinced Nour that they should challenge BBM in a setting of their choosing. That explained the long absence. Persistent Sally had worn Nour down. Now it looked like Nour was having second thoughts.

I was surprised. Sally had always been quick to confrontation, but this was the first time I'd seen her push someone else into the line of fire. I knew that all too well because I was usually the person scrambling to catch up; Sally would be in the lead, taking the greatest risks herself. That difference aside, this couldn't end well. Nour would be raped, or BBM would be humiliated and take it out on someone, probably the women.

"Okay, I'm ready to leave," I announced loudly. A quaver in the voice? Maybe BBM would accept this way out and turn toward the van. No. The only one who seemed to notice was Sally who again raised an eyebrow at me.

Jr., who'd not been engaged in anything to that point, looked from the two women to BBM and back. Then he stared questioningly at BBM. Jr. wanted to watch a rape . . . maybe help himself to sloppy seconds.

BBM looked sharply at Jr., then, with a bark in Arabic, strode over to Nour and grabbed her by the hair. He was a full foot taller. She yelped and tried to push him back, but he tore her blouse open with his free hand, revealing a bra that had Soviet Union Heavy Industries stamped all over it. Jr. wiped the corners of his mouth.

Nour's pants were a greater challenge and BBM didn't seem to know how to proceed so he pulled a pistol from his back pocket and waved it menacingly in all directions. This had an immediate effect on three people. Khalid and Sr. retreated behind the van, and Nour, now trembling, unzipped her olive drab pants and started to slowly pull them down. Her knickers were no more revealing or sexy than the brassiere.

Her pants around her ankles and her hands on her hips, Nour glared defiantly at BBM. My heart went out to her. Exposed, defenseless, and small.

I'd lost track of Jr., but he reappeared beside me, fumbling with the video camera. He had the tripod open and planted in the sand, but was pushing the small buttons on the camera at random.

"May I?" I asked. And punched the *Record* button. What the hell. Let's go with Sally's plan. It was too late for any other.

The next move, BBM's, was scripted in stone. Everyone was waiting for him to perform. He pocketed the pistol, opened his fly, and, after a moment of fumbling, pulled out his penis. Although a large man, BBM didn't appear to be proportionately endowed.

Sally giggled – a stage giggle, to anyone who knew her – and looked away with an exaggerated expression of embarrassment. She was playing her role well, but the risk to her was lower than to Nour.

Nour peered down at BBM's offering, then up at him, her face registering disdain, or maybe disappointment. She looked down again and joined Sally in giggling. A forced giggle, but my admiration for her courage soared. Jr., caught up in the moment, snickered.

BBM's face worked; his shoulders drooped. It looked like he was finished for the day and Nour's virtue intact. I punched the *Stop* button.

That declaration of victory was premature. BBM wasn't finished for the day. He started shaking with rage. Crimson rose in his cheeks above his beard. He charged at Nour, who tried to step away, but with her pants around her ankles, fell backwards on the sand. BBM was on top of her, shouting. Nour was struggling, but no match for the size and weight of the man.

I leapt forward – I think I heard Sally shout my name – but before I'd gone more than two steps I was thrown sideways and landed hard. Jr. had intercepted me. Looking up from the ground I could see Jr.'s attention had already returned to Nour and BBM. Jr. wasn't going to be denied his rape.

With an eye on Jr., I got to my knees, preparing another lunge at BBM when, abruptly, he pushed himself to his feet, leaving Nour half-covered in sand. He was holding his semi-erect penis and shouting in Arabic. Turning to me, he explained, "I will not waste my seed on this whore."

I nodded acknowledgement. BBM's manhood nominally demonstrated, this was a good time for all parties to return to a neutral corner.

Jr's expression could be read only one way: profound disappointment.

Rehearsal

As we rolled along the main track, two thoughts were foremost. 1. BBM had been publicly humiliated; a partial erection had got us out of a bad situation but not much more. There'd be payback. 2. During the two minutes that the Nour & Sally Tragi-Comedy Special had everyone's attention, I should have been looking for the Kalashnikov – Sally's intention. I'd missed the signals.

I needed to up my game.

A third, belated, thought: Although it had been on the verge of going disastrously wrong, grudging kudos to Sally and her leading lady. It seemed unlikely there'd be further rape attempts. And Sally was not through with the BBM. The fires don't burn hot enough in Sally's vision of hell for rapists.

"How are you doing, Nour?"

She looked taken off guard. Of course. Impossible for me to imagine what was tumbling through her head.

"Yes? Oh, I'm sorry, Mr. Brown. Thank you for trying to help me. I hope you weren't hurt when Mohammad slammed you to the ground."

Not what I was looking for; I wanted to discuss strategy. "No, it's my place to apologize, Nour. I let things go too far. I can't imagine your fear. I really admire the courage you showed."

She blushed, then, embarrassed, scowled. Time to move to another topic; I tried a more focused question.

"Did you recognize any landmarks that would tell us where we're heading?

"Oh, we're going into Saudi. They will be safer there. But we are still in Jordan and going east. I think that was El Khazali on our right when we stopped. I camped there once as a child." Her voice sounded distant, detached. Taking refuge in those memories? "Perhaps they want to cross the border where there is no traffic. The smugglers cross further south, and they usually cross at night."

She was long on description, short on analysis. I followed up, "The meaning of this route?"

Again, a surprised expression. Wouldn't a professional intel agent – even one who'd just come through a savage rape attempt – be constantly updating the situation and options?

"Well," a pause as she regrouped, "if they go the well-traveled route our truck would not be so noticed. We would be just another vehicle that might be used for smuggling. The Jordanians are not interested in smugglers leaving the country with empty trucks. Although the Saudis might be more interested in who is coming into their country."

"It sounds, Nour, that since we're leaving the well-traveled route, they're willing to risk detection on this side of the border in order to have more empty space around them when they get across. Right?"

She nodded agreement.

Was I looking for support for the worst-case scenario, execution? If so, there was more evidence close at hand. When Jr. put the video camera and tripod back under the seat, he'd disturbed something else that was now visible: a large rolled black banner with an Arabic inscription in white lettering; the work looked amateurish.

So that's how it's going to end. The banner clinched it. An abrupt, but only slightly premature end of life for Sally. We'd known, without ever saying it, that a viable liver wasn't going to arrive in time. For me, I'd be denied a few more years, but my world had grown small lately; it was Sally, and on rare occasions our daughters. My mind started to rehearse our executions.

In 16th century Europe beheadings were grand affairs because the headliners were household names. Ringside tickets were sought after. Did a good turnout make the condemned feel better about things? In contrast, our audience would be small: Jr., Sr., Khalid (protesting), a video camera, and BBM wielding the sword.

At least our decapitation would go more smoothly than it had for our more famous predecessors. The medieval executioner's axe was a blunt instrument and repeated blows were required to separate the heads from the bodies of those luckless souls who'd displeased their sovereign.

Who would be killed first? Would I be forced to witness Sally's death, or she mine?

I had to find the strength to deny our executioners the satisfaction of weeping, mewling, begging for mercy. What can occupy your mind that will help you hang onto any vestige of dignity in this situation? Famous last words? If I mentioned Mary and Margaret by name, I'd be undone. Say something nationalistic? How out of character. Decades earlier I'd realized the imaginary lines that trace national borders are an unfortunate inheritance of the human race, lines imbued with the superstition that God's grace is found on only one side.

Perhaps I'd be handed a prepared script to read. What incentive could there be to play ball at this point? They could threaten to make Sally suffer, I suppose. If they did, then I would read – with as much irony as could be summoned – for the audiences that caught my act on Al Jazeera and YouTube.

Or maybe I'd read just to prolong life and possibility for a few more minutes.

The biggest challenge was clear: Stand erect. Do not beg for mercy. Try to show quiet defiance, not resignation. *And for Christ's sake, Max, do not blubber and thrash around impotently as you're dragged to the block. That image is not a fitting legacy to leave your daughters.*

I couldn't look at Sally.

From Max Brown's notes on Kohlberg's stages of moral development.

Stage 4+. Disaffection with the arbitrary nature of "law and order" reasoning. This is a transitional stage. The emerging stage, 5, has not been completely integrated into the personality. For the stage 4+ individual, guilt often changes from being defined by society to viewing society itself as culpable.

This reasoning process can be employed to oppose rules that are seen as having been imposed illegitimately. For examples: colonial imposition of western values on nonwestern subjects, or secular opposition to religious law (or the reverse).

At its finest, stage 4+ reasoning can lead to opposition to a system that is rooted in an antiquated and now discredited view of social justice (e.g., apartheid).

At its worst, stage 4+ reasoning provides intellectual cover to flout any system of justice that's personally inconvenient.

Point out to students how stage 4+ reasoning can be confused with stage 2: self-interest/what's in it for me. Describe some moral dilemmas and ask students to provide both stage 2 and 4+ rationales.

Lights out

Sally hadn't spoken since we'd been herded back into the van. I felt she owed Nour a king-sized apology, and, from the looks of her, she felt the same. While I was trying to suppress dark images, Sally slid down the bench to Nour and spoke in a low voice. Nour looked straight ahead and finally said, "No, I am also responsible. I agreed." And made no eye contact.

That's all Sally was going to get.

She's such a good person and so convinced that being in the right will invariably lead to the right outcome that, during our life together, she'd launched us into several difficult situations. In contrast, I'm rarely sure enough of myself to make a bold move. That hesitance had to stop; our prospects were so bleak that any change of course would be for the better. The only option that came to mind was to disable the van. If, as seemed almost certain, they intended to kill us and pin the blame on jihadists, they'd want to get some distance from our carcasses and establish alibis. They couldn't do that on foot and they wouldn't want to be picked up by a passerby who might later identify them and place them close to the crime. They needed the van.

The road less traveled was also less solid. We got stuck again within an hour. While the BBM supervised – cradling the Kalashnikov – we excavated behind all four wheels, placed rubber floor mats behind the rear wheels, and then everyone pushed. A few hundred meters to our right a natural stone bridge formed a graceful arch between two small mountains. Intrepid tourists were on top. They waved, but made no sign they intended to help. Probably best for them.

After another fifteen minutes of slow travel the van lurched to a stop to the accompaniment of excited voices from the front. Jr. threw the sliding door open and jumped out. One hundred meters away five oryx were grazing on a desert bush.

Sally joined in the excitement. "These were extinct in the wild until a few years ago. See how from the side their straight horns look like one? That's where the idea of a unicorn came from."

Nour was whispering excitedly in Arabic with our captors – although not with the BBM. "It's our national animal," she mouthed to Sally.

While everyone was focused on the oryx I slipped around to the far side of the van, opened the fuel filler cap and started scooping in sand. As I was pouring in the third handful there was a slight noise behind me. I turned to see the pistol butt coming down toward my head.

From Max Brown's notes on Frances Kamm's Theory of Permissible Harm.

Kamm's theory states that you may do harm to save someone if and only if the harm is an aspect of the greater good itself. Wait . . . there has to be a better way to say that. For instance, Kamm argued that we believe it would not be permissible to kill one person to harvest his organs (how's that for a personally relevant example?) in order to save the lives of five others. In contrast, it is morally okay to divert a runaway trolley that's bearing down on five innocent people on to a sidetrack where the trolley would mow down only one innocent person.

The math is the same in both examples – one life for five – but the circumstances and intentions are different. If we react to minimize harm we're on safe moral ground. If we initiate the action . . . not so good.

Kamm believed the Principle of Permissible Harm explained the moral difference between these and other cases, and provides guidance regarding what we can do to achieve a good outcome and what we cannot do, such as in the organ harvesting example.

If there were some way to separate getting a liver for Sally from an intentional act to start the process, then that would be morally okay.

But, I'm getting really sick and tired of moral philosophy. I just want my wife to live.

Monaural

"I think he is going to be alright." The words are Nour's; the tearful face hovering above me is my wife's.

Something was wrong. There was intense pain in my head. Expected. Voices were muffled – also a possibility – but something seemed to be enveloping my head. Cautiously exploring the left side of my face, I found cloth where I expected skin.

"It's for your ear, Max. He didn't hit your head squarely which probably saved you from a fractured skull. But the top part of your ear is detached."

Detached? There's an interesting descriptor to apply to a body part. I tried to speak, but the cloth bandage that was holding whatever was left of my ear in place was tight under my chin. I waved a hand to signal disapproval of the arrangement.

"We have to wrap his head differently, Nour."

Nour untied the *keffiyeh* – hers – and as Sally carefully supported my neck Nour wrapped the cloth around my head. As groggy as I was, I couldn't fail to notice that Sally looked away when the damaged side of my head was uncovered.

Able to speak, I slurred, "What's happening?"

"We're inching along. The van will run for a few minutes but then the sand in the tank clogs the fuel filter and they have to crawl underneath to clean it. This is our fourth stop."

"Are we heading back?"

"I don't think so, Mr. Brown. We do seem to be on a popular tourist track. We heard someone asking if we needed help. I don't think we have gone more than a kilometer or two."

The filter had been cleaned and the van rocked as our captors climbed in. After a long period of cranking the engine caught. But it wasn't healthy. Some of the sand had gotten through the filter, or had been spilled into the intake pipe during a cleaning. How would this play out? And, God! My head hurt.

A few minutes later the engine's sounds of distress increased and it died. Time for another cleaning. Loud voices in Arabic that had to be swearing.

"They think that if they do this often enough they will finally get all the sand out. How much did you put in the tank, Mr. Brown?"

"Three handfuls. If it all finds its way into the fuel line this could go on for a while."

I pushed up on one elbow to get my bearings. Jr. had been replaced by Sr. as our guard. I thought he looked almost sympathetic. Did I have it wrong about the beheading? Or wasn't Sr. clued in? The effort required to hold myself up just a few inches was taxing. How much trouble was I in? With a painful effort I inclined my head forward. My shirt was coated in drying blood.

The engine started again, but ran rough. "They're getting faster at cleaning," announced Nour. "That didn't take more than ten minutes . . . wait, feel that? We're backing up. They're turning around."

This was a group that had trouble sticking with a plan. First the backtracking on the path to Mount Aaron, then the retreat from Wu'eira Castle, next the rush out of Sho'bak Mountain, and now this.

The ride over the sand that had seemed silkily smooth before was now jarring. Nour folded her vest and placed it under my head. Only a small improvement. *Please stop the van – stop the jarring.*

In response the engine died.

More swearing. Doors slamming. And ten minutes later we were underway again. The engine was definitely rough. Perhaps sand had clogged an injector. What did that mean? Maybe not enough power to sustain high speeds or climb steep inclines. Why was I thinking about these things? Action. Sr. might still be turned.

"Mohammad, time is running out. If you surrender you can negotiate. If they catch up to us . . ." I wasn't sure who 'they' were in this scenario . . . "there will be shooting. And there definitely won't be leniency in court." In my impaired state I couldn't detune my vocabulary and Nour translated leniency for Sr.

The sympathy in his expression was replaced by impassiveness. I was getting nowhere.

With a theatrical groan I raised up on an elbow and stared directly at Sr. He finally acknowledged by casting a sideways glance my way. "You know, Mohammad, that what they are planning is against everything you believe."

His faced worked and he muttered something. My hearing. never great, was now halved. I think he said, "How do you know what I believe?"

Sr. resumed staring at the floor of the van. Maybe small progress. At least he's thinking.

And . . . detached? How much damage had I suffered?

Intellectual

I've always done it. Maybe it's a good thing. In difficult situations I start to intellectualize. It creates a buffer between myself and unpleasant reality.

I'd tried Kohlberg's stage one moral reasoning on Sr: keep going like this and you'll get shot because your pursuers are more powerful than you. I'd tried stage two reasoning: negotiate for a lighter sentence. And I'd tried stage four: your religion tells you not to do this. Now, I'd just tried stage five: this runs counter to your values.

Was this the right approach? Keep throwing different moral arguments at him until one of them sticks? We were running out of stages.

It sounded like the fuel filter cleaning was coming to an end. I tried to position myself to reduce the jostling and closed my eyes. Maybe sleep? I heard Sally say, "Okay," and then there was movement on the seat.

"There is nothing I can do." The voice was Mohammad Sr.'s. He'd taken Sally's place on the bench seat by my head.

I started to sit up and immediately decided against it. Pain. I looked up at Sr. who was again studying the floor.

"I'm relieved to hear you say that, Mohammad. You seem to be a good man. But, why is there nothing you can do" An attaboy, followed by a challenge.

The response was slow in coming.

"We are trapped by our mistakes."

"Please tell me everything. If I'm going to die, I'd like to know why."

He looked quickly at me, and away.

Another pause.

"We make mistake when Badr throw acid at my niece. He fall off mountain in Petra so I think Allah take justice on him. We do another mistake when we pay poor man to go to prison for Badr. We do biggest mistake when we agree Switzerland doctor can take organ from niece. I do not want her to give organ but Badr talk strong that if niece give organ to others who need organ we can forgive her and welcome her back to family."

"Why did Badr attack his sister?"

"She not his sister. She have different mother and father. She and Badr are cousins. Her name Sumayyah. Badr want to marry Sumayyah but she say no. She tell her friends and hurt honor of Badr. Badr angry and throw acid."

The van lurched forward. Pain. *Have to keep this conversation going.*

"Who talked to you about taking organs from Sumayyah? The big man with the beard?"

Sr. nodded but said nothing. I needed more open-ended questions to keep him talking.

"What do you want to happen next, Mohammad?"

That question took him by surprise. Maybe I should have built up to it but the pain from the bouncing of the vehicle was making it hard to concentrate.

"I do not know. Sometimes I feel I must be punished. Other times I believe this not my fault."

His face relaxed and he looked around the van. For Mohammad the conversation was over. For me, over too soon.

"Um . . . Mohammad, why do you say that?"

"Say what? Not my fault?"

I nodded, and regretted the movement.

"I not want any bad thing. I agree because Badr and nephew say this is what Allah wants. They say woman must respect man. I do not know Holy Koran well. Now I am reading."

"Have you read anything interesting?"

"All Holy Koran interesting." Said with a hint of offense. My mistake.

"Sorry, Mohammad, I meant, have you read anything that helps you make decisions, or see the world more clearly?"

He didn't hesitate. "I know what you want me to say. That Prophet – peace be upon him – say I must help you escape."

I'd rushed it.

"No," perhaps to place in evidence proof of his piety and enlightenment, he continued, "I am reading about women. Prophet say 'Best of men are those who are best to their wives.' He also say, 'Only an honorable man treats women with honor and dignity and only a vile and dishonorable man humiliates and degrades women.' He say many more things like this."

How to use this newfound enlightened view?

"You have two innocent women that you have taken prisoner, Mohammad. Any thoughts on that." A risk. I was pushing him but didn't know how long I could focus on the conversation.

Nour started to say something, but stopped in mid-word. Sally must have shushed her. *Sorry, Nour. Not looking for a confession or contrition here. Trying for a recruit.*

No response from Sr. so I pressed the case. "How does honor and respect of women fit with their beheading?" I tried to keep my voice down; Sally and Nour hadn't seen the banner and may not have come to the same conclusion.

"What?!" from Sally. My voice hadn't been low enough.

"Hypothetical, babe. Let it go." Fat chance of that.

She turned on Sr. "That was the big plan? Behead us somewhere out here in the desert? Make it look like terrorists did it?" Sally's a smart cookie. It's never been easy to conceal the truth from her. "What kind of a Muslim – no, what kind of a *man* would do that!"

Sr. was no better at dealing with Sally's wrath than any other guy I'd met. He sputtered some 'buts', then fell silent.

With difficulty I turned to get a view of Sally. Of course; she was glowering at Sr. Was this going to help? I'd been working on this subtle Socratic approach which, if successful, would lead him to say the things we wanted him to say.

She wasn't finished. "How can you go along with such a plan?!"

"That's just it, Sal. You can see that Mohammad doesn't approve." I looked toward Mohammad – damn it hurt – for confirmation. He nodded yes. Not a full-throated declaration of support, but progress.

We rode in silence, the engine started to lose power, coughed, died, and we coasted to a halt. Angry opening and slamming of doors. The sliding side door was thrown open and Jr. got in, signaling to his uncle that he should leave. Jr. glared at me, inspected his pistol, and glared again. *Got it, Jr. You're just a hair's breadth away from plugging the annoying American who fucked up the fuel line.*

Sr. returned – interrupting his nephews' theatrics – with a small bottle of water and a pill. "Codeine."

These guys had packed for every eventuality.

Did you know that codeine is a sedative, as well as an analgesic? I came out of a deep sleep sometime later, my head feeling better. The health of the van's engine, however, had deteriorated during my absence. We were bucking along; one cylinder was dead and another seemed to be only an occasional contributor.

"Do you know where we are, Nour?" As if it mattered. We were captives in a van; that's where we were.

She shrugged, then, deciding that a Mukhabarat agent should have her bearings at all times, offered, "I think maybe we are going back to Rum village. This truck is too sick to take us into Saudi now and if we leave the track we will get stuck very fast because the motor has no power." To prove her point we could feel the van bog into soft sand, and then, with an heroic effort, pull itself out and forward.

With restored mobility I sat up and took stock. Jr. was slouched against the back door of the van. Sally was dozing on Nour's shoulder. Was it time for her to take more meds? And Nour. I realized I hadn't focused on her. Ever since a meltdown in Thailand two years ago when redoubtable Sally had revealed that she suffered from the same insecurities as the rest of humanity I'd loyally tried to pay little notice to other women.

Nour has a pretty face, although she uses too much makeup. The face is round. Definitely not Bedouin, but she didn't seem Palestinian either. Circassian? King Hussein had staffed Mukhabarat with Circassians as they had no tribal affiliations within Jordan and were known for loyalty and dedication to duty. How old? Thirty, maybe a little more. Married? Probably not and at 30+ time is running out in this society. She so badly wants to be seen as tough and competent but the image of the defenseless girl, half naked in unattractive underwear, came back. I felt a rush of paternal affection for our tough/vulnerable intel agent. That's something else codeine does to you.

I slid down the bench seat to the front. Raised voices from the cab. *Good. Fight it out among yourselves, and success to all parties.* Wait, fighting's no good. We had someone up there who was leaning toward our side.

A shot.

The van coasted to a halt, the engine dead. The sliding door was hurled open and Sr. was thrown in. He was dead too.

Whingeing has its uses

The BBM was silhouetted against the low-hanging sun. Jr. looked at his dead uncle, then at the BBM. With a feral snarl Jr. lunged from the back of the van toward the open door, reaching behind him for his pistol.

The BBM grabbed for the sliding door as Jr. extended the pistol. It was a tie. The sliding door slammed closed on Jr.'s outstretched arm as he got off a single shot. Had he connected with anything? Jr. screamed, and with his left hand pushed the door open. As the door released his forearm it flopped to an improbable ninety-degree angle toward the ground. The BBM had the pistol. With no hesitation he raised it and put a bullet into Jr.'s forehead. The impact of the shot carried Jr. back and across the body of his uncle. The dead Mohammads formed a Christian cross.

Expressionless, BBM slid the door closed. A minute later there were sounds of a key in the lock, then silence.

Nour, Sally and I pressed ourselves against the front wall of the van on either side of the small sliding window to the front cab. BBM seemed to be in a frame of mind to finish off everyone at the scene. Minutes passed. The window didn't slide open; no gun was extended into the back compartment. BBM and Khalid had gone?

"Phones," said Nour. "The dead men have phones. We can call for help."

Looking at the Mohammads for the first time, they appeared peaceful. Is this the justice they deserved? Perhaps Sr. could have been offered a second chance. But in death they might be of use. They'd provide phones to summon help. And even before Nour mentioned the phones, I'd been thinking about another contribution they might make: two fresh livers had just come on the market.

Nour made three calls – one of them to request a refrigerated vehicle – and we settled in, waiting for rescuers to arrive.

"They should be here soon," said Nour. "Mukhabarat will have someone in Rum village who will come or send the police."

She'd no sooner said this than there was a polite tapping on the metal door, followed by, "Pardon? Is anyone in there?"

The accent was southeast England and the accompanying face that leaned through the opening door was round and florid, topped by a few strands of flaxen hair.

Squinting into the darkness of the van, "Damned rascals took our transport at gunpoint, you see. But, kind of them to leave the keys in your door here. Is everyone alright?" The rosy hue went of our rescuer's cheeks when he saw the two bodies on the floor. "I say . . . they aren't . . ."

He couldn't say the word, but Sally could. "Dead as door-nails. Who took your transport?"

The reply was slow in coming. Finding his voice, "Two men. Big fellow with a beard and another older man. Our party was heading out for a drive in the desert, with a Bedouin dinner, when they hailed us. Our driver investigated, and, well, here we are."

They weren't all here. The rest of the tourists, and their guide, were a few hundred meters off, watching us.

"After they took your vehicle, which way did they go?" Nour was back on the job.

"Off that way, I'd say." He gestured while keeping an eye on the two corpses.

"Southeast," said Nour. "Shortest route to Saudi. It will be getting dark." She consulted the GPS on the phone she was holding. "We're only five kilometers from the border." Addressing our Englishman she asked, "How long ago did they take your vehicle?"

"Twenty, maybe thirty minutes. We were in shock and were slow to notice this van. We thought it was unoccupied. I came over mainly because I'd tired of the whingeing of my companions."

Night was descending; Venus appeared above the western horizon. Nour turned on the van's flashers. From the southwest three distant sets of headlights were making their way across the desert toward us.

From Max Brown's musings on a theory of non-cognitive morality.

There are behaviorism theories (our morality is the product of our conditioning). And there are cognitive theories (we reason out the implications and justifications before we act). What happens when there's no time to reason it out and our past experiences haven't prepared us for the situation?

Take the brain out of it and other organs are left in charge, and boy, are they ready! Perceive a hostile action? The adrenal medulla goes into hyper-drive and produces a cascade of hormones that improve fighting ability while simultaneously sending our thoughts and perceptions in a dark direction.

During my time on earth I've shot five bad men without thinking. I've shot two good men without thinking. I pushed a very bad man out of a plane at 19,000', again without moral dithering. I'm a person consciously committed to non-violence and I've done those things. Moral reasoning came after the fact. Is it a luxury available only to those who have time and information?

Daily Journal

Sally Taylor-Brown

5 April
Amman
Jordan Hospital

It's seven AM and the sun is pushing up into a greasy sky and lighting this hospital room. I'm waiting for the transplant procedure and could not be any more nervous. My stomach – how to describe it? No food for ten hours; off the meds that kept the nausea down; and butterflies like you would not believe. I tried to describe it to Max who said we'd reward my stomach later with a large steak and a fine Bordeaux. Food? Talk about food at a time like this? I know he was trying to be helpful, but there are times for a light-hearted response, and there are other times.

Max is big on keeping the mind occupied as a defense against thinking about unpleasant things so I asked him for my Daily Journal and a pen. Then I sent him to look for a left-handed monkey wrench. He got the hint. He's sitting in a vinyl-covered chair thumbing through magazines. They're in Arabic.

We were so drained last night I'm surprised I remember any of it. Mukhabarat had a chopper waiting for us in Rum village. Apparently they try to avoid touching down in the fine sand of Wadi Rum since the stuff goes everywhere, including into the engine. Not to knock that fine sand, though. It's what saved our bacon. During the flight back to Amman Nour was on the phone the entire time, making arrangements, so the chopper brought us straight to the hospital where a surgical-prep team was waiting.

I'm not ready for this. Just a few hours ago it looked like someone was going to chop off our heads in a grisly videotaped execution. Now someone is going to chop out my liver. Things are moving too fast, but I know you can't be picky about the schedule. An unclaimed liver doesn't sit on the shelf for long.

One thing I remember vividly from last night is my conversation with Nour. Funny timing. Maybe she thought I needed a distraction (I did) or maybe she thought we were close enough friends. She told me her life's story.

It's an amazing story and I wish I could tell it all in her own words, but I would butcher it. I guess I wasn't as focused as I should have been. Where I'm sure of her words I'll write them down.

One thing stood out, though. The entire time she was talking I don't think she looked at me once.

Here goes:

"Our family is from Nablus. Maybe you know it. It is just across the Jordan River in Palestine. Mama lived there with her parents and two sisters. Mama had an older brother but the Israelis were looking for him so he wasn't around much. I don't know if he ever did anything or if he just fell into the profile of being a man between the ages of 15 and 45.

"Mama's brother avoided the IDF which reinforced their suspicions, and that meant trouble for the family." She said all this so quietly I had to strain to hear.

Nour's mother told her that the brother could only visit every few weeks, spend a couple of hours, and then slip off into hiding again. Also, every few weeks, the IDF would visit. Always in the wee hours and they would announce their arrival with a stun grenade thrown through a window.

"While mama, her parents, and her sisters were deaf and blind from the grenade, the Israeli soldiers would tear through the house, throwing everything around looking for mama's brother – my uncle, although I wasn't born yet."

A couple of hours after one such raid, as the family was putting the house back together, one of the soldiers returned alone. Nour said he was a Russian who spoke no Arabic and not much more Hebrew.

"This all happened just at the start of the time when the Israeli government was encouraging Russian Jews to come to Israel. The Arabs who were still in Israel were having larger families than the Jews and might become a majority. The Russian immigrants did not integrate into Israeli society very well."

This explanation was followed by a long pause. I wondered if she was going to continue because I had a pretty good idea about what happens next.

"The Russian-Israeli had not come back to help clean up the mess."

Another pause, then Nour told me her mother was very beautiful. She said the soldier raped her mother. He did it twice to show what a man he was. Nour said this without emotion. Then she said in the same flat voice, "Nine months later I was born."

When she told me this I felt sick, even sicker than I feel right now. I had pushed Nour into a situation where she was nearly raped herself. That lady is made of iron.

The story doesn't get happier. The family was ashamed of Nour's mother and kept her out of sight when the pregnancy became obvious. She thought there might be talk among more distant relatives – cousins – that she had done something to bring this on herself and should be made an example of. Eight months pregnant, she took a bus to the Allenby Bridge border crossing and left Palestine forever. She made her way, mostly on foot, to the Baqa'a refugee camp which is about 20 kilometers north of Amman. She saw a sign for a health center and went directly there where she was allowed to stay until Nour was born.

Of course Nour has no memory of her early years but she and her mother lived in the Baqa'a camp, depending mostly on UNRWA handouts for food and shelter. They lived in a tent for a while until UNRWA put up prefabricated shacks. "Winter in Jordan can be harsh," in that same flat, distant voice.

Nour's first memories are in that shack, playing with other children. She thinks there were ten people sharing the two rooms. "I went to Baqa'a many years later to try to find my home but I couldn't be sure."

Then, when Nour was five, a flood of new refugees arrived. Palestinian militants had launched an *intifada* and the Israelis had come down hard. As her mother had long feared, a recent arrival from Nablus recognized her. A few days later her mother thought she spotted her own father – Nour's grandfather – in the camp. Instead of a joyful reunion, she hid. She asked a woman on the Camp Council to see what could be learned. The woman confirmed that there had been inquiries about her – about Nour's mother. The woman recommended administrative detention.

I guess it's better than being killed, but administrative detention is prison. Women that the government fears are in danger of honor killing are simply locked up in a separate ward of a prison.

"My lullaby every night was the screams and rants of women in the criminals' section on the other side of the partition. They had many crazy women there, or maybe prison made them crazy." I think that's the only thing she said that had a touch of bitterness to it.

Nour said they had a few comforts in the prison. An NGO provided sewing machines and material so the women could learn a skill, and there were some toys to play with. The detainees could mingle freely and there were other children. A different NGO organized two closely supervised trips for the children, one to Wadi Rum and the other to Petra. But they had to return to the prison and their mothers could not leave.

The procedure for getting out of administrative detention was logical, but flawed. Every male member of the detainee's immediate family signed a pledge that he would not harm the woman after release. Then they reneged.

"The government realized the promises meant nothing after four women were killed when they were sent back to their families. The only safety was to leave the country. Every month a charity found a foreign place to send a woman or one of us children."

Nour says there were 137 detainees and about half that number of children. When Nour was eleven years old – she'd spent six important years of her life behind bars – a British NGO offered her a place in a boarding school in Cardiff. Arrangements for her mother would be made later.

They jumped at the opportunity. An English boarding school? Much better than prison!

"Actually it was about the same."

She knew little English, was treated as a pariah, the teachers were impatient with her. Misconduct – usually the result of not understanding what was expected – was punished with spankings. Five more years passed.

The letters from her mother stopped when she was 14. "In mama's last letter she said she wanted to see the prison doctor but he did not come very often."

At 16 the same NGO provided her a ticket back to Jordan where she lied about her age, doctored her boarding school record, served two years in the army, then went to Jordan University. After graduation she found employment in Mukhabarat. The intel agency's recruiters spotted the forgeries in her record and said they were impressed by her 'entrepreneurship.'

"Did you go back to Nablus and find your family? You mentioned aunts and an uncle."

"Mukhabarat is my family," she said impassively. "I know what I can expect from them."

She folded her hands in her lap and continued staring out the window at the darkness. That was it. She was finished. After a short silence she turned toward me and asked about our daughters.

"Our daughters?" I sputtered. "Nour, I'm still trying to take in what you've . . ."

"There are many women like me," she interrupted. "It is not a good story. It is not even an interesting story."

I so totally disagree. Nour looked embarrassed and left.

Boogers! Activity in the room. Looks like they are about to roll me off to the OR. Max is as pale as a ghost; his mouth is a forced, rictal smile.

Nothing left to do now but hand him the journal and pen and say, "See you on the flip side, Studly." He'll break down.

Stereophonic

I looked at what my soul mate had been writing. She was right. *"See you on the flip side?"* I mostly held it together until she went through the swinging doors into the OR. She waved.

This had better fucking work!

A hand on my shoulder brought me around. A male nurse had come to lead me off for my own surgery. I hadn't thought about it for several hours. Dr. Zuheir had cleared an operating table in reconstructive surgery to work on my ear.

I opted for general anesthesia, mainly so I wouldn't be thinking about Sally. The last thing I saw as I lay on the table was our guardian intel angel, sitting in the gallery among a handful of earnest looking med students. Her *keffiyeh*, stained with my blood, hung loosely around her neck.

From Max Brown's notes on Kohlberg's stages of moral development.

Stage 5. In stage five laws are regarded as social contracts rather than rigid edicts. The difference from stage four is subtle, but important. In stage four you obey the law because, if you didn't, society would fall apart. In stage five you obey the law because it represents our best thinking and consensus on what is right.

That doesn't mean all societies will arrive at the same consensus. The world is made up of different opinions, rights, and values. Such perspectives should be mutually respected as unique to each community.

Those laws that do not promote the general welfare should be changed when necessary to provide "the greatest good for the greatest number of people". These changes are accomplished through majority decision and democratic processes.

Fast forward

The Dead Sea is the lowest place on the surface of our planet, lying 1,200 feet below sea level. Its most significant tributary, the Jordan River, has been sapped to irrigate crops on both banks and the Sea is disappearing, dropping one meter per year.

With low altitude comes higher atmospheric pressure (five percent higher) and oxygen concentrations (another 4.8 percent). Medical research has been ongoing for years to try to document the therapeutic benefits of the greater salinity of the water (over one-third salt), the rich mineral content of the mud around the Sea, and the relative abundance of oxygen. So far there has been some evidence that tissue – particularly skin – heals more quickly in the denser air. Capitalizing on these findings, a string of luxury hotels lines the receding banks of the Sea, offering sanctuary to recent recipients of face lifts, nose jobs and tummy tucks.

Our presence at the Dead Sea was a compromise. Barely conscious after her surgery, Sally – predictably – was ready to head off in pursuit of the BBM. Wherever he might be. The surgical team were incredulous. They wanted her in the hospital for two weeks and close at hand for another four. I sat on the sidelines as the haggling proceeded. Eventually it was agreed: one week in intensive care, three days in a recovery ward, then an undetermined period somewhere nearby. After two days in the ICU, Sally renegotiated: two days in intensive care (time already served), three days in a ward, and an undetermined period "nearby."

The Möevenpick Dead Sea Resort is a vast rambling maze of two-story rose-colored buildings. Sally and I were billeted close to the lobby, denying us a view of the water, but our location shortened the distance medical staff had to walk when they came down from Amman to check on her. It was the least we could do for them.

Sally was putting up a better front than seemed justified. She had to feel lousy from the drugs to suppress rejection of Jr.'s hand-me-down organ. She had such strong negative feelings about having any part of the man in her that I wondered if this wouldn't slow her recovery.

Acutely aware that time was passing, we sought out distractions, which are limited for people on the mend.

- We lay around the pool. Sally, for the first time since I'd known her, had to forego her bikini in favor of a one-piece that covered the long angry zipper-like scar that ran diagonally across her mid-section.
- We coated our faces with the curative mud that hawkers guaranteed would erase wrinkles and liver spots.
- We experimented with the full range of new-age treatments offered in the spa.
- And we waded uneasily on slippery stones in the shallows of the Dead Sea, careful not to allow the saline water onto our fresh sutures.

On our third day of captivity Nour found us lounging by the pool. Her long absence had been unanticipated; she'd been in constant attendance in Amman. We assumed she'd inveigled someone in Mukhabarat to convince Jordan Hospital that Jr.'s compatible liver could by-pass the Registry; Sally had earned it. She hovered around us anxiously during the hours immediately before and after our surgeries. Then she disappeared. We reasoned that the bureaucratic aftermath of a high-profile case such as ours was keeping her occupied filing reports and briefing her betters. Her unannounced reappearance took us by surprise.

Embarrassed to be caught indulging in the sybaritic distractions of the Möevenpick, Sally and I were slow to get the conversation started.

Nour rescued us. "I apologize for ignoring you for the last few days. I have been required to make statements in the pretrial depositions of one of our captors, Khalid."

"Manal's uncle? They found him?"

"Yes, the person you call the BBM abandoned him in the Saudi desert within a few hours. He was dehydrated and exhausted when a smuggler picked him up and took him to Rum village. He tried confessing his crimes to the health center staff who weren't interested. A policeman's wife had brought her son in for vaccination and heard Khalid begging to be taken off the rehydration drip and placed in custody. The woman summoned her husband who obliged Khalid."

"What a strange man."

"His feelings of guilt are not constant, Mrs. Brown. Now he wants you, in particular, to make a statement that can be used in his defense. If you agree, I have brought a court-appointed secretary and a notary with me."

We were granted time to get dressed, then we both made statements. Sally's went on for quite a while and the stenographer was struggling to keep up. At the end, anyone who based their judgment on Sally's testimony would have nominated uncle Khalid for sainthood rather than sentenced him. Her justification to Nour and me? "Well, he did bring me my meds in Sho'bak." I can't object; her capacity to forgive has often come to my rescue.

Two days later she showed me an email from Gisele.

```
Hi Sally.

Glad to hear you are getting better so
quickly. Here the news is good and bad.
Your Fedhole agent, Henri, seems to be
back on the job - or so he says. He's tak-
en leave for a week to sort things out
with his significant other, but told me he
will have spare time to focus on the
crimes that are centered on this place.

That takes me to the bad. You should be
sitting down for this. Hanan has disap-
peared. I didn't want to tell you until we
were certain. Her husband says she went to
Fribourg two days ago to check the ceme-
tery register herself. She didn't come
back. Agent Henri will see if he can find
anything, but he says he's had run-ins
with the cantonal police in Fribourg so
doesn't expect them to cooperate.
```

Sorry to be the bearer . . .
Gisele

Daily Journal

Sally Taylor-Brown

14 April
Geneva

Yes, we're back in Geneva and you-know-who has his panties in a bunch. Here's the argument we had (abridged version):

> Max: You just had a major operation and the doctors insist that you take it easy.
>
> Me: It wasn't that big a deal.
>
> Max: Sputter, sputter. It was a liver-fucking-transplant, Sal!
>
> Me: No, it was a graft. They only shaved off the one-third that had tumors and glued on part of Jr.'s. That's a lot different.
>
> Max: More sputtering (he's not a very good arguer). It was still major surgery. You were under for half a day.
>
> Me: Three hours. And I feel fine. Are you going to pack, or am I traveling to Geneva alone?

The truth is I don't feel all that wonderful, but sogging by the Dead Sea doesn't speed up your recovery when your friends are disappearing and a savage lunatic is on the loose.

Nour also tried to talk me out of leaving. I asked her what she planned to do next and she dodged the question. Is that because she doesn't know or she's trying to get approval, or what? She runs hot and cold. She was distant after I talked her into the thing in the desert with BBM – who can blame her – but then a few hours later she told me her life story. I had the feeling she doesn't do that often. Maybe I was the first to hear it?

Gisele and Agent Henri are coming for dinner tonight – Gisele is picking up Take-Away Chinese on the way over – and we'll try to figure out what to do next.

15 April
Geneva

We got nowhere in our discussions with Henri and Gisele last night and I was too pooped to write it up afterwards. And frustrated.

We were relieved to see that Henri is focusing on work again and not just his love life. But here's a funny thing: I think maybe his long-suffering girlfriend snapped. Henri has a fading shiner. He declined to explain how it happened. I'll bet she got fed up with his dithering and smacked him. That said, he still looks better than poor Max. Max has always had a good head of hair and the scabby left side of his head is just now showing a little stubble. It looks like it might be growing in white. The ear is looking good, but he has no feeling in the top half. When we start making love again I'll strike that off the list of erogenous zones.

Henri said he got stonewalled by the Fribourg Fuzz. If they're looking into Hanan's disappearance they aren't boasting about it. The clinic doesn't open for business for another week and I don't see us getting any more acid-attack victims when it does. Schwarzherz will be pumping Botox into middle-aged local women, maybe shaving the occasional schnozz.

We chased off our lead in Jordan and the trail was already cold here when we left. What to do?

Crap! This is what happens when you try to come to terms with something detestable. My body is not having Junior's hand-me-down. I haven't bothered Max with this because I wasn't sure, but there's another sign every day: skin is getting yellow, more nausea, tenderness and itching. Just now I noticed my urine has turned brown.

Textbook.

Double crap!

I'll have to tell him tonight, then back into the maw of the medical profession. Fuckity fuckity fuck fuck fuck!

Funny. I hate the thought of telling dear Max almost as much as the realization that I'm back on death row. I feel like I've let him down.

From Max Brown's notes on moral psychology

There's a consistent theme in folk stories from all societies: The highest expression of morality is self-sacrifice – typically giving one's own life to save another.

Moral philosophy theories have been silent on this, but the social psych literature takes it up. People say they're more comfortable sacrificing their own life rather than another's. Experimenters use the runaway trolley dilemma. They ask subjects, "Is it better to throw one naïve bystander in front of the trolley to save five people trapped on board, or should you sacrifice yourself?" The culturally acceptable answer (and most frequently given) is that the subject would sacrifice him or herself.

On the mountainside in Petra I was ready to give my life so that Sally would live. Would she do the same for me? Almost certainly. But, in all honesty, when I made that offer to God(s) there was no expectation that it would be taken up.

Still, there's something there. We're supposed to put the welfare of others ahead of our own.

Prisoner's dilemma

This is not disloyal to Sally. It's practical – and the responsible thing for a husband to do.

I walked Henri to his car after dinner last night and we agreed to work together. He'd noticed how tired and drawn Sally looks. Not that I'll grace the cover of *GQ* with my patched up ear and the side of my head shaved and scabby, but my injuries are cosmetic.

I have some ideas to discuss with Henri. I'll tell Sally I'm going to the Université library to work on that course outline some more. She'll think I'm just sulking because I couldn't talk her out of leaving Jordan.

My first thought is that Henri and I should check out Dr. Levy.

What do cops talk about on stakeouts? Henri and I followed Levy, cruising leisurely in his fancy Jag, to a swanky restaurant. While Levy was enjoying an apéritif and lunch, one hundred meters away Henri and I were forcing conversation. Henri's less than half my age. And a cop. And Swiss. Few overlaps in interests – and, believe me, we looked for them. Is this where the doughnuts come in? Alternatives to conversation?

I was ready to pull up stakes when Levy was joined in the restaurant by – you've seen this coming, right? – Dr. Emile Schwarzherz.

"Could be nothing," cautioned Henri.

I needed to believe otherwise.

Henri found his binoculars under a blanket on the back seat and watched the two men. "This is not a friendly meeting, Max. They are arguing."

Even without binocs I could see it wasn't cordial. Schwarzherz had risen to his feet and was leaning across the table, wagging a finger as he spoke. Levy looked up at Schwarzherz, said nothing, and took another forkful of food. Schwarzherz abruptly left.

"I say we raise the temperature, Henri. Do you have business cards?" He nodded. "Schwarzherz is headed this way. I suggest you intercept him, hand him your card and tell him he might want to talk to you before it gets worse. Then leave."

"Worse than what?"

"Let him imagine the alternatives."

Henri acted on the suggestion. I sank low in the car, just able to view the clinic director's expression of surprise – and then alarm. He didn't protest as Henri walked away. Schwarzherz pocketed the business card as if it were contraband, pulled his hat forward, and hurried past.

After Schwarzherz had left the area, Henri returned. "Now what?"

"Same with Levy. Prisoner's dilemma."

Henri repeated the sequence fifteen minutes later when the well-lunched Dr. Levy emerged from the restaurant, scowling. Perhaps the altercation with Schwarzherz had upset his digestion. When Levy received the card his reaction was different. He studied it as if it were in an unfamiliar script. After a moment's hesitation he tried to catch up with the cop who reached our car ten meters ahead of him. We took off before Levy caught up.

"I think you would make a good police detective, Max. What will happen now?"

"I'm making a couple of assumptions. First, that at least one of them is not good at crime. Probably Schwarzherz. He'll do something stupid, or maybe even sing. If they're both professional bad guys, then nothing. And maybe there is nothing.

"Second, they both will know they're under surveillance and they may think it's a 24-hour effort. That'll make them more likely to warn off anyone they don't want to be seen with. Is there any chance you could look at the record of Schwarzherz's phone calls for the next couple of hours? I have his cellphone number."

Henri called it in to 'Lisa' at FedPol. He also asked her to find Levy's number and get the record of his calls for the rest of the afternoon. From the tone of the conversation it sounded like Lisa's the woman Henri has been stringing along for the past eleven years. Sally said they've been fighting and any guy would recognize the careful way Henri was speaking, expecting a blow-up at any point.

"Anything else, detective Max?"

"Sure, while we're messing with these guys . . ."

I dialed the clinic and got Gisele. "Hey, this is Max . . . yes, Sally's husband." How many Maxes does Gisele know? "Look, this may be just my paranoia, but when I drove by your clinic this morning I thought I saw that big bearded guy sitting in a car across the street. With the road divider it took a while before I could double back and the car was gone. But, it wouldn't hurt to notify Schwarzherz. He might want to get some protection around the place before there's another break-in – or whatever these guys do."

Gisele said she'd tell Schwarzherz and if he wouldn't call the cops, she'd do it herself.

"And Gisele, please don't mention this to Sally. It's important for her to rest up a few more weeks. As you saw last night, she's still not herself."

Henri beamed at me approvingly.

My regard for the man's judgment was going up by the minute.

Daily Journal

Sally Taylor-Brown

15 April cont'd
Geneva

Get a grip, Sally Taylor. There are lots of people worse off than I am. I should be doing something to find Hanan.

No ideas. Maybe retrace her steps? Go to the cemetery in Fribourg and try to get a glimpse at that registry? Trains on that line are frequent. I should be back by early evening.

Distractions

Henri called to say he had the report from Lisa. Schwarzherz made four calls to the same number, and no other calls. The first three were for ten seconds each and Lisa says this is typical of a call to voice-mail. The fourth call lasted for less than one minute. That sounds like the right amount of time to tell someone the heat is on and to lie low. The four calls were to a landline in Fribourg. Lisa's off duty now but Henri says she can get the street address in the morning. It's clear that Henri doesn't want to lean on her.

Levy had made no calls on his registered cellphone. Seems strange for a physician to make or receive no calls for a six-hour period. My guess is he has a burner to use in these situations.

Henri added something intriguing: There had been a request earlier in the afternoon for the phone records of the number Schwarzherz had called. Lisa didn't know – or had neglected to find out – who had made the request. Is someone in FedPol finally moving their ample Swiss ass and looking into Hanan's disappearance? One can only hope.

I'm glad Henri called for two reasons: 1. It sounds like some progress is being made. 2. A distraction. My soul mate isn't home and it's approaching seven PM. I called her cellphone and found it ringing in the next room. She leaves it behind as often as she remembers to take it.

So I'm writing to keep my mind occupied. Sally says I had sold her on the value of writing to get through anxious moments. I don't recall ever recommending that, but it seems a reasonable idea.

It's a reasonable idea only if you have something to write about. It's now eight o'clock and still no Sally. I called Gisele to see if they are together. No.

I feel sneaky doing this. Why should I? It's not an insecure husband stalking his wife. I checked her closet. Her favorite warm pullover is gone so she was expecting to be outside.

A trip to the bathroom. The immunosuppressant meds to prevent rejection of Jr.'s liver were lined up on the vanity. She expected to be back within eight hours.

Just checked the hall closet. Knit hat and gloves are gone. Definitely outside. One more place to look, but it feels like an invasion of privacy. Still, I'd understand if she did the same if I were missing. Perhaps there's something in her Daily Journal. It's not a violation of privacy if I just take a peek at the last entry, is it?

Fribourg. *Holy shit, Sal!*

Should I head up to Fribourg, or sit tight?

She'll show up. Probably just missed a train. She's had enough bad luck for one year.

From Max Brown's notes on Nagel's theory of Moral Luck.

Nagel proposes three categories of moral luck.

Two drivers run a red light. A child steps out in front of one of them and, despite heroic evasive maneuvers, the driver hits and kills the child. The second driver roars, untouched, through the intersection to the accompaniment of blaring horns and obscene gestures.

Society piles opprobrium on the first driver and shrugs off the same error committed by the second. Moral bad luck has fallen heavily on the first driver. We assess the morality of a person's behavior by consequences.

There is also circumstantial moral luck. Germans who, through blind fate, were outside of Nazi Germany during the Third Reich are spared the blame attributed to those who were in the country and who were judged as either complicit or morally negligent for not opposing Hitler. Were those Germans who were fortunate enough to be out of the country more moral people?

How about people who have every break go against them. They become bitter and behave badly. Nagel calls this constitutional moral luck; their response to the world has been baked into them by their life experiences. Should they be held to the same moral standard as someone who has received every break life can offer? Apparently not. Perversely, society is more tolerant of white-collar criminals who steal millions than we are of petty thieves.

Then this arrived

I found the note on the floor, partially under the door, at around midnight.

> Braun we have your wive. To proof she say my name BBM. If you want more proof I can sent maybe ear or finger. Do you want ear or finger? Maybe you belive me.
>
> Stop looking where you must not look. We can keep wive many years. Maybe we sell her kidney for money. Then we have money to feed her. This is a good idea. Do you agree?

I slumped against the wall, then staggered to the bathroom.

BBM's note hadn't warned against calling in the police; perhaps that's understood. I called Henri.

"Can you get Lisa to find that address in Fribourg right now? Sally's been taken. She went to Fribourg and I just got a note saying they have her."

"Max, is this Max?" Of course it is. "Is it a ransom note?"

"Not yet. A warning to stop investigating. We hit a nerve and the BBM and whoever he's working with are thrashing around. Maybe they'll ask for money later. I really need that address."

"Lisa is here. I'll ask her, but . . ."

But? That sounds like discord again. "Jesus, Henri. Let me speak to her."

"No, she will understand the urgency." Let's hope. He was gone for an agonizingly long time. Finally, "The information is only available at the station so she will have to go there. When we have the address I will come to your apartment. We need to go to Fribourg tonight. Switzerland is not an easy country to hide someone. People notice. They may try to move Sally soon."

"I'm already going down to my car, Henri. You'll have to catch up. Give me a call with the address so I can watch the place while waiting for you." I hung up to avoid an argument about the wisdom of going alone.

No time to think until I was on the A1, cruise control set on 130 KPH. All adrenalin and reaction to that point. Shouldn't we call in the police? The cantonal cops might yawn off the disappearance of an Arab Muslim, but a kidnapping note? On the other hand, would they be an asset? And what was Henri's exposure? His main squeeze was surreptitiously getting police info and he was neck deep in an unauthorized investigation – at my urging. It had spun out of control for him. If he didn't call in the cavalry he was negligent, and if he revealed his involvement he was probably unemployed.

A buzz and chirp in my pocket. A text message of an address in Fribourg.

Directions to here? asked the phone.

Fucking A, you digital dimwit.

Sally, Sally, Sally. Why did you do this?

As I entered Fribourg Henri called to tell me he was on his way. No mention of Lisa accompanying him or notifying the cantonal police.

The address was in the southeast part of town. Cyrillic, Turkish, and occasional Arabic alphabets adorned the store fronts. Several shops promised *halal* foods for the devout. An exception: I flashed past a sign to a Christian outpost, the College Saint-Croix. A small irony.

The address Lisa had pulled up was for a shabby three-story brownstone apartment building. I circled the block and found a parking spot from where the front door was visible. Then I pulled out and circled the block again, this time going down the alley to see if there was a back entrance. There was.

Back in the original parking spot . . . what now? Wait for Henri? Storm the gates? Before racing out of our apartment I'd paused for only one thing: my ancient Smith and Wesson .38 caliber Masterpiece, derisively named Roscoe. Which was useless in my hands.

Largely to postpone doing something rash I sent a text message to Nour. She'd want to know what was happening although it was two AM in Jordan.

That occupied three minutes.

Fuck it. Storm the gates. Sally's in there.

From the sidewalk the building looked dark and forbidding. Perhaps a faint glow through a second story curtain. The glow flickered. TV.

The French front doors were locked but a credit card solved that. *American Express. This is why you don't leave home without it.* Not a good sign when your mind wanders to slogans. *Focus.*

In the hallway, six mailboxes indicated six apartments, two per floor. None of the names on the mailboxes said BBM. I retreated back outside, turned the door lock to open, and made a call.

"Henri, did Lisa give you a name?"

"Yes, but please wait for me, Max. I will be there in thirty minutes."

"The name, Henri. This is about my wife."

Silence. Then, with resignation, "Haddadeen. George Haddadeen."

Lama, the disfigured woman in Salt, said 'George' had brought her back to Jordan after her second surgery.

I hung up without acknowledging – still not ready for that argument about waiting – and re-entered the building. A mailbox for an apartment on the third floor bore the name 'G. Haddadin.'

Older buildings have charm, and they have creaking floors. The first step registered an audible protest; I backed down. Older buildings also have high ceilings and it looked like a long way up to the third floor. Lots of complaining stairs to negotiate.

Hugging the wall where the steps and risers might be more firmly supported – and putting weight on the banister – I crept up. It was working. Silent progress. Until the penultimate step, which, like the first, took exception to my weight. *Damn.*

Moving quickly across the hall I flattened myself against the wall beside the door. A person would have to extend his head out of the door to see me.

Nothing. They hadn't heard the steps groan? Asleep? Crouching in ambush?

Neither door was marked. G. Haddadin was in 3B, according to the mailbox, but that information was for the benefit of the postman, not late-night visitors.

The Swiss are, if nothing else, systematic and consistent. They read from left to right; ergo, apartment numbering goes from left to right. Probably.

I squared off in front of the door on the right side of the hall. Shoulder? A flying kick near the latch? Maybe the credit card again? A silent entry is always better. I was pulling out the credit card when the soft sound of the deadbolt turning sent me back against the wall.

Roscoe out. Safety off. Which way is that? I hadn't handled the gun for two years. Maybe I should have waited for Henri.

The doorknob turned, slowly. A clear sign this wasn't a late-night run for brews. I tried to steady the gun against the door molding at eye level, finger tightened against the trigger. A sliver of light spilled across the floor as the door inched open. The light was extinguished, but the door wasn't reclosed.

My hand was shaking. *I really need to learn how to shoot a gun.* The barrel rubbed against the door molding; the noise was soft, but audible in the silent hallway.

Suddenly something rolled out of the door, below my aiming point. I turned to find my adversary in the dark. There he was: the dim outline of a shooter, on one knee and with a pistol trained on me.

I'd know that perfume anywhere. "Nour?"

Night visitors

"Dr. Max. I was afraid it was you." She led back into the apartment and threw the light-switch. There were only a few items of furniture; the sofa and armchairs were encased in clear plastic, reminiscent of the homes of my childhood friends, their mothers preserving the upholstery for the big event that never came.

"Nour, I'm amazed and delighted to see you. But . . . why would you be *afraid* it was me?"

"They left a few things behind. I was hoping one of them would come back."

"How did you know to come here? And how did you get here?" Perhaps her presence explained the inquiry into the apartment's phone number that Lisa had seen.

Nour deflected the questions, "I have not been here long," and turned away to resume her exploration of the three-room apartment.

The number and kinds of dirty dishes in the sink convinced her there had been four people in the apartment. A half-consumed package of sliced ham in the refrigerator led her to announce, with satisfaction, "Christians." The amount and distribution of used duct tape on the floor around two kitchen chairs were evidence that two of the four people in the apartment had been captives.

She headed toward a door, presumably to the bedroom. "Prepare yourself," she said over her shoulder.

"Sally?" I croaked.

Nour shook her head. No. Not that bad. Even before the light came on I could make out the blood-stained sheets on a narrow bed. Gauze in the wastebasket, some of it also blood-stained. A black leather doctor's bag half under the bed contained antibiotics, wound disinfectant, a stethoscope, and a rolled kit of basic-looking surgical instruments.

"This," pointing to the bag, "is what you thought someone might come back for?"

Nour nodded.

"Nour, this looks like post-operative care. Everything we've learned so far indicates the organ removal has to be done in an actual operating theatre if they're going to have a marketable organ. The blood on the sheets and these bandages might just be dressing changes. They've had Sally for twelve hours at the most so . . ." a sentence I couldn't finish.

"So you are concluding that your wife is safe for the moment and what we see here is from surgery on another person?"

I'm *concluding* that's not her blood? Hell no. Hoping.

I nodded, numb. Recovering my voice, "Perhaps the victim is a woman who works in the clinic and came to Fribourg six days ago."

"The doctor's bag is a mystery. Unless the doctor expected to return soon."

"Or didn't want to be seen carrying it around in this neighborhood." My abiding faith in the vigilance/nosiness of Swiss burghers.

My phone vibrated. Henri.

"I went into the apartment, Henri. Already gone. There's a Jordanian intel agent here. How far out are you?"

"Just entering Fribourg. Maybe ten minutes."

"We're on the third floor."

I hung up and turned to Nour to explain Henri's involvement when she put a finger to her lips and turned off the lights.

"Front door," she whispered. This was followed by the same creak of that first step. "Is your friend already here?"

I shook my head. Pistols out, we listened to the creaks of flooring as someone made their laborious way up the stairs. It wasn't anyone concerned about detection. He or she paused on the second landing. Maybe not coming our way? Then the slow climb resumed. BBM seemed in better physical condition than this. That last step of the staircase issued a prolonged complaint. I took a shallow silent breath.

The door was pushed open. Nour threw the light switch, and standing between us – our pistols leveled at his temples – stood Dr. Emile Schwarzherz.

Misdirection

Schwarzherz jumped, then slowly extended his hands above his head. "Mr. Brown – what are you here for? And a pistol?"

Schwarzherz looked alarmed – and intimidated by the guns – but he didn't exhibit the guilty panic that might have been expected.

"Since we have the pistols and a degree of leverage, Doctor, let's turn the question around. What are you doing at a crime scene?"

"My God! Crime? I received a call to look in on a surgery patient and change dressings if necessary." He opened a paper sack to show us the packages of gauze and tape.

"Then you should go into the bedroom and check on your patient. We'll let you know when to return." I pulled back the hammer on the pistol for emphasis.

As soon as he was out of the room, "I don't get it Nour. I'm pretty sure this guy plays some role in the organ harvesting, but he's as cool as a cucumber." Would she have learned that phrase in boarding school?

She smiled. Noteworthy, since Nour had favored us with few smiles during our acquaintanceship. "Not so cool. I'll show you.

"Doctor," she called. "Come back."

Schwarzherz warily re-entered the room, standing sideways to us.

"Turn toward us, Doctor." He slowly pivoted. Nour pointed. Our clinic director had pissed himself.

Schwarzherz raised his arms in defeat, incriminated by a weak bladder. "It was never supposed to be like this," he blurted. "I became involved with only the best of intentions. You have to believe me."

"What was it supposed to be like?"

Schwarzherz looked at the ceiling, then rushed to explain. "Six months ago a charity approached me, offering to help with our acid-attack women after I operated on them. They said they had a physician on call and trained nurses. I only had to notify the charity of women who might need assistance as they recuperated."

The fact that he hadn't informed anyone else at the clinic of this arrangement was evidence he knew something wasn't right.

"Several times I was asked to perform follow-up surgery. The charity provided the OR and another physician scrubbed in and stayed with the patient after I'd finished."

"When did you figure out what was happening after you'd left the OR?"

Schwarzherz declined to answer.

Nour shook her head. She didn't understand.

"What the doctor isn't telling us, Nour, is that the "charity" paid him directly to conduct the surgery, and maybe even for the leads. That's why he kept this arrangement to himself. He was useful in getting women back into an OR. They would come voluntarily if they were told Schwarzherz wanted to improve their looks. Sometimes Schwarzherz actually did that and after he left the OR the other physician cut out whatever organs were on order. When Schwarzherz wasn't available, I imagine they'd improvise. If the victim put up a fuss there was always someone there to hold her down while she was gassed."

Nour looked at Schwarzherz savagely.

"Another stab, Emile. This charity was given access to the patients' records, right?"

"Well, yes. That is standard practice in medicine."

"And those records contained interview notes with the patients so this 'charity' could identify which women were less likely to be missed by family and friends if they disappeared."

A grunt and negative headshake from Schwarzherz.

"Do we have the main points right, Emile? You served up Arab women – okay, maybe unwittingly at first – to Levy, who mined them for marketable organs."

He didn't respond. Was he regretting his rush to confess?

"We'll take that as a yes. Now, there's your presence here tonight. Would you care to illumine us?"

Apparently not. His expression had changed from embarrassed to truculent.

"Then I'll take another guess. At some point you figured out the organ harvesting part. Maybe when you learned the women were dying after you performed minor cosmetic surgery. Maybe you went back to the OR for some reason and found your reconstructive surgery patient opened up. It's not important; we can let the details of your epiphany come out in court. But you did wise up. You also realized you were implicated and that's why you're here tonight."

Still nothing from Schwarzherz.

"Or I could be understating your involvement. You could be the loathsome villain who cooked this all up."

That got a response, "No, I was unaware until the women started dying. I had no part in the removal of vital organs."

"And you did nothing."

The statement seemed to anger Schwarzherz. "No. I objected in the strongest terms."

"But didn't go to the police. Why not?"

Nothing from Schwarzherz.

Things were falling into place. "Ah. That's when they trashed your clinic. A warning, something to pique your paranoia. Maybe that explains why you kept a gun in your house and were blasting blindly into the night.

"Refresh my memory, Doctor. Does Switzerland invoke the death penalty?"

A snort of disgust from Schwarzherz. It wasn't a credible threat as no civilized European country kills its own. Another tack:

"There may be a path opening to a shorter prison sentence. A FedPol agent will come pounding up the stairs any second now to take you into custody. If you help us rescue Sally and Hanan you might do better at sentencing."

Another snort, but he was thinking.

I summoned Nour into the hall. "It's not adding up. I'm pretty sure Schwarzherz is in this just as I described. But why would they let him come here? Is he the fall guy? Makes no sense, Nour. They sent him to us and they have to assume he'll sing."

"Maybe misdirection? Your doctor will lead us one way while they are going another? It's a common tactic used by terrorists in the Middle East. Or it could be a simple test. If your doctor found no one here it would be a sign that we weren't on their trail yet."

"That makes as much sense as anything else." I told her about our encounters with Levy and Schwarzherz earlier. "If they find that we're closing in, then sending us down the wrong path is the best – and maybe only – thing they can do at this point. The last known location of any of them was Geneva when someone slipped a note under my door two hours ago. But as you know, these guys are constantly changing plans and direction. And this looks like Haddadin's work. Levy definitely wouldn't want us talking to Schwarzherz."

We went back into the apartment; Schwarzherz was searching through the kitchen drawers, probably for a knife. "Time for you to side with the angels, Emile. Here's what's happening: Your friends sent you here – while they skedaddled – so that you could send us off the wrong way. They get out of the country and leave poor Dr. Emile standing alone before the judge. With no one else to share the blame I'm guessing the court will come down hard on the one perp they have."

Schwarzherz flinched at the word 'hard'. Perhaps because I smacked my fist on the table.

"If you want to do yourself any good you'll tell us the obvious place they'd go, and then try to think of an alternative hiding place they might have. We think it's the second choice that Haddadin is headed to."

"I know nothing of these people." A defiant glare. Embarrassment over wet trousers had precipitated a confession. Now he thought he could stonewall?

"Disingenuous, Doctor. You knew where to find Levy at noon. You know something. Their habits. Where they stay. As I said, if Haddadin didn't want you giving us unhelpful information he wouldn't have you here. And, if you haven't figured it out, your debt of loyalty is cancelled. Haddadin served you up."

We didn't have a lot of time to coax information out of Schwarzherz. With each passing minute Sally was moving further away. Increased pressure was next. Perhaps Schwarzherz' own surgical instruments could be put to good use. Based on Mukhabarat's reputation, Nour might have some creative ideas. With Sally's life in play I certainly had no qualms and was warming to the irony of using Schwarzherz's own tools to slice away at sensitive parts of him. I turned to Nour and raised my palms in exasperation.

That inattention was Schwarzherz's signal to make a break for it. He pushed me hard backward over a chair. As he lunged toward the open door Nour dropped to the floor and kicked hard at his ankles. Schwarzherz toppled forward onto his chest.

Nour was up and behind his prostrate body. A savage kick to the nuts. *My my, Nour! I'm disappointed. Not in you. It's just that that's what I wanted to do. You beat me to it.*

While Schwarzherz was occupied I salvaged the second-hand duct tape and hog-tied him, face down on the floor, two arms behind his back to one raised ankle. Nour, perhaps in a reaction to her recent assault on Schwarzherz's masculinity, had flipped over to the far-feminine side of the spectrum and was fussily collecting unused tape and carrying it to a waste basket in the bathroom.

Someone coming up the stairs. Henri was due. I turned to greet him. "Hi, Agent Hen . . ."

The BBM.

The Magic Door

A hazy – and unsettling – memory from early childhood is of a series of bedtime stories my mother read about a magic door. As recall serves, the child in the story could –

a) go bravely through the door to adventure (and peril – occasionally defeat – the child had to fill in the blanks; was defeat death?), or

b) approach the door timidly which always led to denied entry, or

c) stand indecisively near the door until, inevitably, something unpleasant tumbled out.

If there was a moral – and children's stories always come packaged with a lesson – the publisher believed the best option was to charge forward toward uncertainty, and in most cases, glory. Entertaining as these stories were, it was never clear to me that the odds favored rushing forward.

I'm telling you this to try to understand my paralysis. There, only a few feet away, framed in the magic door from which Nour and Schwarzherz had emerged, stood my wife's abductor. And then he was gone. I hadn't moved an inch.

"Dr. Brown. Did someone just come up the stairs?"

"Shit, Nour. That was Haddadin . . . BBM."

We rushed toward the door and collided. Recovering and vaulting down the steps, we burst through the French doors into the street to see a car skid around a far corner.

"Sally may still be in Fribourg, Nour."

I was searching my pockets for keys when, "Max, I find you in the street. Is something happening?" Agent Henri had arrived one minute too late.

"Henri, where's your car? The bad guy just took off in an old Peugeot."

"A block away. If you are thinking hot pursuit maybe it is too late to go for my car. What happened?"

Nour told Henri about the events of the last few minutes. I was stunned by the near miss. We had BBM right there and I froze. Henri nodded thoughtfully as Nour briefed him; he hazarded only the occasional glance in my direction. I'd fucked up.

When we got back up to the apartment, Schwarzherz was struggling against the duct tape and was close to freeing himself. Almost casually Nour kicked him in the crotch for a second time and reattached the tapes. Payback for the Russian-Israeli who'd raped her mother?

"This man is our remaining lead, Henri. We thought Haddadin had set him up as the fall guy who would send us off in the wrong direction, but now I'm not so sure since Haddadin came back."

Henri studied Schwarzherz as if something could be learned by analyzing the surgeon's facial features. He didn't kick him.

Then Henri and Nour conferred. Professionals. My counsel was not wanted.

At length Henri turned to me, "A new theory, Max." Nour nodded concurrence. "They left something behind. More than a doctor's bag."

At this announcement Schwarzherz resumed struggling against the duct tape.

"Ah, Emile. You're really no good at this bad-guy business, are you? You just signaled that you know something. Would you care to share that? Or should Nour continue to play soccer with your nuts?"

Nour moved into position. Henri looked uncertain.

Schwarzherz was sweating. "There's only one possibility but I don't know where it is. Someplace not too warm. A box 30 centimeters on each side." Nour stepped away.

It seemed clear what that described. "Nour, Henri, these idiots left the harvested organ behind."

Henri was the one to discover the organ container in a cupboard against a cold exterior wall. "It looks like a kidney," he announced, reclosing the lid.

"Whose is it, Emile?" I assumed Hanan.

"I don't know. I never saw the donor." Donor? "I was asked to check the sutures. This is the first time I have been here."

Henri was making room in the refrigerator for the organ box. "They're only viable for 10 to 12 hours after removal." He really had read up. "I'll call the Registry and they can put it to good use."

"I'm all for the kidney finding a home, Henri, but if we move fast maybe it can be returned to its rightful owner – the person Dr. Schwarzherz refers to as the donor."

"Any thoughts on where we might find Haddadin and his captives, Emile?" Schwarzherz closed his eyes and grimaced. Bracing for another kick.

Before the two pros, Nour and Henri, could resume their private confab, I offered my own assessment. "If Sally's clinic is the only source of organs, the low turnover means the red-marketing operation can't support a large staff, perhaps just Haddadin, Schwarzherz and Levy. If that's right, then Haddadin has to keep the hostages with him, or dump them." I closed my mind to how they might be dumped, and continued. "They had a fresh kidney that needs to be used tonight. Sally could be held somewhere near the scheduled transplant facility. The only place we know of is Levy's clinic in Lausanne. Although there's less point in going there now, we still might find clues or even a person waiting for a new organ."

Nour interjected, "Without the kidney Haddadin is free to take his captives anywhere."

Everyone wanted to chime in. Henri prevailed, "Not really. In this country you cannot move around without someone noticing. Haddadin needs to go somewhere familiar and secure. Will he keep the hostages alive?" Jesus, Henri; can't you put it better than that? "The answer depends on whether they are more of a burden on his freedom of movement or whether he believes they can be bargaining chips. Unfortunately they can identify him so he is not likely to just abandon them somewhere. Kill them or cash them in for a ticket to freedom." Henri looked pleased at the turn of phrase.

I nodded at Schwarzherz. "That brings us back to you, Emile. Where's Haddadin's base? Don't deliberate too long. I can see Nour's kicking foot starting to twitch. And I wouldn't mind having a go."

Nour didn't wait. Another savage kick and Schwarzherz gasped, turned red, and let out a long plaintive howl.

"My turn," I announced brightly.

"No," wheezed Schwarzherz. "Wait." We waited. "I only know Levy's clinic. That is where everything is done."

"That's not enough, Doctor," and I pulled my foot back.

"Stop. I am not certain of anything. Sometimes I think Haddadin stays in this area. The license on his car is from this canton."

"Of course he stays in this area. We're in Haddadin's apartment. You just gave us nothing. Does he have some other place where he keeps the women or he can go to hide?"

Henri, who apparently didn't approve of torture, pulled me away from Schwarzherz. "Max, perhaps you are looking for information that does not exist. You said yourself that this is a small operation. There is this apartment and there is Levy's clinic."

Henri was probably right. "What do you think, Henri? Go to Levy's clinic?"

"I have no better idea. I will ask the Fribourg police to keep a watch on this apartment. Perhaps they will cooperate without demanding an official request."

"What about him?" nodding toward Schwarzherz.

"I have two sets of handcuffs. I can secure him in my car."
Henri's eyes moved down to the dark stain on Schwarzherz'
crotch, regretting his offer to allow the doctor onto his immaculate seat covers.

Our departure was more leisurely than the urgency of the
situation demanded; growing panic over Sally's situation was
taking hold again. Schwarzherz was understandably slow hob-
bling down the stairs. Then Henri wasted time experimenting
with different ways of shackling Schwarzherz into his back seat,
finally settling on cuffing the doctor's wrists to the door pulls.
And more time was lost in a discussion of whom Nour should
ride with: With Henri to keep an eye on the doctor? Or me, for
old times' sake.

Nour seemed to want to go with me, so I settled the issue
with a declaration.

Finally underway, I brought Nour up to date. She had information of her own, but seemed slow to release it. Spy men-
tality.

"If you are wondering why I am here in Switzerland," – of
course I was wondering – "it is because . . ." Then a long pause
while she considered what she could say.

"C'mon, Nour. I'm not Mossad."

"Mukhabarat has taken a stronger interest in the killing of
Jordanian women. There are rumors that someone very high up
wants progress. It might even be Her Majesty."

Sending a junior agent didn't seem a sufficient response if
the royals were getting involved, and we'd noticed a tendency
among many Jordanians to imagine the king or queen had taken
a personal interest in their endeavors. This royal support was
illusory; the palace was famously slow to endorse any cause for
fear of alienating someone.

"Are you the only agent here?"

"Mukhabarat has a permanent presence in Switzerland, like
they do in most other major countries. I don't know how many

agents or where they are. Perhaps some are in the Jordanian Embassy. That, by the way, is not a secret I am telling you." She looked uncertain about that. "Everyone has their agents here. I hear that the largest number of intel agents is from Mossad."

I'd heard that too, but long ago when Mossad was orchestrating some of their Nazi hunting from Switzerland.

Nour was wandering off topic, probably concerned that she'd been talking out of school.

"I think you were about to tell me why you're here and, perhaps, you have some information that will help us."

That refocused the conversation. We'd just joined highway E27 and were heading south to Lausanne.

"Yes. We've received information that Mrs. Brown's clinic has someone working there who plays a major role in the red market."

"Yes, Schwarzherz, of course. You've just made his acquaintance." I pictured the savagery with which Nour had hammered away at the surgeon's jewels.

"Yes, of course him. But he's just a prop. He provides the bait to bring the women back for more surgery. No, I'm talking about someone who provides the contacts, recruitment and coordination."

"In Sally's clinic?"

"Yes. A Jordanian woman who lives in Geneva. You have mentioned her to me. Hanan al-Tafile."

Denial

Francis Bacon wrote, "The human understanding when it has once adopted an opinion draws all things else to support and agree with it."

Screw you, Mr. Bacon. There was nothing selective about my defense of Hanan. There was no possibility she was on the wrong side. Just look:

- Hanan was the first to take the disappearances seriously.
- She went looking for the first victim – the one whose charred remains were found near Fribourg.
- She had been locked up at the time the clinic was trashed.
- She'd discovered the gutted corpse (although that might be used in evidence against her).

On the other hand . . .

No . . . no 'other hand.'

"That's nuts, Nour. Hanan has been the most active in trying to stop this." Nour shrugged. "Who told you she was working for the other side?"

She shrugged again.

"This is important, Nour. Sally came up here looking for Hanan. If what you're saying is correct, Hanan could have been part of a scheme to trap Sally. If you're wrong – and I'm certain you are – then both women are prisoners."

Still nothing.

"Did this come from Mukhabarat's own sources?" I watched her face for signs. She was probably too well trained to betray anything.

"Or maybe this is what you were told by Fedpol this afternoon when you asked for Haddadin's address."

Aha! There was a sign. Nour's mouth tightened. I couldn't continue studying her as the car had drifted onto the warning strip along the edge of the highway.

Bonfire of the verities

Henri was standing in the parking lot of Levy's clinic, trying to snatch something from a fire smoldering in a fifty gallon drum. The fire wasn't burning rapidly but Henri was unable to reach down into the drum far enough to grab anything substantial. He had on one winter glove which wasn't thick enough to risk more than a second or two near the flames.

"Records, Max. Someone was burning records here." We'd picked up the smell of burning paper a block away. At three in the morning positive explanations for the fire were few.

Nour kicked the drum over onto the gravel. As the contents spilled out, they blazed up, but some of the records – Manila folders that had been at the bottom – were curling from the heat but had not ignited. She pulled out the most intact folders and scooped sand and gravel on them to extinguish the small flames that were eating at the edges.

Henri extracted one and gingerly examined it. "Patient records." He flicked the file with his fingertip. "What an idiot!" Henri expects a higher level of intelligence from his adversaries.

I picked up a folder. The patient had been seen half a year ago; the name and gender hadn't been entered. The notes were in standard indecipherable physician scrawl, but it seemed likely a careful reader would find they described reconstructive surgery, and, if our quarry truly was an idiot, something about thoracic surgery.

"I don't understand. They can't be this stupid. Keep a record of their crimes?"

"I think I do, Henri. Look at the date. Schwarzherz had just been recruited. He'd expect that some kind of a medical record would be made. This may be his handwriting if it's only about reconstructive surgery. Levy needed to know blood type in advance – you can see that part is filled in – to match up the 'donor' to a waiting recipient. These records were filed and forgotten until this evening."

I turned them over in my hand. What sorrows were not recorded? Perhaps they'd be useful in court someday. Not in finding Sally tonight.

"Have you already checked to see if anyone's in the clinic?" Henri shrugged. "Ah shit, Henri. Don't tell me you need a warrant to take a peek inside?" He shrugged again.

Nour's face was a mask, but it was easy to guess what she thought of FedPol's timidly correct methods in a country where property is more important than human life. With no ceremony or warning, she landed a solid kick on the lock of the clinic's back door. It held. I eased her aside and took a lick at the door myself. Still nothing. Her turn again. She pulled her gun and placed two shots through the latch plate. The door swung open.

"Good God!" Henri sputtered. "Right now fifty Swiss burghers are dialing the police station, reporting gunfire. We have to leave."

Nour was unaware of Henri's extra-official involvement. He couldn't be found here, breaking into a clinic. And fat Schwarzherz, shackled in the backseat, presented another difficult explanation.

"Sorry about that, Henri. Nour didn't know. I suggest you scram. We'll take a quick tour of the clinic to see if Sally and Hanan are here." We ran through the door without waiting to see if the cop acted on the suggestion.

The back door led into the records room. Shelves from floor to ceiling sagged under file folders. Levy must have been in business for a long time. Nour looked behind the shelves on the left; I on the right. No bound captives. The supply cupboard stood open and a few items had fallen out on the floor, but then, tidiness may have been low on Levy's list. It did suggest he'd passed through here in a hurry.

Leading with her pistol, Nour pushed into the reception area. The receptionist's counter was as I remembered. The waiting area was not. The straight-backed chairs that encircled the waiting room were now occupied by the wraiths of women who'd died in the clinic. Nour ran down the short hall that led to four doors: two examining rooms, Levy's office, and a small surgery. I checked each in turn.

"Dr. Max, did you see something?"

I must have looked confused by her question.

"You recoiled out of the operating room as if you had been pushed."

It was too easy to picture what had happened there. And once the projector was running, impossible to suppress the images. The narrow, padded table that trusting women had gone to sleep on, cheered by the belief they would awaken, their beauty restored.

"Sorry, Nour. Lots on my mind. Are we missing something?" Levy's clinic had been a long-shot – our only shot – but I couldn't surrender the hope it would pay off. "From the outer dimensions of the building, is there some area we haven't discovered?"

Speedy Nour was outside, then back in. "We have to go. Sirens."

My lousy hearing; the cops would have been tumbling through the door before I'd pick up on it.

"Okay. If they're coming in response to your shots, they'll conduct a thorough search of the building."

Reassured anyone still in Levy's clinic would be discovered by the Lausanne police, we ran to the car and drove sedately away, briefly pulling to the curb to allow three police cars to race by in the opposite direction.

Nour spotted Henri's car in a service station. He and I hadn't had an opportunity to talk. But about what? We were at a dead end.

Henri could be seen inside the station, making a purchase and fumbling with his phone. I checked Schwarzherz who sat erect and quiet in the backseat. An ugly lump on his left temple was oozing blood. He'd provoked the cop.

My phone buzzed. "Max, it's me, Henri. I think Schwarz-herz is ready to cooperate."

Waterboarding v 2.0

Henri's purchase was an adhesive bandage which he gingerly placed over the angry lump on Schwarzherz's temple. The slight pressure got a wince. If the doctor had more information, it was going to be easy to extract.

"Emile," Schwarzherz moved his eyes in my direction, but not his head, "Agent Henri says you've reconsidered and have some ideas to share with us." Schwarzherz was silent. He'd reconsidered again. "Time is no one's friend. If you think it can't get worse, it can. Right now you're withholding information from an officer of the law regarding the abduction of two women. You're just piling on the number of years you'll spend in the slammer."

Schwarzherz was no good at this game. He'd let us know he had info, and now he was withholding it. It was an invitation to enhanced interrogation, and Nour was ready to ratchet up the pressure.

She reached through the car window, smacked the bandaged lump hard, and asked, "Is that sensitive?" Schwarzherz grimaced but, uncharacteristically, was silent. "Your face lacks symmetry, Doctor. Perhaps a matching lump on the other temple? Although," she paused and stroked her chin, "it is a tricky area to work on. As a doctor you know that, of course. Too hard a tap with my pistol butt and that might be it."

Nour had climbed into the front seat of Henri's car and was leaning over the back, facing the shackled surgeon. She held her pistol by the barrel and tapped lightly on Schwarzherz's right temple, as if sighting in on the target. She swung her arm back and Schwarzherz blurted, "Saint-Cergue."

Nour looked disappointed. "I shouldn't waste time talking. I miss too many opportunities." Was she putting on an act? I was impressed.

"Isn't Saint-Cergue where you live, Emile?"

"No, the other one, in Switzerland."

I knew the Alpine village well. Sally and I had hiked around there several times as it was a short drive from Geneva. We usually took the trail that followed the ancient Roman road. That route imbued the outing with greater purpose: walking where Caesar had walked. *Will we ever go hiking there again?*

"An address?" And I reached in the car to restrain Nour's arm – which was again cocked to signal the stakes.

"I don't remember the street name. We were invited a year ago. An old chalet west of the village. I think I could direct you. Levy said it had been in his family for three generations."

"Isolated?" asked Henri.

Schwarzherz chose this moment to clam up again. Tiresome.

Henri signaled we should move away from the car. "I don't like it, Max. This guy was sent to us by your BBM. Can we trust anything he says?"

Nour's misdirection theory.

"Nour and I were thinking the same thing, Henri. There may be another place they can hole up that Schwarzherz doesn't know about or wouldn't think of. Let's press him. Nour, you still may get an opportunity to rough up our surgeon."

Henri looked away and shook his head. "I think while you "press" him I will go back into the store. Maybe buy cigarettes."

"I didn't know you smoked."

"I might take it up," and he walked away.

Nour and I returned to the car. "Emile, let me start by saying I hope you don't cooperate. My concern is that Swiss justice will fall far too lightly on someone who was an accessory to killing Arab and Muslim women. Because of that concern, it seems entirely appropriate to mete out a little justice of our own. Try to focus your mind on what an experienced interrogator might do to you, an interrogator who is, herself, an Arab-Muslim woman. As for me? Every second you delay, my wife moves further away. I would be happy to help with the torture.

Got the picture? Good. Now let's go back to our conversation in the apartment. Is there a second option for the kidnappers? Someplace they have access to but isn't as directly associated with them?"

Silence. This seemed to please Nour.

"Dr. Max, would you get soda water and towels from the store? There is a form of water-boarding I have heard of but never had the chance to practice. They say the soda bubbles exploding in the sinus cavities are excruciating."

"Wait!" from Schwarzherz. "I am trying to think."

Ignoring him, I asked Nour, "How much soda water?"

"No, no. I really am trying to help." Schwarzherz knew of this kind of torture? He was buying into the excruciating part.

"I really am trying to think."

I started toward the store.

"Yes, wait. I remember something. When we were working on a patient Levy mentioned his wife's family has a place in Chamonix that they go to since no one else does."

Progress. I signaled to Henri it was safe to return. Schwarzherz was shaking. What a strange man: momentary flashes of courage amidst a general pattern of physical cowardice.

Henri glanced at our captive, perhaps checking for new signs of damage, and listened impassively while I explained the Chamonix lead.

He checked Schwarzherz again. "Well, Lisa will be back at work in three hours. She can find out who Levy is married to and then trace through property records from there."

The sky was growing lighter in the east. Three hours was a long time. *Sally.* Nour had moved a few steps away and was speaking Arabic into her phone. The conversation was short. "They will call back," she announced. Presumably 'they' were Mukhabarat.

In less than a minute her phone rang. Her participation in the conversation was limited to grunts, *tamams, tayibs,* and a *shokran* at the end. Given the quick response, it looked like Mukhabarat couldn't help.

Nour continued to study her phone. It bleeped. "And here is the address." Looking up at us, "Levy's wife is Lisette Schmidt. Her family has two properties near Chamonix, France. One is a time-share and currently is rented to someone. I just received the address for the other. Do you want GID to send us a map, or can FedPol manage that much?"

She didn't need to say that. Intel services rarely have an opportunity to strut their stuff and the speed with which Mukhabarat had gone through Swiss and French records was impressive, but a put down?

Perhaps to re-establish we were on FedPol's turf, Henri took charge. "We have two addresses. Schwarzherz can provide directions to one and since he is in my car, I'll go there. You and the Jordanian woman (Henri's organizational pride *had* been offended) can check out the Chamonix place." Without waiting for acknowledgement, he turned and got in his car.

As he sped off I turned to Nour.

"I'm sorry, Dr. Max. So many missing Arab women in Switzerland and they have not even started files on them."

"I know, Nour. Henri's one of the good guys. He's doing this unofficially and it might cost him his job." Silence from her side. "Okay, let's head for Chamonix."

My phone buzzed.

"Max? Henri. Sorry to leave so abruptly. She just . . ."

"I know, Henri. She's used to different rules." And a deeper level of concern for Arab women.

"I realize we, FedPol, haven't done very well here, but the real reason I wanted to talk to you . . . if you find something in Chamonix, call and I'll be right there. The French, for all their personality flaws, will mobilize quickly for a kidnapping. Wait for backup. Do not – I repeat, do not try to take these people on alone."

"Of course I won't, Henri."

If he believes that, he's a lousy detective.

The penny drops

The address Mukhabarat gave us was just past Saint-Gervais-les-Bains, a village sprawled along the western flank of Mont Blanc, well short of Chamonix. From what we knew of Levy, it was no surprise he'd told Schwarzherz he had a place in the more prestigious town. If St. Gervais was less chic than Chamonix, it had the advantage of being closer and time was short. Rush hour was approaching and Levy's mountain hideout was at least two hours away.

We'd cleared Geneva and were approaching the French border when Henri called again.

"Max, I called the St. Gervais police. They just got back to me. They found no one at that address. The man who called also said it didn't look like anyone had been there recently, although he didn't explain how they concluded that."

"Fuck. Dead end."

Nour was signaling that she wanted the phone. To insult FedPol again? I put the phone on speaker to monitor the exchange and handed it to her.

"Mr. Henri? I wanted to ask about information I received at your offices yesterday. I met with a Captain Méchant who told me the Federal Police are following up a lead that a female employee of the clinic is involved."

"That is new news for me. Méchant is aware of everything in the department, but I am surprised to hear of this. They did take Hanan al-Tafile into custody for a while, but I heard that there was no evidence."

That's when the penny dropped; the scales fell from my eyes; the light dawned.

"Henri, you told me that the wife of one of your senior officers received a liver transplant rather quickly. Was that Méchant's wife?"

Silence.

"Can you hear me, Henri? I was asking if Méchant's wife received a donated liver."

After a pause, "Hello . . . Max . . . hello? You're breaking up. If you can hear me, I'm continuing to Saint-Cergue with the doctor." The connection was terminated.

"Nour, that call seemed clear as a bell."

"You cannot blame him, Dr. Max. A good junior officer will continue to protect his superior until the evidence is overwhelming. He gave us as clear an answer as his conscience permits." She took out her own phone and called Jordan. One name stood out in the Arabic: Lisette Schmidt Méchant.

We pulled into a mall parking lot, still empty at the early hour.

"I don't know how he'd pull this off, Nour, but Méchant has planted the story that Hanan is the central figure. If he can kill her in circumstances that are consistent with that story he may direct attention away from his own involvement."

"He has two problems: We suspect that Hanan has given up a kidney. Not something the ring-leader would do. Second, there's Sally."

She didn't have to spell it out. Sally would know too much to be allowed to live.

I had no response. Nour's phone buzzed.

Again, she listened gravely; a few acknowledgements. "They apologize for the slow response. The medical records were a challenge. The captain's wife, Lisette Schmidt Méchant, did have a series of medical appointments last summer. The reason for the visits is unknown, but the later ones were with a hepatologist. I believe that's a doctor who specializes in the liver." I was murmuring appreciation when she continued, "They are texting the policeman's address . . . here it comes now."

The Méchants lived in an apartment building facing the Rhône River, not a low rent part of town. Morning traffic was picking up and we didn't arrive at the address for half an hour. I circled the block and then widened the orbit, searching for Haddadin's old Peugeot.

"He would be a fool to leave his car on the street, Dr. Max. We have passed several parking garages."

"I know, Nour, just checking." For what? *Focus, Max.* "Méchant's apartment building must have a garage but I didn't see an entrance." A car vacated a parking space down the block and we took it.

As we got out of the car Nour surveyed me. "I don't see your gun. Remember the business these people are in. Our organs might be on sale this afternoon."

I retrieved Roscoe and we entered the alley behind Méchant's apartment building. A door opened; Nour pulled me back, flat against the wall. We could hear the lid of a garbage bin being opened and closed. Then the door slammed shut.

Nour was off like a shot. I caught up as she pulled bloodstained gauze and bandages out of the garbage bin.

"Did Mukhabarat tell us which apartment they're in?"

Nour looked embarrassed.

"No time to ask now."

I tried the door that had just been used. Locked. "Please, no gunfire, Nour," and I tried the American Express card. No success; there was a security plate blocking access to the catch. Then we noticed a driveway that sloped down from the alley into an underground garage. As we approached, the metal tambour door started to rattle up. It was my turn to pull Nour back. The door complainingly ascended to reveal the bumper and grill-work of a vintage Jag, waiting to leave.

"It's Levy's car. He's the corrupt surgeon who removes the organs."

That's all Agent Nour needed. She ran down the driveway, slid under the slowly ascending door, and when I caught up, had her pistol pressed into Dr. Levy's temple.

Levy looked at us contemptuously. "You're too late."

Late

"We need to get upstairs, and now. What do we do with him?"

Nour knew exactly what to do with him. She brought the butt of her pistol down hard on Levy's collar bone. Even a lay person like me would understand what the soft snap signified.

"Bitch," Levy screamed. "What are you doing?"

"Getting your attention. I could cheerfully smash every bone in your body and still have an appetite for more. Perhaps I will finish the job later when we have more time."

Levy's contemptuous sneer was gone.

"Now, Doctor, what floor."

With no hesitation, "Fourth. They have the entire floor."

"Open the trunk," commanded Nour.

Wincing with pain, Levy reached for the release under the dash. The Jag's trunk popped open a few inches.

Nour went back to inspect it. I held Roscoe on the surgeon. Could I abuse him as casually as Nour did? It was tempting to experiment and I tapped Roscoe's barrel on the injured shoulder. Levy grunted with pain. No, not my thing.

"Out of the car," commanded Nour. Levy was slow to comply so she grabbed his arm and jerked him through the door. This elicited another howl and a string of invective. Nour pulled him toward the rear of the car and toppled him into the Jag's large trunk.

"A disadvantage of a classic car, Doctor. No trunk release on the inside. I suggest you relax and breath shallowly. Your new accommodations might be airtight. Cellphone please?" Levy handed Nour the phone and jerked his hand in as she slammed the trunk closed.

"Shouldn't we ask him who's upstairs?"

"Would you believe anything he said? It's in his interest for us to proceed with our guard down."

She was right. I grabbed the Jag's keys from the ignition – this seemed as good a place to leave the car as any – and Nour took them away from me. She slid behind the wheel, started the car, and drove it forward until the trunk was beneath the tambour garage door. She studied the control box beside the garage door, and after a false start, had it clattering down toward the trunk. I winced as the door sank into the car's polished metal.

Nour surveyed her work. Satisfied that Levy was trapped, she pulled wires from the control box, producing a cascade of sparks. Then – finally – she steered me toward the stairwell. "An elevator might announce our arrival."

I could learn a lot from this girl. But shouldn't we have been thundering up the stairs to the rescue instead of farting around with the car?

Maybe there's one thing she didn't know. "Most of these buildings follow the French custom," I announced. "The bottom floor is the *rez-de-chaussee*. Méchant's apartment is the fifth floor." Her flat expression suggested this was not new information. And why was I trying to impress her? She led up the stairs. I consciously did not look at her as we ascended.

The door from the stairwell at the fifth floor was locked. This time the credit card worked. Nour pushed me aside and eased the door open.

The door led into a small foyer. The elevator was on the right, a door into Mechant's flat on the left, and a reproduction of Monet's *Water Lilies* filled the wall directly across. The lighted numbers above the elevator door indicated it was descending. I was taking this in because I'd ceded the crime busting to Nour.

She listened at the door to the flat and shook her head – presumably no sounds from inside. A tentative turn of the knob . . . locked. She studied the latch. "Dr. Max, you can put more weight into it. Please kick the door just here." And she pointed to a spot above the knob.

I backed away from the door, anxious that I'd fail. Why? Not rescue Sally, or not impress Nour?

I missed the target, my heel hitting the knob and twisting my ankle sideways, but the door gave and swung open. Nour was immediately through it, her pistol preceding her. I hobbled behind and headed into a room to the left while Nour went to the right.

A minute later we met in the kitchen. Piles of discarded duct tape – the restraint of choice – and broken dishes littered the floor across from the china cabinet. Had Sally done this? Not like her to throw crockery around.

"Nour, I wonder . . ." It seemed too implausible to voice.

"I know, Dr. Max. It's like the old cartoons. An angry wife breaking dishes."

"Could be that Madame Méchant wasn't aware of what was going on until this morning."

"I know you and Mrs. Brown say he's a weasel. But a police captain broke the law to get an illegal organ for his wife?"

"Kohlberg stage 3."

A puzzled look.

"He's fulfilling his primary obligations, in this case to his wife, and he's less concerned about the larger picture." No need to tell Nour my own moral reasoning was locked at the same stage: Save my wife at any cost.

The metallic burp of a siren rose from the street. We rushed to a front window – colliding again – and watched an ambulance make a majestic departure, lights flashing, siren now silent.

"Fuck! We did just miss them. Come on, Nour," and I dashed out the door and down the stairs as rapidly as an unreliable ankle permitted.

Even before we reached the garage level we could hear Levy's screams which had attracted a small boy. The boy was mutely watching the trunk, a skateboard propped up on his foot.

"Those aren't shouts for help, Nour. Those are screams of panic. Levy's claustrophobic."

Nour tapped on the trunk, which got a muffled, "Thank God. Get me out of here."

"Cooperate and we might. Where was the ambulance going, Doctor?"

"I don't know. I just change the dressings." A familiar lie.

"Perhaps you need to relax to think more clearly, Doctor. I'm going to tape these gaps around the boot closed. A lower oxygen concentration might help your own mental concentration."

Nour, of course, had no tape to carry out her threat, but it was enough. It sounded like Levy was blubbering.

"I can't tell you anything. These are ruthless people."

"Doctor, Doctor," cautioned Nour. "You should save what little breath remains to tell us something that might improve your chances for survival."

What great lines. Had she rehearsed? Does Mukhabarat have a course on this for their agents?

"He'll kill me."

"You prefer the more peaceful death from asphyxiation. I understand. Of course, theirs is a probable death. Ours is a certain one. Consider the odds one more time before unconsciousness makes the decision for you."

"Just let me out and I'll tell you everything."

"It doesn't work that way. You're wasting precious air. Feeling faint yet?"

Isn't the power of suggestion great? Levy started to choke and gasp for air. "There's a small surgical clinic near HUG.

We're able to reserve it for procedures. Sometimes they'll even provide support staff but we don't need extra hands if it's a removal and not a full transplant like today. There's a client there waiting for a liver and Schwarzherz confirmed that Mrs. Brown's is compatible. Schwarzherz had her blood ty . . ."

"Where's the clinic." Nour had to ask the question. I'd just lost the power of speech.

"I think Rue Cingria, down a short ways from Jean-Violette. I know how to get to these places; I don't memorize street names. I'm supposed to meet them there. I'm scrubbing in. These procedures require three surgeons, although four is better. We could only line up two surgeons and Haddadin insisted I . . ."

He was still rambling on as we ducked under the tambour door and ran/limped toward the car.

Late again

"We have time, Dr. Max. It sounds like they can't start without Levy."

"I'm afraid they can. Organ removal is simpler than a transplant, but let's hope they wait until they have a full team. I suspect they'll want the 'donor'," I couldn't say Sally's name, "unconscious before the transplant surgeons arrive. I have to believe that the other members of the surgical team are hired guns, and not involved in the racket. They pick up their fee and don't dwell on the implications of a transplant conducted in an unusual setting."

Although Rue Cingria was only two miles away, rush hour traffic reduced our speed to a crawl. I called Henri.

"I'm afraid your boss, Méchant, is involved. He may have gotten mixed up with Haddadin and Levy in his desperation to get an organ for his wife."

The phone was silent; I had to confirm Henri was still listening.

"We're trying to get to this clinic on Rue Cingria, but your cop friends can get there faster. They're about to cut Sally open."

"I understand," flatly. "I'll put in the call and head back to Geneva."

Two minutes later we heard police sirens in the distance.

When we finally turned into Rue Cingria we were confronted by flashing lights and a barricade. If there was a siege, it was over; the cops were strolling around, chatting. I ran toward the door of the clinic and was grabbed by a policeman. "My wife's in there. They're going to kill her!"

"Are you Monsieur Brown?" I nodded. "Come with me." Nothing in his manner indicated good news was just around the corner.

We entered the clinic – the door jamb was splintered – and encountered a grave looking Captain Méchant, briefing two junior officers. He ran his hand repeatedly through his hair – his security blanket – as he talked. Acknowledging our arrival, Méchant turned toward us. "Ah, Mr. Brown. Dolorous news. I was unsuccessful in apprehending the butchers. Sheer happenstance that I averted what I could." It took effort to control my features. Nour was better at maintaining a flat expression.

"My wife and I were on our way to the hospital to visit an acquaintance." He motioned toward a parked car occupied by a grim-faced woman." We were parking on this side street when I thought I saw suspicious activity. Two women – one perhaps your wife – were being taken into this clinic. It appeared that one of the women was resisting. As I approached to question them, sirens alarmed the men and they escaped out the back. I believe they still had the two women with them."

The cops weren't going to challenge a plausible account from a senior officer. Nour and I ran through the clinic. The alley behind it was empty. As we came back through we passed a small operating theatre with two tables; one of them was occupied by a frightened looking woman who wasn't going to receive a new liver today. Had she been told that it might not be a Premium Grade body part? Any senior medical personnel who'd been present had melted away; if the circumstances hadn't seemed irregular, the arrival of the police would have erased any doubts.

Nour was eager to expose Méchant's inventions and was trying to question the one nurse who'd stayed behind and whose English was imperfect.

"Forget it, Nour. Méchant's story will fall apart when Levy is brought in. We have to see if we can pick up the trail."

There was no sign of the ambulance. Had its duties been completed and sent away? Or were Hanan and Sally strapped to gurneys, one of them recovering from a kidney removal. I dialed the phone, a task slowed by the tremor in my hands.

"Henri, Max again. Haddadin slipped away with his captives when he heard the sirens. Méchant is still here, spinning a yarn, but I suspect he's just trying to buy time for Haddadin to get a head start. It looks like Méchant has his wife with him. I get the sense she didn't know what her husband was up to. That aside, Haddadin, Sally, and Hanan may be in an ambulance, or Haddadin's old Peugeot."

"Neither is good, Max. Lots of old Peugeots on the roads, and the police will be reluctant to pull over an ambulance, especially if the emergency lights are on. Still, it's easier to spot."

"That takes me to the next point. How do we get the cops into the hunt. They're receiving a line of bull from Méchant. He won't send them looking for the right vehicle."

"Our splintered system is useful for something. Go see which vehicle Méchant tells them left with the captives – we can be sure it's the other one – and then try to identify the branches of police who heard his story. I'll try to mobilize a branch that isn't present. I don't want it to come down to my word against the captain's."

Nour and I returned to the surgery's reception area where Méchant was holding court, lamenting his failure to apprehend the perps, the junior officers reassuring him he'd gone beyond the call and should be commended.

"Captain," Méchant looked at me sharply, "we saw Haddadin and his captives just minutes ago. They were traveling in an old Peugeot and an ambulance. In which one did they leave here?"

Méchant started, then recovered. "You saw them?"

"Yes, we tried to follow them from an apartment building on the Rhône. We lost them in traffic and were guided here by the sirens."

Too early to let on we knew who lives in the apartment. Better to let Méchant believe that he can still play for time.

"I think a sedan . . . perhaps Peugeot."

Back on the phone. "Henri, Méchant says they're in the Peugeot. The shoulder patches were for Geneva city police – maybe some canton cops as well."

"Okay, then it's the ambulance. If the EMTs resisted, Haddadin put a gun to someone's head. He's on the run, looking over his shoulder. But the stakes keep getting higher. His captives are just slowing him down. Unless he thinks he'll wind up in a hostages-for-freedom negotiation soon he'll want to ditch them."

Maybe just fatigue, but Henri was becoming less sensitive in his choice of words with each utterance.

Dealing

"Think, Nour. I can't." We were back in the car and I was slumped over the steering wheel. Should I cry? Lose control? A cathartic meltdown that would restore balance and clarity?

"We'll find them, Dr. Max. They have nowhere to go. The ambulance is very visible. I'll see if Mukhabarat can find out if Haddadin or Levy requested a transfer ambulance this morning. We can give identifying information to the police."

A phone call in Arabic. Followed by a long wait for the return call.

Nour's phone rang. The message was brief; Nour barely spoke.

"Nothing," she said apologetically. "Ambulance requests come in by phone and are put into the computer when the dispatcher has time or the inclination to do so."

Outside the car Geneva was doing what Geneva does every morning: going about its many businesses with a municipal air of self-importance and disdain for those not involved. Do any of these smug Genevois know what evil is underway in their midst? Would they care?

I was blaming a city for my problems.

My phone rang. The number was unfamiliar.

"Max," Sally's voice! "I don't know if I can believe this, but BBM wants to cut a deal."

"Oh, babe, you're alive. How are you?"

"Passable. That's not the issue. Haddadin wants safe passage somewhere – he's not clear on the destination – and he wants you to arrange it. If everything goes well Hanan and I will be freed."

And if everything doesn't go well . . .

"I need more to go on, Sal."

Haddadin had taken the phone. "You are doctor and I believe you also rich man. If you are smart you will think of way for me to escape. First you must tell me honestly who is looking for me."

What to say? Nothing that would jeopardize Sally and Hanan. Make him believe the noose is tightening? Or, should he be led to think he has nothing to fear so he'll lower his guard?

The truth. It's simplest to keep track of and it might build trust. "As of right now I can tell you that Schwarzherz is in the custody of a FedPol agent. I imprisoned Levy in the trunk of his car but no one but me knows that. Méchant's involvement has not been revealed to the police. He should be safe from arrest for several hours."

"I ask who looking for me."

"I don't know the details, but I believe one branch of police are looking for an ambulance."

"Then you must bring different car."

"Where?"

"You bring car to IKEA parking garage. Call when ready. And bring lots of money." He hung up. Things were moving too fast for Haddadin; he hadn't even come up with a ransom amount. And he was asking *me* to devise a workable escape plan?

"Dr. Max, we won't make the vehicle exchange in a parking garage. An ambulance may be too high to enter and there's usually only one exit. Haddadin should understand he could be trapped."

"It's a strange location. Right by the airport. I wonder if that's significant." Did Haddadin expect I'd arrange his extraction via an international airport?

"What's he angling for, Nour? He's getting more people involved. Any exchange will reveal his location – even if it's just to collect the money. I wouldn't do it this way. He has two advantages: first, he has hostages and, second, no one knows where he is. Is he going to give up both of those?"

"Maybe. The GID profile has him as not very smart. They don't think he's the brains of the operation. I, personally, think it's this Dr. Levy." Her features tightened. Wishing she'd done more damage than a simple fractured collar-bone?

"Haddadin has gotten this far through brutality and intimidation."

"I can understand why he'd like to ditch the ambulance, Nour. But, why the IKEA garage?"

"Didn't you notice, Dr. Max?" I don't notice a lot of things. "His bedroom furniture is from IKEA. Since he lives in Fribourg this may be one of the few places in Geneva where he knows his way around."

"Well, aside from that we're getting nowhere trying to find the logic in his actions. You can add to your profile that he's erratic, violent, and hot-tempered. And we're just doing whatever he says. We should be taking the initiative, Nour."

"Unfortunately, that's the way it usually is in hostage situations. We comply with the kidnapper, and watch for an opening."

Nour should know, but still, dismal counsel. "Alright. We can make one small change. We need a bigger vehicle than this car. I'll rent a small van at the airport. I want Haddadin to have the option of keeping all of his hostages with him. I'm afraid of what he would do if he had to dispose of some."

While I drove north toward the airport against on-coming rush-hour traffic, Nour got on the phone and reserved a van. Then she called Henri. After a brief argument, Henri agreed to step back. The IKEA meeting was ours. He could not, however, call off the police search for the ambulance.

"Which police did you notify, Agent Henri?"

Silence. Embarrassed?

"The tourist police." Who patrol central Geneva on bicycles. Do they even have cars? "They were the only ones not already compromised by Méchant's story."

The parking garages at Cointrin Airport weren't full and, in fairness, Swiss efficiency has its uses; within fifteen minutes we were in a Renault minivan with seating for seven. A kilometer to the west the blue and yellow IKEA sign jutted above the others.

I hate IKEA. Correction: I hate going to IKEA. It's where Sally and I fight. Nowhere on the long list of our areas of compatibility and complementarity will you find home décor. We arrive at IKEA, apprehensive; we leave sullen and empty-handed – unable to agree on a coffee table.

How strange those emotions could surface in the current circumstances. I called back to Haddadin's number.

"Haddadin, we're in a grey Renault van and we're approaching the IKEA parking garage from the airport side. What next?"

"The money. Did you get lots of money?"

"You weren't specific. I have 2,000 francs, the maximum I could get out of the cash-point at the airport. Any more would take time."

"Enter garage and go to most low level."

We wound down the parking levels. Nour had been wrong; the ceiling of the decks was high enough for an ambulance. The store was just opening and there were few cars parked. By the time we got to the bottom level, there were none. The ambulance sat at the farthest corner. *Sally. Sally is in that ambulance.*

I picked up my phone to call Haddadin again; there was no signal.

"Dr. Max, Haddadin doesn't know I am here. How can we use that?"

Why ask me? She's supposed to be the pro. The question had been rhetorical. Nour had an answer.

"He will transfer the hostages to this car but keep Mrs. Brown with him at all times. She provides the most leverage. Then he will walk with her to this car. Perhaps I can get a shot. He stands much taller."

"Are you that accurate?"

"From close range, yes. Don't worry, Dr. Max, I will not attempt a shot if there is any danger of hitting your wife."

I drove the minivan slowly behind a large support column and Nour dove out the door. Continuing forward, I parked ten meters from the ambulance. Nothing from within. A tap on the horn and the ambulance's large rear doors inched open. A young man, an EMT, peered out.

The ambulance door opened further on one side. The young EMT got out and turned to assist someone: Hanan, her wrists duct-taped together; blood had soaked through her blouse. The EMT held Hanan's arm, steadying her as the two walked to the minivan. She climbed into the van and lowered herself slowly onto a center seat. No eye contact.

"Hanan, it may be small comfort now, but we did find your kidney." No response.

The EMT looked back at the ambulance uncertainly. A pistol was extended through the partially opened door, waving him back. The young man looked at me – the uncertainty in his expression progressing to terror – then turned and walked unsteadily to the ambulance.

Had Nour moved to a better vantage point? The column she'd got out at was over thirty meters away. At that distance I wouldn't have been able to hit the ambulance, much less a man's head.

The distance wasn't going to be the obstacle. The ambulance started to slowly reverse toward us until one of its large doors grazed our car. The ambulance jerked to a stop and both rear doors were swung open by momentum, slamming into the side of the minivan, creating an enclosed passageway between the ambulance and van.

I could see her at last. Sally was sitting on a gurney, wrists duct-taped together; the tape continued around her waist, immobilizing her arms. The BBM stood behind her, gripping one arm.

The BBM turned away from us and fired two shots, almost casually.

I looked at Hanan.

"Mr. Haddadin said he did not want loose ends. There were two men in the ambulance." She showed no emotion. Was this what happened to the holocaust victims? They experienced so many horrors that finally nothing could shock them?

Haddadin prodded Sally with his pistol and the two made the short journey to the minivan – no clear shot for Nour. They climbed into the minivan, taking the rearmost seats.

Haddadin was taking inventory of the minivan with a scowl of disapproval. Had I selected the wrong model? Sally kept her head down. Finally she looked up, much of her face hidden by the mop of hair that she couldn't push back. There was something pleading in her expression. Expecting a clever rescue plan? Could we reason with Haddadin? How? There'd be no appealing to his better nature. And the long trail of bodies he'd left on two continents ensured no judicial authority could offer leniency for our release. *There has to be a lever somewhere. Think, Max!*

"Now we go to airport. This woman and I want to take airplane ride together. We go to France side of airport." I must have hesitated. "Now!" He slammed the minivan's sliding door closed for emphasis.

As we headed up the ramp I could see Nour in the rearview mirror. She'd stepped out from behind the column, her gun held limply in her hand. The picture of defeat.

Then she straightened, turned, and ran toward the stairs.

No plan

Geneva Cointrin airport is unique in that it serves two countries. Switzerland, of course, but the airport's northern boundary lies along the frontier with France. There's a smaller terminal on that side as well as French emigration control. It's rumored to be lax; perhaps the French want to stand apart from the uptight Swiss. Lax or not, could Haddadin get on a plane with a hostage and a gun? It seemed unlikely.

What did seem likely is that once Sally and Haddadin got out of the minivan Hanan and I would be 'loose ends.' We had to abort this plan.

"Haddadin, if you're thinking of buying two tickets and getting through security screening, it won't work."

"I already order you think of escape plan. You have better idea?"

I had zero ideas.

We emerged from the parking garage. I looked in the mirror at Sally. The morning sun was slanting through the van's windows, the lines of fatigue casting narrow vertical shadows around her mouth and eyes.

"Babe. Your skin color . . ." I hadn't seen her in a bright light for two days.

She examined the backs of her hands, looked up toward the rearview mirror, and slowly nodded. "I'm sorry."

Sorry? For being the victim of a callous and capricious universe?

What's the point? What, please tell me, is the fucking point? My knuckles white on the steering wheel, Sally's yellowing face in the mirror. Would she get a shot at another liver? Somewhere in my reading there'd been mention that a person who'd rejected one transplanted organ was not a promising candidate for a second one. There are no sentimentalists at the Registry. One strike and you're out.

There has to be a lever somewhere. Think, Max! Tell Haddadin if he finds a liver for Sally we will be guilty too and won't be able to accuse him? Another look in the mirror at Sally. *I'd do it. I'd trade my soul for one good liver.*

And become like Haddadin, Levy, and Schwarzherz.

If Hanan weren't in the car I'd drive into a concrete abutment and end it.

And it's thoughts like that, my friends, that fuel reckless action.

Nour said Haddadin was not smart. Roscoe was still in my pocket, testimony to Haddadin's mental limitations. If he could be distracted maybe I could get the gun out and shoot him before he reacted.

Wishful thinking. A) I'm a bad shot. B) I was facing away from the target. C) Haddadin's gun was pressed into Sally's side, probably cocked. Still, in situations like this is an unworkable plan better than none?

As we entered the tunnel that passed under the airport to the French side a sedan passed us and slammed on the brakes, forcing me to do the same. A BMW, driven with the discourtesy for which the mark is famous. The Beemer accelerated, then hit the brakes again. *Dammit. We have enough problems.*

I checked the mirror. Haddadin had taken the pistol out of Sally's side and was pointing it in my direction. Another cycle of accelerate – brake. Haddadin was clinging to the center seatback. "Stop this!" he shouted.

I slowed. The sedan did the same. We were now backing up traffic.

Of course. The driver had to be Nour. She must have heard Haddadin's demand to go to the French side of the airport. She'd 'borrowed' a car in the parking garage and tailed us. What's her plan? This didn't seem to be leading anywhere.

"Go around," shouted Haddadin.

Not an option. There were no breaks in the on-coming traffic. Then, abruptly, the sedan accelerated and was well ahead of us when we emerged from the tunnel.

"Go now to terminal." The overhead blue and white signs ushered us into the right lane for the departure terminal, but the exit ramp was blocked. The same BMW was positioned across it and three cars were already lined up, their drivers honking. Join the queue?

No. "Continue on road," ordered Haddadin. We did.

The BMW pulled out of the exit ramp and followed us.

"I will kill all of you if that car follows us more."

Sally spoke, for the first time. "That's not a useful threat. The driver of that car can't hear you. Kill us and you have no hostages."

That got through. Another check in the mirror. Haddadin's brow was knotted. He turned and pointed his pistol through the rear window. Nour was following closely. I swerved the van slightly from side-to-side while trying to fish Roscoe out of my pocket. Mental note: modify at least one pants pocket to make it shallower.

"Drive straight," shouted Haddadin. He was still trying to steady his gun for a shot at Nour's car. I eased the van over onto the warning strip. A useful jostling.

"Sorry," I shouted over my shoulder, and swerved back out into the lane. A good speed bump would be welcome, but they're never where they're really needed.

Still wrestling with Roscoe. The hammer was hung up on cloth. Haddadin noticed. "Put hands where I can see."

Now he was focused on me. No pulling out the gun and getting a surprise shot off. Disable the vehicle? It had worked once. I tilted the still pocketed pistol toward the engine compartment and fired three times, tapping the brake pedal in time with each shot.

"Ohoh! Did you hear that? Something's wrong with the motor." Would Haddadin buy that explanation for the noise?

A bullet had found something vulnerable and the minivan lurched. This was followed by a small pop and smoke came up from around the pedals.

"We're on fire!"

This was too much for Haddadin and he pointed his gun at Sally, then Hanan, then me, undecided who to kill first. I had to give him another option before he started shooting in desperation.

The minivan was slowing of its own volition, the smoke intensifying. "Haddadin, we have to get off the road, but I have another plan." I didn't.

An exit was only a short distance ahead. Lurching, the van rolled through the exit onto a single lane road. We'd gone a few hundred yards when the engine died. The smoke continued.

"We need to get out before this thing blows," shouted with intensity to convince doubters.

Haddadin didn't need convincing and was already fumbling with the handle on the sliding door. He was the first one out and gesturing with the pistol for Hanan and Sally to follow. I jumped out of the car, eager to remain seen as an indispensable member of the group. But, where was Nour?

A different sedan, a Volvo, came up the road and slowed to a stop. The driver, an elderly Frenchman, judging by the national soccer team's jersey he was wearing, eyed the smoking minivan. Haddadin was fast. He had the pistol through the car's open window, pressed against the driver's temple. I was sure he was going to shoot the man, but Haddadin motioned for him to get out.

With hands raised, the Frenchman backed away from his car.

"In car," the pistol directed at my midsection. "You drive." It looked like no one was going to be dropped from the group.

I'd been most worried about Hanan. She understood her diminishing value and quickly got into the front passenger's seat. Sally and the BBM in back.

I had put the car in Drive when the owner started to protest. This display of ingratitude, after having spared the man's life, was too much for Haddadin. He swung the pistol out the window and aimed it at the old soccer fan . . . when providence intervened. The minivan erupted in flames, followed seconds later by an explosion. Our car rocked and the Frenchman was thrown to the ground. Not seriously injured, he scrambled to his feet and bolted across the field. I floored the accelerator before Haddadin could re-aim and fire.

"Go back now to big road." A U-turn, and we were headed back, past the smoldering minivan, toward the main highway where Haddadin instructed me to turn south toward Geneva. If I had the plan, why was he issuing the driving instructions?

Hot pursuit

'Hot pursuit' is permitted across national borders throughout Europe, but what are the rules when the perp is headed *toward* police, not away from them?

This legal technicality would only trouble Agent Henri Verteux. An excerpt from his statement:

```
At approximately 0925 I had just delivered
a kidney in its transport box to a clinic
in the ELITA network when the radio report-
ed that a dangerous criminal with three
hostages had fled into France in a Renault
minivan via the Cointrin Airport tunnel. We
- I had a prisoner secured in the backseat
of my car - were two km. from the airport
and I proceeded in that direction. The next
radio transmission was that the criminal
and his hostages had reversed course and
were now headed back toward Geneva in a
green Volvo sedan. I later learned that
this information came via a Jordanian in-
telligence service. Federal and Cantonal
Police were preparing a roadblock at the
Swiss end of the tunnel. I assumed that
FedPol would have notified French security
services in an attempt to trap the sedan in
the tunnel.

Upon arrival at the tunnel, I saw that Cap-
tain Méchant was directing the roadblock,
which consisted, at that time, of only one
police car and a motorcycle. I had been re-
cently made aware that Captain Méchant was
compromised through indirect association
with the criminal when the Captain obtained
an organ outside of regular channels for
his wife.

As I approached the roadblock on foot, dis-
playing my credentials to the Cantonal Po-
lice, the green Volvo could be seen enter-
ing the tunnel at the far end, still on the
```

French side of the border. The Volvo
stopped, suggesting the driver was uncertain what to do. At that moment Captain Méchant mounted the police motorcycle and
started toward the Volvo. I shouted that we
had no jurisdiction as the criminal had not
entered Swiss territory and we were not,
technically, pursuing him. I regret making
this statement as it may have contributed
to indecision and hesitation on the part of
the Swiss security personnel present. I also believed, in my defence, that time
should be allowed for the French gendarmes
to arrive and seal off the exit from their
end of the tunnel. Only then could a successful confrontation be made on the criminal in the Volvo. I understand now that
French police had not been notified.

———

In the green Volvo, we all stared at the flashing blue lights at
the far end of the tunnel. I was awaiting instructions from Haddadin, which was pointless. No mastermind there.

There was movement among the blue flashes. Someone was
coming toward us on a motorcycle. Helmetless. As he got closer
we saw it was Méchant – no mistaking that billow of grey hair.
Was he coming to join forces with Haddadin? I gave the BBM a
questioning look. Haddadin desperately wanted an ally. A hope-
ful expression spread across his large face.

Let's extinguish that hope pronto. "Haddadin, Méchant isn't
coming to your rescue. It's more likely he wants no witnesses to
his crimes. Not you, not Sally, not Hanan, not me. He doesn't
know we have Schwarzherz and Levy. He thinks that if he can
start a shootout – he assumes the other police will be right behind him – he can get out of this unscathed as long as there are
no survivors on our side."

Haddadin wasn't buying it. He needed to believe an ally was
coming to his aid. That's when Méchant made his first mistake.
He pulled out his service pistol and took aim at our car. Had-

dadin looked uncertain. I was certain, however, that we shouldn't hang around. I slammed the gear lever into Reverse and started backing toward the exit. The car slewed back and forth, barely within control. I turned the wheel hard and hit the brakes. Would we spin around, or roll? I didn't care.

The Volvo spun 180 degrees. Dropping the gear lever into Drive, we shot forward, away from the motorcycle. The rear window exploded as the first shot – Méchant's second mistake – passed over our heads.

"Understand, Haddadin? He doesn't want anyone in this car left alive to talk."

The BBM was slow to come to terms with this obvious truth, but, perhaps to test it, he turned and leveled his gun at the motorcycle, now 50 meters behind us and gaining. No friendly wave from the cop; Méchant fired again.

Haddadin was convinced. "Go faster!" and he squeezed off a shot.

We came out of the tunnel. *Where were the French fuzz?* A car roared out of an entry ramp, almost clipping our rear fender. I watched in the rearview mirror as the driver – Nour, of course – kept her car between us and the motorcycle. After making feints to the right and left, Méchant tried to pass Nour on the right. Nour's car nudged the speeding bike, sending it off the road into a plowed field. The motorcycle bounced across the furrows, a skipping pebble; Méchant kept it upright for a few seconds, but lost control and the bike toppled over onto its side. Would that luxuriant pile of hair – his only admirable attribute – protect him from injury?

One down, and our side had the ally.

Not for long. Haddadin fired at Nour's car and hit something vital. I watched Nour fight for control as the BMW fishtailed – perhaps a front tire was gone – and slowed; she was out of the chase. Our situation had swung back to the same level of peril as one minute earlier.

But wait. The cavalry, in the form of a Swiss police car, shot out of the tunnel. Another chance.

No. The police car stopped and I watched in the mirror as two cops ran across the plowed field to the aid of their downed comrade.

Haddadin ordered me to turn onto the same side road we'd gone down before. Comfort in a known setting? We flashed by the blackened minivan.

As if he'd been waiting for this moment Haddadin extended the pistol toward me. "You say you have plan. We now again in same place. What is plan?"

A bad plan

An excellent question. Maybe if I reasoned it through . . .

Ahead of us lay villages and vineyards. We had to get out of the car where it would be more difficult for Haddadin to control the situation, but he wasn't going to allow that in a populated area. I pulled off the road and turned toward him.

"Here's my analysis: People are starting to look for you. Within a few minutes they'll be looking for this car. Your only ally among the security forces, Méchant, doesn't want you captured alive. You just saw that having hostages didn't stop him from firing. He wants you dead and he might be able to persuade others that would be for the best." I paused. Where to from here?

"That is not plan."

"No," with exaggerated patience, "the plan comes next. Hostages are not helping you any longer. But – and my personal interest is obvious – killing us will just mean the police will have to dedicate more resources to capturing you."

Haddadin looked unconvinced.

"Look, Haddadin, right now the police – if they know anything at all about you – think you're someone who's been illegally selling the organs of foreign women. That's a crime, but it's not an immediate threat to public safety. If you kill three people – and the cops know you have us – then the frightened public will be clamoring for the police to do something. Every cop within 100 kilometers will have only one assignment: to find you."

"I still do not hear plan."

"Okay, let me spell it out: A) This car is marked. B) We're slowing you down. You need to get rid of us and the car in a place where *we* are not able to contact the police and *you* can get a head start." That sounded plausible, so I plunged on. "See the Jura mountains to the north? There's a wildlife park there. To the west of that is a nature preserve. Lots of places to drive the car into the forest where it won't be found. We can be tied to trees until hikers find us."

What the fuck was I saying?! This really might work for Haddadin and hikers might not find us in time. Hikers are admonished at every turn to not stray from the prepared paths. Not only would Haddadin tie us up, he'd probably gag us as well. We can't count on him to be so stupid he'd leave us able to shout for help. But, compared to our current circumstances . . .

Would this closely reasoned argument get through to Haddadin?

"Go to most near forest."

Two small villages later we were traversing up the switchbacks toward the Wildlife Park of Haut-Jura. The Taylor-Browns had explored the side roads fifteen years earlier when the girls were small. Which roads had been opened to development since then, and which not? A cable hanging loosely between two posts across the entrance to a dirt road signaled one possibility. Stopping, "How about this, Haddadin? Closed to traffic and it looks little used."

"Go."

Which way? Up the hill or onto the dirt track? I drove through heavy brush around the post and onto the dirt road. Haddadin didn't object.

After less than a kilometer bouncing along ruts, the track turned right, steeply uphill. Years of water cascading down the road had carved deep channels. I steered the left wheel into a channel, and the Volvo dropped on its suspension. Ride over.

"This looks like a good place, Haddadin." It didn't. He and I got out of the car to examine the situation. The car was immobilized. To the east traffic could be faintly heard on the highway. "Now you have to figure out how you want to restrain us." Said matter-of-factly. Two workmen, solving small technical problems together.

"I shoot you all in legs." Said simply, and clearly not up for negotiation.

No one said a word. This was better than some possible outcomes, but I hadn't considered maiming, perhaps being permanently crippled.

"Uh, nothing to tie us with? Shots will be heard." Still trying to keep that neutral, problem-solver note in my voice.

Haddadin dug in his jacket pocket and produced a silencer which he twisted onto the pistol.

"Better I shoot you in car. More comfortable for you to sit." A humanitarian gesture.

"Would you allow me to remove the tape from Sally and Hanan. They might need to put pressure on the wound so as not to bleed to death."

The absurdity of this conversation was lost on Haddadin, who gave the request serious consideration.

"First you get in car." He understood the dangers of allowing us out where we might surround him.

Hanan started to weep softly. There'd be no rescue and I had agreed with the BBM on how the game was going to end. Wheelchairs – with luck.

Haddadin positioned himself by the left front fender from where he could watch his three hostages. He looked relaxed. There was a plan in place that he understood and could execute: Disable us, and walk through the woods to safety. It was, after all, a pleasant day for a walk. He reloaded his pistol – how many bullets did he think he'd need to put into us? – thumbing cartridges into the clip and scanning the tree line on the west side of the dirt road. There were several breaks in the brush.

While Haddadin was occupied, I climbed into the back seat with Sally and started fumbling with the tape on her wrists. "Oscoe-ray, ocket-pay."

She looked at me with alarm. Had the woman not learned pig Latin as a child? Softly, "Roscoe's in my pocket." I freed her wrists. The blue flesh where the tape had chafed the skin contrasted with the yellow of her hands.

I leaned forward over the seatback to free Hanan, my pocket accessible to Sally, out of view of the BBM. Sally needed no urging. Her hand was in my pocket . . . she slipped the pistol out.

I pulled the last of the tape from Hanan's wrists. "Don't be frightened, Hanan. Things will work out."

Sally was ready. "Sit back down slowly, Max. Don't alarm him . . . and keep your arms out of the way."

I looked up at Haddadin to indicate I was finished, and fell back into the seat, my hands above my head with a loud, "Oops, sorry!" Sally fired.

The windshield shattered and a bullet tore into the car's hood. The BBM threw himself to the right, and rolled toward the trees, jamming the magazine into the grip of his pistol.

"Damn," from Sally. She reached across me and fired again, showering Haddadin with dirt. The BBM was scrambling for the cover of the trees, shooting over his shoulder.

"Only one bullet left, Sal. No shoot out. Out of the car, Hanan."

Hanan was ahead of us and by the time I'd clawed across the seat she was into the trees, with Sally close behind. We ran through the woods toward the highway, the women outpacing me, despite their recent ordeal.

————

Statement of Agent Henri Verteux:

French gendarmes reported two women and a man attempting to stop traffic on Route D1005 north of Gex. One of the women was armed. I proceeded to the scene and found M. and Mme. Brown, Americans, and Mme. Tafile, a Swiss national. They were un- harmed. After a brief discussion the gen-

```
darmes allowed me to take Mme. Tafile
back to Geneva so that she could go into
immediate surgery and her recently re-
moved kidney could be restored to her. As
I was later informed, unfortunately the
kidney was no longer viable. M. and Mme.
Brown were held for questioning by French
Securité for three hours, then released.
```

———

I had questions of my own for Sally: "How could you miss? You never miss."

"You're a great one to accuse, Studly. My hands were stiff and sore."

"But, babe. You aimed so low! He's a big guy; you could have easily shot him in the chest."

"I was going for his balls. For Nour."

Daily Journal

Sally Taylor-Brown

11 May
Geneva

I started this story in my journal, not expecting it would turn out the way it did. I wish Max was writing this, but that's not an option.

How to tell you?

We had barely caught our breath when Max embarked on a campaign to whip up interest in hunting down Haddadin. I think it was that "keep the mind occupied" thing he's mentioned. *Le Temps* and *Le Tribune de Genève* ran second-page stories, with mugshots, but it led to nothing. The BBM might be stupid, but he did know how to hide.

With no sign of Haddadin, Nour went back to Jordan. I had mixed feelings about her leaving. I admire her and we owe her a lot, but I think she was sweet on Max and that's a complication no middle-aged wife needs.

She stays in touch. A few weeks ago she texted that Haddadin was not in Jordan and we should keep our guard up. Part of his profile at Mukhabarat includes "vengefulness and an abhorrence of loose ends." Abhorrence? She's starting to sound like Max.

Henri was put on administrative leave without pay. He and Lisa took off on a vacation. Méchant's career is over, but he isn't doing time. A court found that his dabbling in the red market was "understandable"; he was only trying to save his wife's life. Bull hockey, Judge. Méchant was giving those butchers cover.

Anyway.

The two docs are in the slammer awaiting trial and good riddance. Schwarzherz is facing ten years; Levy is likely to get life. Of course that means our little clinic is closed, but Dr. Zuheir in Amman stepped in to handle the acid-attack cases from the Middle East. It should have been that way all along.

Our donors say they will support Zuheir, but I suspect the money will drop off. The donors have always liked stopping by the clinic to see where their money is going, get a glimpse of one of the patients, be showered with gratitude by our staff.

As for Max and me, you can probably guess about my boy. After the unproductive press blitz, he went to work feverishly writing up everything that happened from when we were in Petra at the Monastery right up to the last set-to with the BBM. Maybe the people who read his books don't appreciate it, but he has always put in a lot of work, revising, changing a word or a section.

He also went a couple of times to talk to a priest he'd met at the Université, but he never told me what that was all about. At the time I assumed it had something to do with the course he'd been preparing on morality.

Anyway. Two weeks ago he was 'polishing the turd', as writers like to say, when the doorbell rang. I was closest so I answered. Standing on the stoop was the BBM, minus the second B (for beard, if that's not clear). He wasn't selling Girl Scout cookies.

I didn't see a gun, but his hand was in his jacket pocket. I must have screamed since Max came running. He'd picked up a letter opener on the way out of our little home office. Haddadin did have a gun which he was pulling from his pocket just as Max pushed me out of the way and hurled himself at Haddadin and plunged the knife into the big man's solar plexus. Max reeled back with an expression of horror on his face. The letter opener was buried to the hilt in Haddadin's chest. The BBM looked down at the knife with surprise, then slowly went over backwards.

Haddadin lay on his back, his feet twitching. I can picture that perfectly, those two big shoes, their worn soles facing us, jiggling like he was trying to learn a new dance step.

Max dropped to his knees in the doorway; his eyes were turned away from the dying BBM. He started trembling – in time to BBM's feet jiggles? – and mumbling, "Jesus, no. Jesus, no. Jesus, no."

I put a hand on his shoulder, too stunned to speak.

"Why can't I stop killing people, Sal? Is it me or is the universe setting me up."

"He had a gun. What were you supposed to do? You saved our lives."

"We don't know that. Maybe he was here to apologize."

Seriously? But I didn't say that. Max was too upset. He's killed a lot of people, including his own father, and it's just kept getting worse for him.

"Max, honey, you saved us. Remember how many women died because of Haddadin? He had it coming."

Max started shaking his head violently, trying to dislodge a demon. I knelt down beside him and held him tight.

"You're a good man, Maxwell Brown. Knock this off. There *is* evil in the world and you can't negotiate with it and you can't reform it. Most people try to avoid it." No response. Did he even hear my voice? "A few stand up to evil and try to remove it. Maybe you're lucky. You've been given the opportunity to reduce the amount of evil that's around."

Not a great speech, but I'd thought about these things a lot. Max always understood there was evil. He just never understood why. His fear – he told me this often – was that every time he stood up to evil men he became more like them.

I don't know if Max had time to figure out Haddadin's motives, but Haddadin made them clear. He was not there for any noble reason. While I held my dear, over-wrought, over-moral husband, Haddadin raised his pistol and shot Max in the back.

Evil won.

I pushed the door closed with my foot and cradled Max in my arms. "You're a good man, Max. A good man. A good man."

I was still repeating it when the police arrived.

Five days later we had a memorial service. A nice turn out. It makes me think that everyone should try to go to as many funerals as they can. It helps the grieving family when they see they are not alone in mourning the departure of a loved one.

Margaret and Mary, for the first time since they were born, were at a loss. I didn't know Mary was so emotional. She cried almost constantly. Part of that may have been due to my appearance which is the other loose end I need to tidy up.

You get one shot at a transplant. That's not to say that a repeat definitely won't work, it's just that the odds are not as good if your body has already kicked out one alien organ. My oncologist explained this all to me. Since transplantable livers are in short supply they go to the people who are most likely to benefit from them. I understand that.

I tried to reassure the girls and sent them back to London. They're not dummies. They know that a person with liver cancer gets three to six months without a transplant. I've had five.

And I've had things to finish up, since time is short. The main thing is to put what Max and I have written together into one – I hope readable – narrative. I found Max's notes on moral philosophy and I've inserted those. They seem to fit. He also took pride in the glossaries he's added to each book, so you'll find that starting in a page or two.

A lot of tears, reading his words. Now all that's done there's still one decision hanging: Do I wait, or should I take matters into my own hands? Roscoe is standing by in the nightstand. If a miracle cure was just around the corner someone would have mentioned it, don't you think? Life without Max is not really life at all. But no decision yet. I have to consider how my suicide would affect the girls.

I have no religious beliefs. Afterlife? I'll soon find out. Hoping there is, of course.

Enough. I can see I'm starting to ramble. Goodbye, everybody. Sorry to end on such a downer. Max and I have had a fairy-tale life, but all lives come to an end. Now I've accomplished something I never thought I'd do: I've written a book. Well, half of it. The party's over. But not without one shout out to a really good guy:

See you on the flip side, Studly.

Glossary

Al Jazeera. A satellite TV news station based in Qatar. Famous in the Middle East for tweaking the noses of the region's despots, and in the West for airing the pronouncements and videos provided by terrorists. In the news world, a contender; Al Jazeera boasts the second largest newsgathering network in the world (BBC is #1).

Canton. A state of the Swiss Confederation. There are 26.

Asclepius was the Greek god of healing. The rod of Asclepius, a snake-entwined staff, remains a symbol of medicine today.

Cointrin airport. Perhaps I'm alone in my interest in the dual nationality of the Geneva airport. Undeterred by that possibility, and expanding on the comments made in the text . . .

French access to the airport was the result of a deal in which France ceded a few acres to Switzerland to allow for a longer runway. In return, the Swiss have allowed France to operate an independent embarkation and debarkation point. Not all airlines have baggage check-in facilities on the French side so the traveler might get a boarding pass on the north side of the airport and have to schlep luggage to the south side. One consistent advantage of the French side: car rental rates are lower.

Federal Police. Switzerland is a confederation which means the cantons have considerably more authority than those of us who live in republics or federations are familiar with. Fedpol, as a result, is a comparatively small national police force and typically enters a case only at the pleasure of the cantonal police.

Franc. Swiss currency is the Swiss franc (CHF) which has been trading at around one franc to one US dollar.

Golden rule. "Do unto others . . ." Interesting how ardently this low level of moral reasoning (stage 2 for Kohlberg) is promoted by so many religions.

Buddhism: *Hurt not others with that which pains yourself.*
Confucianism: *What you do not want done to yourself, do not do to others.*

Hinduism: *One should always treat others as they themselves wish to be treated.* This, by the way, may date back to 1900 BCE; the Christian Golden Rule is not a new idea.

Judaism: *Thou shalt love thy neighbor as thyself.*

Zoroastrianism: *Whatever is disagreeable to yourself, do not do unto others.*

Halal. What is permissible in Islamic law; often applied to food and drink.

Honor crimes. I may have muddled things – I wasn't myself when I wrote that chapter. Honor crimes cover a range of violent acts against (almost always) women. The common feature is that honor is invoked as the justification for the violence, although the motives of the perpetrators may be quite different. A second common feature is, obviously, the very low value placed on a woman's life.

The textbook case arises when a family believes its honor has been impugned by the behavior of a member and that person must be brought to account, often killed. The family – the male members, anyway – decides. Estimates of the number of deaths range from 5,000 to 22,000 women per year.

The motives behind acid attacks – in my observations – are more often the result of the rage of one affronted male: a cuckold, or jealous husband/fiancé/boyfriend, or a man deeply uncertain about his appeal or . . . you get the idea; fear of sexual inadequacy figures somewhere. 'Honor' is slapped on, but it's rarely the primary motivator. Am I any clearer here?

Hot pursuit. Most European nations permit police to pursue a fleeing suspect (for serious crimes) across their border, but not to arrest them. Local police have to be summoned to make the arrest. An extradition request is needed to get the perp back, even if an escaped convict.

IDF. Israel Defense Forces. Includes the army, air force and navy.

Imam. Muslim prayer leader. Imams conduct religious services, are often leaders in the Muslim community, and provide religious guidance.

Intifada. The first *intifada* ("shaking off") began in 1987 as a Palestinian response to Israeli occupation and repression. The Palestinians' twin strategies were resistance and civil disobedience. The Israelis' stated response – not their finest hour – was a policy of "might, power, and beatings" and "breaking Palestinians' bones." During the first two years, over 25,000 Palestinian children required medical treatment as a result of IDF beatings. The outcome was generally regarded as a moral and political victory for the Palestinians, but at the cost of high casualties.

Jebel Harun. AKA Mount Aaron and Mount Hor. The burial site of the Prophet Aaron, Moses' brother. The site is marked by a mosque – the tiny dot on the highest peak in the picture. There was the usual family bickering between Moses and  Aaron which you can read about elsewhere. The significance to Sally and me can be seen in this photo: not easy to get to. But reportedly Moses and Aaron went up there from time to time. And they were wearing sandals.

Keffiyah. A scarf that can be wrapped around the neck, face, or head. The color is politically significant. Palestinians adopted the black and white *keffiyeh* as a symbol of national identity and solidarity. Nour's red and white *keffiyeh* is found on all security personnel in Jordan to signal their apartness from the Palestinians, despite the fact that Palestinian refugees and their descendants now make up 72 percent of Jordan's population.

Kohlberg, Lawrence. The developmental stages of moral reasoning are described in the narrative. Here are some scraps about the man's life:

Born too late to participate in WWII, he signed on to a ship contracted to *Haganah*, a militant Zionist organization, to smuggle Jewish war refugees past the British blockade into Palestine. The ship was intercepted and Kohlberg was imprisoned by the Brits on Cyprus. He escaped and went to Palestine to join the struggle for a Jewish homeland. He refused to participate in the fighting, focusing on non-violent activities.

In 1948 he returned to the US and earned a BA in psychology at the University of Chicago in one year. Students could earn full course credit by passing an exam for the course. Evidently Kohlberg was a pretty bright guy. He followed a more leisurely path to a PhD (still at Chicago) after which he bounced around academia, finally settling on the Harvard Graduate School of Education where he remained for the rest of his career.

His theory was a direct challenge to the behavioralist tide that was running strong in psychology at the time. Moral <u>reasoning</u> is, by definition, cognitive, and not the product of conditioning influences. Over time he made minor adaptations to the theory, as research data dictated the need. Stage 4+ is a case in point; that sub-stage was a response to the finding that many of his research subjects would slip back a stage as they grew older. We've all seen it: The moralistic young liberal who, thirty years later, is shouting, "Get off my lawn."

Kohlberg was not without his critics. Prominent among them was Carol Gilligan who argued that the morality of women was more care-based and Kohlberg's justice-based stages ignored that aspect of moral development. Feminists rushed to embrace Gilligan.

As Sally notes, he picked up a parasitic bug while collecting data in what is now Belize. The disease caused him intense abdominal discomfort and depression. On January 19, 1987, Kohlberg parked at the end of a dead-end street in Winthrop, Massachusetts. He left his wallet with identification on the front seat of his unlocked car and walked into the icy Boston Harbor. The car and wallet were found within a couple of weeks. Kohlberg's body was recovered months later when the tidal marsh across the harbor thawed.

Méchant, Verteux, Schwarzherz. What's in a name? Méchant is French for nasty, wicked, villainous. Verteux (Henri's family name) is French for upright, virtuous, which Agent Henri Verteux is to excess. Schwarzherz is German for black heart. Did their family names predestine their character? Or reflect it?

Mossad. The Institute for Intelligence and Special Operations: Israeli Intelligence. They take a rough and ready approach to their job; Mossad is most famous for a *long* list of assassinations. Are they allowed to do that? We don't know. When formed, Mossad was the only part of Israeli society declared exempt from national law. There's a special set of laws governing Mossad, and they're conveniently secret.

Mossad initially targeted the more reprehensible officials of the Third Reich. National governments, where the assassinations occurred, would tut-tut, but there was no serious effort to curtail the killings, given who the victims were. That laissez-faire attitude started to change as Mossad turned its deadly attentions to thinning the ranks of Hamas and Hezbollah. Switzerland even jailed a Mossad agent for wiretapping a Hezbollah operative.

Mukhabarat. The General Intelligence Directorate (GID) of Jordan. After Britain's MI-6, Mukhabarat is the CIA's closest ally. They're very effective, but tales of torture are too widespread to ignore.

How effective are they? In 2001 Mukhabarat got wind of a planned terrorist operation in the US, employing hijacked aircraft, and called "Big Wedding." They notified US authorities through multiple channels but were ignored by the newly installed Bush administration. Big Wedding, of course, was Al-Qaeda's code name for the 9/11 attacks.

NGO. Non-governmental organization. Usually a charity or political-action group. The big international NGOs you might have heard of include Doctors without Borders, CARE, Amnesty International, Save the Children, and Greenpeace. Small NGOs – e.g., Sally's clinic – rely on local fund-raising or one dedicated backer with deep pockets.

Oryx. A medium-sized member of the antelope family that can survive for long periods without water. The pointy horns are lethal and will dispatch an ambitious lion.

What works against lions doesn't work against guns. The oryx were hunted to extinction in the wild; game safaris of 300 or more vehicles carted Arab princes and their guests around to

blast away at the animals. In the 1980s they were re-introduced into the desert from zoos and have, ten-tatively, taken hold. There is still some poaching, trophy hunters being – we all agree – irredeemable assholes.

Panglossian. Dr. Pangloss was a character in Voltaire's *Candide* who was remarkable for his unshakeable optimism. It is to Professor Pangloss that we owe, "All is for the best in this best of all possible worlds." He maintained this position even as he witnessed, and justified, acts of cruelty and evil.

I became interested in the character – and added the word to my vocabulary – when fascinated with theodicy many years ago. (See my first book. Available on select remainder tables and at fine yard sales everywhere.) Voltaire's novel was a satirical attack on Leibniz's optimism which was founded on theodicy. Consistent with theodicy, Leibniz maintained all is for the best because God is a benevolent deity.

Petra. If you don't know about Petra, perhaps a listing of awards will whet your interest:

- one of the Seven Wonders of the New World,

- a UNESCO World Heritage Site, and

- the Smithsonian has told us that it's one of the 28 places we *really* need to visit before we die (those admonitions have always seemed patronizing).

It's a sprawling city carved out of solid rock that dates back past 300 BC. The founders, Nabateans, were especially accomplished in creating water-collecting systems; useful knowledge in the desert. Also useful knowledge, they figured out how to divert the flood waters that roared down off the rock faces that surround Petra, an inundation guaranteed by every rainstorm. Chief among the drainage conduits is *Muthlim Siq* along which our hardy band entered Petra.

One picture: the Monastery. Recall that it's over half a football field in height. To create it the Nabateans removed the rest of the mountain with hand tools. Think about that for a minute.

Prisoner's dilemma. If two accused prisoners – held in isolation from one another – <u>don't</u> rat each other out and don't confess, they both receive a light sentence. If only one rats out the other, the ratter receives an even lighter sentence and the rattee receives a heavy sentence. If they both rat out the other – without confessing – they both receive intermediate sentences. While cooperation (silence) is best for both, they can't count on the good intentions of the other so, when the options are described to them, they both tend to rat out the other.

Roman forts. These were cookie-cutter affairs. Each was garrisoned with 200 men. Watch towers were placed a fair distance away to monitor approaches to the fort. Here's a picture of the one Nour led us to.

Roscoe. Slang for a handgun in the '30s and '40s.

Saladdin. I'm a big fan – as far as I can admire a professional soldier. He was a Kurd, not an Arab, who initially embarked on a life of religious study. Pulled into military service, he rose up the ranks through demonstrated ability, family connections, and shrewd political alliances. He figures most often in literature and movies today for three things: 1) The taking of Jerusalem where he treated the inhabitants with extraordinary generosity; he's the guy who let the Jews back into the city (the Crusaders had kicked them out). 2) His standoff with Richard the Lion-hearted. And 3) Raynald de Châtillon. This is the one man Saladdin sought out to personally execute – and did. De Châtillon's murder of pilgrims, his attempt to attack Mecca, the (unconfirmed) capture of Saladdin's sister – it was all too much for the normally chivalrous Saladdin.

At the height of his rule he controlled Egypt, Syria, Upper Mesopotamia, the Hejaz (west side of the Arabian peninsula), Yemen and large parts of north Africa.

His generosity was legendary. When he took Jerusalem he demanded only a token tribute payment from the inhabitants ($50 in today's money). For those who couldn't pay, Saladdin anted up their tribute from his personal resources. When he died he had one piece of gold and forty pieces of silver – not enough to cover burial expenses. He had given everything else to the poor among his subjects.

Sho'bak Castle. This is one of several castles built around 1115 by Baldwin I of Jerusalem. The network gave him control over the caravans that crossed the area on their way between Damascus and Cairo. In building Sho'bak Baldwin was acquiescing to a plea from the Christian monks who held vigil at the shrine on Jebel (Mount) Harun (Aaron). The monks had complained that the Saracens were threatening them.

Our old acquaintance, Raynald de Châtillon, obtained the castle
through marriage and
immediately set upon
the caravans – both
commercial and reli-
gious pilgrims – that
had previously pas-
sed through un-
molested. There are
no epithets strong
enough for the guy.

The distinguishing
features of Sho'bak
were cisterns and the steep descent (355 steps) into the mountain to a spring and pool. Reliable access to water enabled the
Christian defenders to hold out for two years against a siege
mounted by Saladdin. Saladdin had become deeply fed up with
de Châtillon's thuggish behavior. The defenders bartered their
wives and children to Saladdin's forces for food. When the castle finally fell, Saladdin returned the women and children, un-
harmed.

Shokran. Arabic for thank you.

Stun grenade. It produces a bright flash and loud noise that
temporarily blinds and deafens those near it.

Sumayyah. The name of the Karaki acid victim who was sub-
sequently killed in an organ harvest. It's also the name of Islam's first martyr, Sumayyah bint Khubbat. Although the
Prophet's followers were a tiny minority in Mecca, the local
powers came down hard on them. Sumayyah was alternately
tortured and cajoled but she held fast to her faith. In a rage her
inquisitor (Abu Jahl, for the record) shoved his spear through
her. Some parallels, don't you think?

Tamam, tayib. Arabic for okay, right, or fine.

UNRWA. The United Nations Relief and Works Agency was
formed to provide relief and support to Palestinian refugees dis-

placed from their homeland. Today it provides support to more than five million registered Palestinian refugees in camps.

Vejovis. The Roman god of healing.

Wadi Rum. No 2" x 2" grainy picture will do Rum justice; you have to experience it for yourself. However, you have already seen the majestic desert in movies, going back to *Lawrence of Arabia* where Rum is featured as itself, up to *The Martian* where Rum is cast as Mars. And many other films in between, whenever a vast unearthly backdrop has been needed.

Wu'eira Castle. One of several castles the Crusaders built to control commerce in the area. In its day it was regarded as impregnable, thanks to its location perched atop high cliffs. Today it's close to rubble (hence, no picture).

Author. Michael Bernhart is an award-winning author who has published extensively on international development and healthcare quality. The *Max Brown Tetralogy (+1)* examines the many faces and well-springs of evil as the novels trace the arc of one man's life.

Acknowledgement. A large debt of gratitude is owed to Jill Cobb who painstakingly reviewed the manuscript and patiently advised the author.

Inspiration. A small component of a women's healthcare program that Dr. Bernhart managed in Jordan addressed the rampant violence practiced against women. It would be a stretch to attribute any improvement in the well-being of Jordanian women to that meager effort. But, sometimes you just have to try.